THE AMISH HEIRESS

Patrick E. Craig

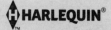

Recycling programs
for this product may
not exist in your area.

ISBN-13: 978-1-335-45493-5

The Amish Heiress

Printed in U.S.A.

HARLEQUIN®
www.Harlequin.com

Part One

The Key

Rachel, my darling girl, how can I tell of the joy you give me. In the dark days when we thought we had lost your papa, I was adrift in my grief but you were my ray of sunlight. In all those years when Jonathan was gone, you were my rock, the one person I could turn to that always had an uplifting word or a loving gesture. I know your heart ached as mine did, but somehow you held yourself above the pain and were always there for me. And for such a long time, you were the one who believed your papa would come home someday. That is why it surprised me when it was so hard for you when your papa did come home. You were fourteen, you were becoming a woman, and Jonathan had missed such a big part of your life. I think that you had finally reconciled yourself to Jonathan being dead—you had moved on. And then when he came home, you had to learn that relationship all over again. We were so close, the two of us and then there was another person in the house, a man who in many ways was a stranger to us both, especially on his "bad" days. I think you felt like he came between us. So when the opportunity came for you to go, you were ready, too ready...

Rachel—From The Journals of Jenny Hershberger

Chapter One

Trouble in Paradise

"I won't do it!"

"You will do what I say!"

"I'm eighteen, Papa, and my own person. You can't make me do anything anymore!"

"Rachel, Jonathan, please stop shouting at each other."

The voices pushed out the open front door like a symphony orchestra with every instrument out of tune. A girl stood in the doorway pointing her finger back at someone inside. She spoke and this time her voice was low and icy.

"Mama, I hate him. Ever since he came back, my life has been...hell!"

"*Dochter*, you don't mean that. Please, apologize to your papa."

"I won't apologize to someone that's...that's *verrückt*!"

"Rachel!"

"So, I'm crazy, am I? Well, we'll see. Go on. You want to leave, just go. Get out of my house."

"Your house? Your house? I've lived here longer than you. You come back and think you can just take over and order us around. Papa, I don't even know you. I'll go, and maybe I won't come back!"

Rachel swung around, slamming the screen door in the face of the man who was following her. She ran down the steps and out onto the lane before her papa could catch her.

Jonathan Hershberger opened the door and watched his daughter run away through the field. His wife, Jenny, came out and watched their daughter go. Jenny's face was pale and her eyes were red.

Jonathan put his hand to his head. "My head hurts, Jenny. Help me inside."

Jenny dabbed her eyes with a handkerchief. "You are not supposed to get angry. The doctor said you could have a stroke."

"I know, Jenny, but I can't help myself. There is something in Rachel that pushes me over the edge."

"In her, Jonathan, or in you?"

It was a cold, wet, March day in Paradise. The predominant color was brown—brown stubble, brown earth, dead grass in the front yard. The small swale beyond the pasture fence was filled with runoff from the winter snowmelt, and the leaden surface drearily mirrored the gray clouds gathered above the Hershberger farm.

Rachel Hershberger trudged down the path. Her feet sank into the soft mud, and the edges of her dress soon bore the stains of her ill-advised trail breaking. Her face was red, and a single tear streaked her cheek. She spoke out loud to no one in particular. "Why did he have to come back? Everything was fine without him."

Now the tears began to flow freely, seemingly eager to mar the loveliness of her face. Her dark auburn hair was held tightly in a bun beneath her *kappe*, and the wool jacket she wore over her plain dress kept out the March chill. But nothing eased the chill in her heart.

The squishing of her boots, an occasional sob and the rippling sound of the little creek off to her right played a strangely discordant concerto that jarred against the serenity all around her. She came at last to the main road. As she walked, Rachel was absorbed in her sorrow and did not pay attention to the soft clop of the horse's hooves behind her until the small buggy pulled up next to her.

"A bit chilly for a walk in the mud, isn't it, Rachel?"

Rachel looked up into the kindly face of Daniel King. He sat on the buggy seat with a quizzical look on his face.

"Go away, Daniel. I don't need your indefatigable good nature right now."

"Indefatigable! *Ja*, now there's a fifty-dollar word. Come on, Rachel, hop in and I'll take you wherever you're going and keep you tidy at the same time."

Rachel stopped and looked up at Daniel. His handsome, beardless face smiled at her from under the black hat, and he sat straight and tall. Rachel's shoulders dropped and she sighed. She wanted to be by herself, but her hike through the mud had worn her out. She climbed up on the seat next to Daniel.

"You and your papa fighting again?"

"Yes, if it's any of your business!"

"Look, Rachel, don't go there. You have spoken with me many times about Jonathan, so it's not a secret. What was it this time?"

Rachel slumped down in the seat. "I signed up for another animal husbandry class, but my papa told me to drop it."

"Why, because Amish girls are supposed to stay home after eighth grade and learn to be obedient little servants?"

Rachel looked at Daniel in surprise. "Something like that."

She looked again. Daniel wasn't smiling. He was staring straight ahead, and his face was set in a stern mask.

"Why, Daniel, you surprise me. I wouldn't expect anything like that out of you."

Daniel shook the reins over the back of the horse and relaxed. The smile returned to his face, and he looked over at Rachel. "There's a lot you don't know about me. I'd be more willing to share it if…if you'd let me court you."

Rachel turned away abruptly and stared out at the brown fields of Paradise, Pennsylvania. "Don't, Daniel. You're my friend, but that's all. Besides, I don't want to get married. I have…other plans."

The barbed remark didn't ruffle Daniel's calm demeanor. "So what will you do, Rachel? Run away to the city and become an animal doctor? Couldn't you find work here?"

Rachel turned back to Daniel, and now there was excitement in her voice.

"Don't you see? It's not the 1800s anymore, it's 1990. There's so much more to life than an Amish farm in Paradise, Pennsylvania. There's music and art and museums—the whole world to see. I want to see the pyramids. I want to go to the Louvre and stay there for weeks. Daniel, don't you ever want to go, to see, to do?"

Daniel looked down at the reins in his strong hands. "No. I want to work with my papa, and then take over the farm someday and raise the finest horses in Pennsylvania."

Rachel gave an exasperated sigh. "And that's why we could never be together. I want to be part of something bigger, and in order to do that I... I..."

"Can't stay Amish?"

Rachel looked at him. The answer lay heavy between them in a silence broken only by the soft clopping of the horse's hooves.

When Rachel banged back through the door, Jenny was sitting on the sofa. Her face was sad. She lifted her finger to her lips.

Rachel pulled off her coat. "Where's Papa?"

"He's sleeping, Rachel. He got a bad headache. You know that it hurts him physically when you fight with him."

Rachel looked down. She felt bad, but she wasn't going to back down. "Mama, is he the only one who lives here? Why do we have to tiptoe around all the time?"

Jenny motioned for Rachel to come sit beside her. Rachel plopped down stiffly beside her mama. Jenny's arm circled Rachel's waist. She pushed through the stiffness and pulled her daughter close. Rachel finally relaxed and put her head on Jenny's shoulder. Soft sobs began to shake Rachel's body. Jenny reached over and stroked her daughter's cheek.

"I know it's difficult...to have Jonathan home. He

still struggles with what happened on the boat. He watched his parents die and it hurt him so."

"I know, Mama, and I feel sorry for him, but he's so hard to live with."

Jenny turned Rachel's face toward her. "Rachel, your papa was a different man for eight years. He lost any memory of being Jonathan Hershberger, of being an Amish man, of you and me and our home here in Paradise."

"I know, Mama, but—"

Jenny put her fingers softly on Rachel's lips. "Let me finish. Before your papa converted to the Amish faith he was an atheist, or at least an agnostic. He had tried drugs and different religions. He thought he was going to be a famous musician, and if he hadn't met me, he probably would have been. When he lost his memory, he went back to what he knew—playing music. He became famous and made a lot of money."

Rachel stirred. "I know, Mama, but it doesn't explain why he's so strict with me."

Jenny sighed and put her hand to her face to brush away a tear. Rachel saw the involuntary movement and her heart softened.

This really hurts my mama. She also wishes things were not this way.

Rachel's arms crept around Jenny. "Oh, Mama, I'm sorry. I know this makes you sad."

"Yes, *dochter*, I am sad. Sad for the years we missed, you and I, with your papa. Sad for the pain that your papa went through, and I am sad that you and he are not close like you were. But I am also grateful. I thank *du lieber Gott* every day that Jonathan came back to me…to us. I thank Him for the miracle He performed when my heart was broken beyond hope. Your papa and I were made for each other. We are two lives and one heart. It is a very special thing that *Gott* does. That is His plan for marriage, and someday I hope you will find the same joy. Jonathan and I had ten wonderful years together. When he disappeared and I thought he was dead...."

Jenny paused and dabbed her eyes. "Rachel, when your papa came home, he did not really know who he was. Sometimes he goes back to being Richard Sandbridge, and that is what confuses you. One minute he is a strict Amish man and the next he is an easy-going musician. The only thing that has saved your papa is the *Ordnung*. He clings to them like a life preserver, because some days that is the only way he knows who he is. So he tries to live by them as best he can just to stay Amish. That's why he is so strict. He believes that keeping the *Ordnung* will make him all right with *Gott*. He forgets that the *Ordnung* can't save us."

Rachel took her mama's hand and kissed it. "I'm sorry, Mama. I don't understand this sometimes, but I do love Papa. I'll try to do better."

"And I love you and will try also, *dochter*."

The women looked up to see Jonathan standing in the doorway. He held out his arms and Rachel rose and went to him. She held onto him and hid her face against his chest.

I hope so, Papa. I truly hope so.

Chapter Two

A Longing

Rachel was unhappy. Even though the sun was shining and the muddy fields around her were beginning to dry up, and the first faint breath of spring touched the air around her with a promise of the fragrance to come, Rachel didn't notice. The weather had changed for the better, but it hadn't changed the gloom in her heart. She pushed her scooter down Leacock Road, headed for the Old Philadelphia Turnpike.

After the fight with her papa, things had been quiet for a week. But soon Jonathan seemed to forget his promise and started riding her about little things again; the way she did her chores, the way she wore her clothes, her devotion to Bible study or lack thereof. Everything seemed to touch a sore spot in her *daed* and bring forth a caustic comment or a curt instruction. That is, when he was her papa. At other times, he seemed confused and disoriented, looking for the telephone that wasn't there or asking where his guitar was.

It had been four years since Jonathan returned to

Paradise. He had been gone for eight years, and the day of his return, though miraculous and joyous, had been the first day of the most confusing and vexing time in Rachel's life.

As Rachel pushed her scooter along, she tried to remember the days before the accident, when she and her papa had been so close. But the memories were hard to come by, like fragments of a wonderful dream that seems so real in the safety of slumber, but, upon awakening, can only be recalled in bits and pieces, finally to dissolve in the shadows of forgetfulness. And that was Rachel's remembrance of her papa—a dream that could not be recaptured, a golden time that had somehow been replaced with the reality of a confused and angry man who did not seem to care if Rachel loved him or not.

At last, Rachel came to the crossroads. She turned right and began to walk along the side of The Old Philadelphia Turnpike. She loved the houses along this road. They were grand and palatial—so different from the Amish houses—and Rachel wondered what life was like for the people who lived in them. She could only imagine what it might be like to be the daughter of one of these wealthy families, attending a private high school and then having to decide which college to attend. She dreamed of all the things that rich girls would do—things like dating and proms, playing sports and owning a car, taking long vacations to romantic places.

I feel like a foreigner. Look at me, pushing this stupid scooter down the road in this silly outfit, wearing this dumb hat. Why can't I just be like everybody else?

Rachel wondered if it was a sin to think that way.

If they only knew what really goes on behind the four walls of a typical Amish home. We are just the same as everyone else. We fight, we treat each other badly, we can't figure out our relationship with Gott, *or even if He's real…*

Rachel stopped and looked up. She had never thought about the reality of *Gott* in this way and it made her nervous. After an anxious moment, she walked on, trying to get her thoughts back to romanticizing the lives of the people who lived in the mansions along the Pike. But somehow her thinking about *Gott* got in the way of her dreaming. She was tense and ill at ease, and suddenly she felt like she might throw up. She wanted to take the scooter and fling it into the ditch. She wanted to pull off this silly *kappe* and let her long auburn hair flow free in the wind. She felt her heart racing so she stopped and took some deep breaths.

I have to do something. I have to get away from Papa…

"Rachel?"

She jumped involuntarily and then turned. Daniel King was sitting in his buggy a few feet away. "Lost in your thoughts?"

Rachel felt a surge of anger toward Daniel. "Oh my goodness, Daniel, *sie erschraken mich!* Why are you always sneaking up on me? What are you doing here?"

Daniel frowned and then he lifted his hand to silence her. "Rachel, your *maam* told me you would be coming this way—I need your help."

Suddenly Rachel felt foolish. She blushed and lowered her eyes. "What's wrong?"

"One of my mares is foaling and the baby is positioned wrong."

"Have you called the vet?"

"Yes, but he's not available. He's away over on the

far side of Lancaster, and my papa is in Hallam. I can't wait for them. The mare might die. That's why I'm asking you to come help me."

Rachel lifted her scooter into the buggy and climbed up on the seat beside Daniel. He turned the horse and started back toward the King farm. Rachel sat on the seat with her head down and her cheeks burning.

After a while, Daniel spoke. "I'm your friend, Rachel. I only want the best for you. I came to find you because, next to the vet, you're the best person with sick animals that I know."

"Yes, and if my papa would let me go to college, I could be a vet."

Daniel chucked the horse again and replied, "You're eighteen years old. You can make some decisions for yourself."

"Yes, but the *Ordnung* forbid girls going to school past the eighth grade. What about that?"

"The policy toward extra schooling is not as harsh as you think. Often girls are allowed to continue if the elders see that there will be benefit to the Amish community. In your case, the benefit would be a good, non-*Englischer* vet to help the Amish farmers. After all, Rachel, like you said, it is 1990, not the middle ages anymore."

"But you don't understand. I have a dream. I don't want to just become someone who works for a vet. I want to go to Cornell University's College of Veterinary Medicine."

"But that's far away, isn't it?"

"Ithaca, New York, to be exact."

Suddenly Rachel was excited and she reached in her pocket and pulled out a folded up piece of paper.

"It's the very best college of veterinary medicine in the whole county. They have two hundred and eleven faculty and seven hundred and thirty-two non-academic staff members for only three hundred and sixty students. They have an incredible graduate studies program where you can work toward either a Master of Science or Doctor of Philosophy degree. There are internships and residency programs. Oh, Daniel! Wouldn't it be wonderful?"

Daniel sat quietly and then smiled. "You must have that brochure memorized. Does Jonathan know about this? And how are you going to get in? You only have an eighth grade education."

Rachel slumped down in her seat. "I know, but I got straight As in school, and Papa did let me take some courses at the Junior College in Lancaster. I did really well there. And... I've already written a letter to the Dean of Admissions explaining my situation. Maybe they would let me in as a hardship case."

Daniel shook his head. "You have a lot to overcome. It might be very difficult."

Rachel felt a twisting inside her. She wanted to scream at Daniel.

You just don't understand, Daniel. I don't want to be Amish, I don't want to be married, I just want this!

They sat in silence. When they arrived at the King farm, Daniel drove straight back to the barn, and they climbed out and hurried in. The mare was lying down on her side in a stall. Her legs were sticking out straight and stiff. Rachel could see the muscles contracting as she pushed to get the foal out.

"Get a bale of grass hay and spread it all around

the stall. And then get me a clean bed sheet. Quickly, Daniel!"

Daniel ran to get the sheet as Rachel knelt beside the mare.

She shouted after the retreating Daniel. "And bring a blanket, Ivermectin, and Banamine, if you have it. Oh, and a squirt bottle of iodine!"

Rachel turned back to the mare and gently caressed her face, rubbing around the ears.

"Come on, mama, we are here now. Don't worry, we will help you get this baby out."

The mare continued pushing. She was grunting softly and her tongue flicked in and out. Daniel arrived back with the supplies.

"Give me the sheet, Daniel!"

Rachel spread the sheet under the mare's hindquarters and examined the mare closely. "I see the birth sac and I can feel the foal's nose, but it looks like the shoulder is wedged inside. I'm going to reach in and grab a leg and shift the baby."

As she did that, the mare moved and suddenly the foal's nose and two front hooves emerged. Rachel tore away the sac and grabbed the front legs.

"Help me pull, Daniel, but only pull downward, just one tug."

Daniel took hold of the foal with Rachel and together they gave a quick tug downward. The head and shoulders popped out and Rachel smiled.

"Things will happen rather quickly now."

And then the foal was out and lying next to its mother. Rachel squeezed the liquid out of the tiny foal's nose with a gentle downward motion. The foal and the mother lay quietly, still connected by the umbilical cord. The foal shifted and the cord broke.

"Squirt the iodine right on the navel stump, Daniel. Now give me the Ivermectin and the Banamine."

Rachel estimated the mare's weight and gave her an oral dose from each bottle.

The little colt tried to stand up. It struggled for a minute and then suddenly stood up on shaky legs.

"It is a filly, Daniel, strong and beautiful. Put the blanket around her and keep her warm."

Daniel looked at Rachel with admiration in his eyes. "You were wonderful."

Rachel smiled at the praise. "I'm surprised that you didn't know more about birthing. You love horses so much."

"I have watched many times, but my *daed* always has the vet do it and he helps. You did a great job. My papa will be pleased and grateful."

Daniel paused. Then he put his arm around Rachel's shoulders. "You have a gift. If you want to go to college, then I support you in this."

Rachel stared at Daniel for a moment and then threw her arms around him. "Thank you, Daniel."

Daniel's arms wrapped around Rachel and they stood that way for a minute and then Rachel realized what was happening. She pulled away, her face burning hot. Daniel's hands fell awkwardly to his sides.

"But how will you do it, Rachel? Isn't it very expensive? And how will you convince your *daed*?"

"I do not know the answers to those questions, Daniel. But I know this. If I can get the money to go, I'm going whether Papa gives me permission or not."

Chapter Three

The Inheritance

Augusta St. Clair marched into the offices of Murray, Peterson and Lowell. Augusta was a formidable looking woman with perfectly coifed white hair wearing an obviously expensive, charcoal business suit. The extremely handsome young man beside her had a look of extreme boredom on his face. Behind them trotted an older woman who tried to intervene. "Maybe we shouldn't go in Mrs. St. Clair. I think—"

"Shut your mouth, Eva," Augusta snapped. She pushed her way past the startled secretary into the inner sanctum of the prestigious law firm. Several pieces of paper were clutched in her hand.

James Lowell looked up from his desk. His face paled. "Augusta, I can't see you right now. I'm in the middle—"

Augusta St. Clair cut him off with an imperious wave of her hand. "You will see me right now, James."

James Lowell sighed and looked over at the two men in the chairs facing him. "Well, gentlemen, it seems we will have to discuss this matter later."

One of the men stood. "This is a five million dollar deal—"

Augusta cut in. "Mr. Carrington. I could buy your crummy factory and shut it down today. If you don't want that to happen, I would suggest you come back another day. Goodbye."

She turned to the man behind the desk as the chastened visitors slunk out the door. The young man found a chair and started to light a cigarette. At a warning look from Augusta, he put the pack back in his pocket. Eva stood waiting for a command.

Augusta flung the stack of papers down on James Lowell's desk. "Just what is this?"

Lowell swallowed hard, picked up the top document, and adjusted his glasses. "Oh, you got my letter."

"Don't play games with me, Jimmy. I want to know what this means."

James Lowell put the sheaf of papers down. "I thought I made myself very clear, Augusta. I have looked over everything and I have concluded that I must deny your request."

"You have concluded?" Augusta laughed. "You little pipsqueak! You don't deny anything; you do what I say. Now you call the trustees and tell them to sign the papers, or you will wish you had never been born."

A bead of sweat formed on Lowell's forehead.

"I can't. They won't have it. The inheritance directives are over four hundred years old and there is not a person on the board who will deviate from them— not one inch!"

"Oohh!"

Augusta's face began to turn red. Eva touched her shoulder.

Augusta turned sharply. "What is it, Eva?"

The woman's face went pale. "Please, Mrs. St. Clair, you know what the doctor said. Your heart…"

Augusta's face worked convulsively. Finally, she took three deep breaths. Her voice was evenly modulated and low.

"You're right, Eva. I don't want to have a heart attack." She turned back to Lowell. "I wouldn't want to die before Jimmy does."

The young man tried to mollify things. "Threats won't help the situation, Grandmother."

"I'll tell you when to speak, Gerald."

Gerald closed his mouth and kept silent.

Augusta leaned on James Lowell's desk. "No, James, I wouldn't want anything to happen to you…" Augusta paused meaningfully while Lowell turned even paler.

Then Augusta smiled and patted James Lowell on the hand. "Oh, I'm just playing with you, Jimmy," she said, but her eyes told a different story. "Now, tell me exactly what the board said."

Lowell wiped the sweat off his brow, adjusted his glasses again, and pushed a stack of papers toward Augusta. "It's all in here."

Augusta ignored the papers. "Just give me the Cliffs-Notes version."

Lowell looked helplessly at Gerald. "You can keep your trust, you can keep the house and the estate, but no one inherits the bulk of the money unless they are a direct descendant of the oldest son and have the Key. That's the bottom line."

"The Key? And what is the Key?"

James Lowell shrugged. "I don't have the slightest

idea. I would suggest you contact Michel Duvigney. He's the director of the board of trustees."

Augusta walked toward the door. Without glancing back, she spoke to Eva. "Eva, get the pertinent information from Mr. Lowell and set an appointment with Mr. Duvigney."

"Yes, Mrs. St. Clair."

Augusta opened the door and then stopped and looked back at James Lowell. "When I settle this, I will settle with you, Jimmy. Nobody stands in my way. It's a bad decision. Come, Gerald!"

With that, she turned and stomped out, her grandson and secretary trailing along.

Three days later, Augusta sat in the office of Michel Duvigney. It was small and cramped with red cherry wood bookshelves lining the walls. The desk was the largest piece of furniture in the room. Pictures of Duvigney with well-known people, including three ex-presidents, hung on the wall. Dim afternoon light tried to force its way through the drawn venetian blinds, but the only real illumination came from the small lamp on the desk.

Duvigney was old, but somehow the lines of age had not marked themselves too deeply on his features. His white hair and crow's feet around his eyes were the only giveaways. Augusta sat stiffly while Duvigney went over the paperwork in front of him. Finally, he lifted the whole pile, tapped the bottom twice on the desk to even the documents up, and set it aside.

Then he spoke in a quiet, sibilant voice. "I'm sorry, Augusta, but there is no other decision that can be made. The directives for the succession of the St. Clair inheritance are quite explicit. Only the direct descendants of an eldest son can inherit. It can be male or female as long as it can be proved that the eldest son was either father or grandfather to the heir."

Duvigney took a folder from the pile and opened it.

He scanned it for a moment. "I see that you are the widow of Jerod St. Clair, the younger son of Maximillian St. Clair. Jerod was killed in World War II in a mission over France. You had one son with Jerod…"

Duvigney glanced down. "… Ah, yes, Francis, who is also deceased, as is his wife."

"They died in a skiing accident in Switzerland, an avalanche…"

"Yes, I have the details here. So, Augusta, even though you are the sole beneficiary of your late husband's will, which entitles you to his portion of the St. Clair trust, the house you are living in, the property in Connecticut, and the townhouse in London, you persist in pressing your claim to the bulk of the estate which is in trust for the true heir, a claim that is without merit."

Augusta twisted in her chair.

"Well, if I'm not able to inherit, what about my grandson, Gerald? Shouldn't he be considered?"

Duvigney's voice took on a tone that sounded like a snake hissing. "Augusta, you don't seem to be following me. The St. Clair family is over eight hundred years old. The precedents for preserving the lineage and the inheritance were established hundreds of years ago in Europe. You, as a relative newcomer to the family, cannot seem to grasp the significance of the St. Clair traditions."

Augusta stiffened. "Excuse me, Michel, but my family has a very old and proud name. We are descended from the royal families of Russia. We have traditions as well."

Duvigney smiled again. "Excuse me, Augusta, but your family is not descended from the Romanovs. Your grandfather was a Yugoslavian immigrant named Alexzander Bošnjaković who was a cheese maker in New York. Your father was a used car salesman who changed his name to Bosnan so his customers could pronounce it. Your real name is Francine Bosnan, and you were born to a lower middle class family in The Bronx. Compared to the St. Clairs, your family doesn't have traditions, it has habits."

Duvigney's face cracked for a moment at his attempt at humor. The effect was not pleasant.

He glanced down at the dossier. "You met Jerod at a USO dance in Manhattan in August of 1944 and began seeing him on a regular basis. You arranged to become pregnant before he was sent to England in February 1945. Jerod married you three weeks before he left and, *voilà*, you were the wealthy Augusta St. Clair, possessor of a proud name and a mysterious background, a background which you invented."

Duvigney smiled in a patronizing way that infuriated Augusta, but she held her tongue.

"Sadly, Jerod was killed on a bombing run over Germany a week after he arrived in England. Your son, Francis, was born three months later in June 1945."

Michel picked up a pencil and tapped it a few times on his desk. "You see, Augusta, we do our homework. It was your husband's older brother, Robert, who was the true heir to the St. Clair fortune. It has come to our attention that he was also married and had a child, but the wife and child disappeared."

Augusta stared at the old man. "How did you find out about Robert's wife and child?"

Duvigney showed the first signs of exasperation. "Ms. St. Clair! For years we believed that Robert died without an heir, and so Robert's trust was a closed account waiting until we could take action to declare a new heir. When you came forward to press your claims, the case was re-opened, and during that new investigation, certain facts came to light, including a copy of a marriage license issued to Robert St. Clair and Rachel Borntraeger, dated September 15, 1946. We also found a birth certificate for their daughter, Jennifer Constance St. Clair, dated January of 1947. Robert St. Clair was killed in a car accident, but the whereabouts of the wife and daughter remains unknown. Our representatives are conducting a search for them. If we find her or the child and they can prove relationship to Robert through DNA testing, or if the daughter has the Key, then they will be invested with the bulk of the trust estate which totals…"

Duvigney reached over and pulled out a spreadsheet. "…around forty billion dollars in investments and properties."

Augusta clamped her jaw shut to keep from gasping. Finally, she spoke. "May I ask you a question, Michel?"

"Yes?"

"What is the Key?"

Duvigney's face took on a serious mien. "The Key is the St. Clair Key. It is a birthmark that was found on the first St. Clair in 1123. It is a red, key-shaped mark that is located above the heart. This birthmark has determined the heir for centuries. It sometimes skips generations but it has always followed the line. Your brother-in-law, Robert, had this birthmark, but your husband did not.

If we find an heir that carries the Key, there will be absolutely no question as to the validity of their claim. They will be immediately granted title to everything."

"Even if they are female?"

"A woman may inherit if she has the Key, but only to the second generation from the direct heir. If no heir is found, then fifty years after the heir's death, the board of trustees will follow the other lines of descent and name the closest St. Clair male the new heir. This prevents internecine strife."

"Internecine strife?"

"Family members killing each other for the money. It seems that in the fourteenth century, certain of the St. Clair brothers attempted to murder each other, so strict guidelines were set in place by their father."

"So you are saying that Robert's daughter could inherit, if she has the Key, or his granddaughter or grandson. But if they could not be found, then the fortune would go to the next St. Clair male which would be Gerald?"

"Not exactly, Augusta. Robert died forty-four years ago. Gerald would become the next in line six years from now, but only his heirs could inherit. Gerald would have to have a child who reaches the age of twenty-one. Then the estate would be invested in that heir. And so the line would continue."

Duvigney glanced at his Rolex. "I'm sorry, Augusta, but that is all the time I have. I'm afraid there is no further use in your pursuit of this claim. Now, if you will excuse me—"

A door behind Augusta opened and a large man stepped into the room. The signal was clear. The meeting was over.

As their limousine cruised up Park Avenue, Augusta sat in the back, fuming. "Why that pompous, overblown secretary! Who does he think he is?" Augusta knew she had to make a plan. She picked up the car phone from the armrest next to her and dialed a number. A man's voice answered.

"Gordon Randall Security."

"Randall, this is Augusta St. Clair. I need you to do some work for me."

"What do you need?"

"I need you to find a little girl; well, she would be grown up now. Her mother was married to Robert St. Clair. She was from Lancaster, Pennsylvania and she was Amish. Her name was Rachel Borntraeger. That's about all I have. I'll leave the rest up to you."

"Fine, Mrs. St. Clair. Any other instructions?"

"Yes, Randall. Other people are looking for this girl. It is imperative that you find her first."

"Fine, Mrs. St. Clair. Consider it handled."

Chapter Four

Painful Days

The grey-green sea rolled in long, choppy swells beneath the boat, the waves moving toward him out of the mist. It was dark, so dark, and the smell of the salt water was terrifying. A stiff breeze drove the icy spray off the tops of the waves into Jonathan's eyes, blinding him. The chill of winter…the gulls circling behind the boat…the plaintive cries whirling away on the wind. The sea, ominous and dead…

He stood in the gloom and the cold spray and the endless waves, rolling, rolling, rolling by, and where were they going? He was lost, gone, alone on the bridge of a ghost ship. He looked through the window into the wheelhouse, but there was no one to pilot the boat. Where was the captain? Then he felt a hand touch him. He turned to see his dad standing there, but Dad was dead, dead as the grey-green waves.

Jonathan's dad smiled. "Thank you, son." And then Dad was gone, gone like a breeze that touches the face on a desert day and then slips away, leaving only regret behind.

But I'm not in the desert. I'm on this boat on the ocean and I'm alone and lost in the shadows and I'm freezing. Dad! Dad! Help me, please.

Then the explosion! The huge boat twisted like a snake, and the abrupt distortion threw Jonathan to the deck. As he lay there, stunned, his mother came out of her stateroom.

Mom! But she's dead, too! What's happening?

Then there was fire and smoke and another explosion. And then he was deep in the water, and above him the waves churned. It was so cold, and he couldn't breathe. And then he was swimming, swimming upward toward the light and the fire on the water. His head broke the surface and he gasped for air. Burning diesel fuel covered the waves and he felt the fire burning his face, burning, melting, reaching for his eyes…

And then he saw his mother and father again, not twenty feet away on the boat, and they were smiling. *"Dad, Mom!"*

Dad looked straight into Jonathan's eyes. He reached his hand toward Jonathan but he wasn't afraid. Jonathan couldn't hear him over the wind, but he saw his father's mouth forming words.

"Son, I believe!"

At that instant, the *Mistral* exploded with a roar. Jonathan struggled in the water. He was in the fire and the water, burning and drowning. The grey-green waves rolled over the deck and Mistral sank. Within seconds, there was nothing left except some floating pieces of wreckage driving west before the howling wind.

Jenny! Jenny!

"JENNY!"

"Jonathan! Jonathan! Wake up!"

Jonathan groaned and rolled over. He opened his eyes and stared into the face of the lovely woman beside him in the bed. "What? Where am I? Who are you?"

"Jonathan, it's me, it's your Jenny. I'm here, beloved, right here. You were dreaming."

Jonathan clutched at the woman's arm. "I've got to find Jenny and Rachel. I'm lost and I can't find them. Help me."

The woman placed her hand over Jonathan's eyes. Her skin was warm and alive, not dead like the horrible, killing sea. He heard her voice from a long way off.

"Close your eyes, Jonathan."

Jonathan closed his eyes beneath her hand.

"Now see your Jenny in your mind's eye. See her face, her red hair, the love for you in her eyes."

A face, beautiful, framed by unruly golden-red curls… A white *kappe*, the eyes filled with love and compassion.

Jenny, it's you, my Jenny.

"Do you see her?"

"Yes, I see her. She's coming to find me."

"Now open your eyes, Jonathan."

He opened his eyes. They were still covered by the woman's hand. Slowly, she lifted it away, pausing to lightly caress his face. He looked at her. The beautiful face with age lines showing but still her face, the curls with a touch of white among them, but still Jenny's curls…

It's Jenny, my Jenny.

"Jenny, Jenny…"

"Yes, beloved, it's me. I'm here, I'll always be here."

Peace flooded Jonathan's soul. He was with his Jenny in his house in Paradise. He pulled her tight against him. He breathed the fragrance of her against his cheek. There was life here; life and safety and home. They lay quietly together.

"Was it the dream, Jonathan?"

"I was back on the boat. My dad and mom... I watched them die but they were smiling. They weren't afraid."

"Yes, dearest, because you gave them Christ, and they went to be with Him. That was your gift to them, Jonathan. That was why God took you to see them one last time."

"But then it took me so long to get home and I get confused. Some days I wake up and I think I'm late for work and I look for my guitar and...oh, Jenny! Will I ever get well?"

"You were gone for eight years, Jonathan. I don't know why God did that, but he worked everything for good while we were apart."

"But what about your folks? They died while I was gone. I never got to see them again. I loved them."

"I know, and they loved you also. My papa was so proud of you. He saw how *du leiber Gott* worked in your life, how much you loved me, and how precious Rachel was to you. It was as though you were Amish all your life. You belonged to us."

Jonathan released his wife and swung his legs over the edge of the bed. He sat for a while, his head in his hands, quiet. Jenny reached out and began to rub his back.

Jonathan gave a deep sigh. "I am sorry that Rachel and I are having so much trouble. I don't want to be hard with her. When she starts talking about going out in the world, I get frightened. I know what's out there, and I fear for her."

Jenny was quiet for a few minutes. Then she spoke.

"When I was a little girl, I came to live with my mama and papa in Apple Creek. I did not know who I was. I remembered but a little bit about my real mama. Then you helped me find out about my parents."

"Yes, but what—?"

Jenny put her fingers on his lips. "Don't you see, Jonathan? *Gott* sent me to Apple Creek to fill a terrible, empty place in my mama's heart."

"… After your sister, Jenna, died."

"Yes, and that was a wonderful thing. But if I never came to Apple Creek, we never would have met, there would be no home in Paradise, there would be no Rachel."

"But that doesn't answer my questions about me, Jenny, why I act this way, why I am so harsh."

"My papa struggled with the same things for many years. During World War II, he rejected his faith and joined the Marines. He ended up on Guadalcanal. He had to kill Japanese soldiers. It did something to his heart and his mind. My mama told me that when he came home he was different. He rejoined the church out of fear. He felt as though he had committed a terrible sin during the war, and he believed that if he just kept the rules of the church, somehow he would be allowed to go to heaven. It was because he was so strict that my sister, Jenna, died. It was a terrible thing, but *Gott griff nach seinem Herzen. Gott* was reaching for his heart."

Jonathan turned to look at Jenny's face. "Do you think the same thing has happened to me?"

Jenny paused. "In a way, yes. When you became a Christian, you understood that the church doesn't save us. Only Jesus can do that. But there were other parts of your life that you found difficult to surrender to God— your love for music, your gifts as a songwriter. You never sold your guitar, and sometimes I would hear you out in the barn playing softly so no one would hear you."

Jonathan grinned. "You heard me?"

"Yes, dearest. I never said anything because I love your songs and your wonderful voice. It was your song that led me to you when I found you again in that nightclub."

Jenny smiled with the memory. Then she went on. "That may have been what the Lord was reaching for in your life—to surrender everything to Him so that if you did play music it would only be for His glory, or even to set it down altogether so that there would be no idols in your life that were above Him."

Jonathan's brow furrowed. "So you think He might have let me live as Richard Sandbridge so I could see what my life would be like if my dreams came true?"

"Were you happy then?"

"No, Jenny. Even when I had hit songs and lots of money, there was always something missing—something I would have traded everything for."

"Like the pearl of great price that was found in the field?"

"Yes, Jenny, exactly. And when you found me at that nightclub, when all my dreams were coming true, it was so easy to put it all down and come home. This farm, this land, this is who I am. And you and Rachel are worth more to me than all the gold records in the world. But then I get frightened."

"When you have the dream?"

"Yes, the dream. I'm lost and floating on the sea. I'm clinging to a piece of wood and the waves are crashing on me, and all I want is to come home, to sit by the fire with my wife beside me and my little girl on my lap."

Jenny put her arms around Jonathan. "So maybe the *Ordnung* are like that piece of wood that you clung to all those days in the ocean. And perhaps that is why you are so strict—because the *Ordnung* are like a life preserver for you. They keep you centered and hold the world at bay."

"Yes, Jenny, you are probably right."

"So even if they are that way for you, maybe they are not that way for Rachel?"

Jonathan thought for a moment. "So I am forcing my fears on Rachel?"

"Yes, it appears that way."

Jonathan stood up and went to the window. Outside, the air was bursting with the clean, strong smell of the fields—his fields. The first growth of the spring planting was beginning to show green against the brown earth. Jonathan saw a small bird sitting in a tree. It had black feathers on its topknot with brilliant yellow underneath. It trilled a short song and then flitted away.

That was an Oriole. I've never seen one on the farm before.

A breeze shook the flowers on the plum trees and the pink petals drifted down in a magical shower. The clouds above were showing golden as the day began to grow.

"I think I understand what you are saying. I will try to remember, but sometimes it is so hard, Jenny. I will be working at something, and then I'll be staring at the tool in my hands, wondering how to use it. It's as though I'm standing outside my body, observing me and wondering what I am doing. Thoughts come to me and I can't unlock them, and I know that if I could just get back inside me, everything would be all right again."

"I know you struggle, Jonathan. The doctors have told me that you still suffer from the effects of your injuries. They said you might never be well, but I am trusting the Lord for that. I know that you will be healed, and until then, I will take care of you."

Jonathan turned back to Jenny and pulled her up into his arms. The smell of her was like a beacon in a black night, the feel of her body pressed against him was like a breath of air to a drowning man.

"I am so grateful for you, my darling Jenny. I want to be healed from this. I just hope I don't drive Rachel away before I am."

Chapter Five

The Search

Gordon Randall sat comfortably in the chair across the desk from Augusta St. Clair. He was looking at a few sheets of paper in front of him. A crooked smile broke the harsh contours of his hawk-like features.

"So what have you found out, Randall?" Augusta asked sweetly.

"You may not know some of this, Mrs. St. Clair, so I'm going to bring you up to speed."

Augusta leaned back and folded her hands in her lap, with the fingers intertwined. "Go ahead."

"As you know, Augusta, your brother-in-law, Robert, married a young girl on September 14, 1946. At that time, he was living in Lancaster, Pennsylvania. The girl's maiden name was Rachel Mary Borntraeger. Rachel Borntraeger was born in Lancaster County, Pennsylvania, May 12, 1928. A midwife filed the birth certificate. I have the certificate here. She was eighteen years old when she married Robert St. Clair. Robert was twenty-six. Robert and Rachel had one child, Jennifer

Constance St. Clair, born in January of 1947. The interesting thing in all of this is that Rachel was Amish."

"Amish. Yes, I heard that from my mother-in-law. When Robert told his parents that he had gotten the girl pregnant, Max, my father-in-law, told Robert to pay off the girl, but Robert refused and married her. Max believed that Rachel Borntraeger had deliberately failed to take the necessary precautions in order to hook a wealthy young man into marriage. Max never forgave Robert but Margaret, my mother-in-law, was heartbroken. She loved children. She was such a sentimental old fool."

Augusta paused. "I met the girl, you know."

Randall was surprised. "When was that, Mrs. St. Clair?"

"In the spring of 1950. After Robert was killed in the car wreck a young woman showed up on the doorstep of the city house with a toddler. She said her name was Rachel St. Clair and the youngster was Robert's child. She wanted to see Max or Margaret. Max had passed by then and Margaret was getting senile. I felt it was my duty to protect Margaret so I sent them away."

Randall made a note on one of the sheets of paper. "And then what happened?"

"The woman persisted in contacting us. She came to the house a second time and I had the police escort her off the property and warn her not to continue disturbing us."

"Did she stop?"

"No. She called again and said that she had documentary proof that she and Robert were married and the baby was Robert's. I refused to see her or let her bother Margaret. I was only fulfilling my responsibility as a dutiful daughter-in-law."

Randall grinned, although the grin was hardly friendly. "Can I be blunt, Augusta?"

"Speak your mind, Randall."

"You were never a dutiful daughter-in-law. The truth is, you are not who you pretend to be. You are not descended from Russian royalty, you are the former Francine Bosnan, who married into a fortune, and you have been protecting yourself ever since."

Augusta scowled. "Duvigney knew about me, too. Somehow my life has become an open book."

Randall went on. "It's my guess you knew exactly who this girl was, and she represented a threat to your status in the family. So you took swift action against Rachel Borntraeger St. Clair."

A look of mock dismay crossed Augusta's face. "Why, Randall! How can you accuse me of such a thing?"

Randall laughed. "You can stop blowing smoke in my ear, Augusta. Just tell me what you did to the girl."

Augusta tried glowering at Randall. He didn't bite. Finally, she spoke. "I sent the police to her hotel to find the documents."

"By police, do you mean the cops you own in the Manhattan NYPD?"

Augusta glared at Randall. "It is important for a family of our stature to have connections in the right places."

"Uh-huh. And what happened when you sent the boys round to steal the documents?"

"They found some evidence, photos of Robert and

the girl, things of that nature—but no wedding or birth certificates. She must have hidden them."

Randall looked at his notes. "And what other action did you take?"

"What makes you think I took further action?"

Randall sighed, put the notes back into the folder, and started to get up.

"Where are you going, Randall?"

"Look, I don't have time to play games with you. Just give me the facts or I'll go. I have other clients, you know."

A flash of anger crossed Augusta's face. "How dare you speak to me in that manner? I can have you taken care of with a phone call."

Randall put his hands on the desk, palms down, and leaned forward. "Augusta, don't try threatening me. Maybe you've forgotten how this works. If you attempt such a course of action, there are certain files that would be immediately sent to the police and the feds. You're in way too deep with me. And you should know that along with a record of our activities, there are certain incriminating materials I've gathered. I'm very sure you would not want those materials to be made public. So let's just play nice. What did you do to the girl?"

Augusta shifted stiffly in her chair and motioned for Randall to sit back down. "Point taken, Randall. All right. I had the woman put out of the hotel. She took up with a heroin dealer named Joseph Bender. She stayed with him for a few months. Then Bender and his brother were involved in a bank robbery. The brother was captured during the holdup but Joseph Bender escaped and disappeared. I assume he took Rachel St. Clair and the baby with him, because they never returned to Bender's apartment. I was unable to track him down."

Augusta got up and went to the bay window and looked out. Then she turned and sat on the oversized sill. "My people talked to Bender's mother but she said she didn't know anything. I never heard from Rachel Borntraeger again. Since no heirs had come forward in forty years, I was sure that my claim to the estate would be undisputed. Now I find that only an heir in the line of an oldest son can inherit the principal trust, which represents billions of dollars. That's how the fortune came to Robert's father, and it would have come to Robert if he had lived."

"Can it be inherited by a female?"

"It can be inherited by a woman but only if she has the Key, and she can be only two generations away from the elder son. If the older son leaves no heirs, the trust is held for fifty years and then a younger son or the son of another branch of the St. Clair family would be nominated as the principal heir."

"What is the Key?"

"It's a birthmark, a key-shaped red mark above the heart."

"So let me get this straight, Augusta. The daughter of Robert St. Clair or his granddaughter or grandson could inherit but only if they had this Key?"

"Yes. It is the one irrefutable proof."

"And what about Gerald?"

"At this point, he could not inherit, being the second generation of a younger brother, my husband, Jerod. Robert died forty-four years ago. There are six years left and then Gerald would come into the line, but there are conditions. Gerald would be the heir, but he would not receive the money. He would have to have a son, and then his son would inherit when he reached the age of twenty-one."

"Why the long gap in determining another heir?"

Augusta smiled. "They didn't want the boys killing each other for the money."

"So unless Robert's wife is still alive, the little girl that came to the house in New York with her is the heir, if she has the Key?"

"Yes, she or Robert's grandchildren, if there are any."

"Why don't you just find the wife and Robert's little girl and eliminate them so that Gerald could be in line for the inheritance?"

Augusta got up from the window bench and returned to her desk chair. "You don't seem to understand, Randall. Gerald will not come into the line for another six years. But only Gerald's son can inherit. Gerald doesn't have a son. If he had a son tomorrow, which he won't, I would have to wait twenty-six years to get the money. I'm sixty-eight now. I would probably be moldering in the grave by then, or so old I wouldn't even know what money is. I can't wait for the fools on the board of trustees to dilly-dally around. I want that money, and I want it now!"

"So if I find Robert's wife or daughter, what are you going to do with her?"

Augusta scowled. "First of all, I don't think you will find Rachel St. Clair. She was very determined to prove that she was Robert's wife, but I have not heard a thing from her for forty years. I believe that she is dead. As for the little girl, she may be alive and if she is, I need you to find her."

"Why is it so important for you to have all that money, Augusta?"

Augusta's face narrowed and she pursed her lips. "I want it because I want it. The St. Clairs have always treated me as a second-class citizen. It will do my old heart good to take all their money and see them come begging to replenish their trusts and pay their bills."

Randall considered Augusta's words. "The only solution is to find the girl. If she is still alive, she should be about forty-three years old. But it won't be easy. You met her in 1950. That was forty years ago. A lot has happened since then."

"Randall, you are the only hope I have in this situation. We must find that girl."

"You say the man that Rachel St. Clair ended up with was Joseph Bender?"

"Yes."

"How did you know about the bank robbery?"

"Well…"

"Augusta?"

"All right. My contacts paid Bender to keep the woman addicted to drugs. He didn't know I was involved. He just knew that someone wanted the girl out of the way. Then he disappeared and I never heard from them again."

"What about the brother?"

"Sammy Bender went to Sing Sing for shooting a bank guard and a teller in the holdup. My people have the information."

Randall put his notes back into the folder and slipped it into a leather briefcase. He closed the latch and stood up. "I will need to speak to your contacts. Have them call me today. In the meantime, I will go to Pennsylvania and see if I can find any Borntraegers that might know of Rachel or her daughter's whereabouts. And I will check with Bender's brother, but this will not be easy."

"If you can solve this, Randall, you'll be rewarded beyond your wildest dreams."

Randall smiled unpleasantly. "Augusta, you just said the magic words."

Randall turned and walked to the door. Augusta stared after him.

Randall stopped and looked back. "I hope I live to spend it, Augusta, for your sake."

Then the door closed behind him.

The private line on Michel Duvigney's desk rang once and then stopped. Duvigney pulled a notebook from his pocket, checked a number, and then dialed it. A cold voice answered.

"Randall speaking."

"You have some information for me?"

"Yes. I spent some time with Augusta today and will be following some leads she gave me. It will be hard but not impossible to find the girl. I'll be checking a source tomorrow. Hopefully, they'll give me some information that will set me on the right track."

"'Hopefully' is not a word in my lexicon, Randall. Either you can find the heir or not. There are a great many issues here, Randall. They go far beyond the disgusting St. Clair woman's greed. She is the lesser daughter of a Yugoslavian car mechanic. It would be a shameful thing if the old tart got her hands on the trust. And there are other issues."

"What other issues?"

"That is no concern of yours, Randall. Let's just say that if Augusta St. Clair gets any further, there will be hell to pay."

"I understand."

"On another note, does Augusta have any inkling of your, ah, divided loyalties?"

"At this point, no. But we'll have to play the game carefully, for my sake, if not for yours. You may have access to a lot more money than she does, but she is just as ruthless as you. If she knew you were doing an end-run around her schemes, she'd become a formidable foe. And I would be caught in the middle. A very delicate situation, as you can see."

"Just play it straight with us, Randall, and make sure that we get all the information before Augusta. If you do, you will be handsomely rewarded, I assure you."

"That's the second time I've been promised a big reward today. Things are looking up."

There was a click and the line went dead. Duvigney stared at the receiver in his hand.

Enjoy it while it lasts, Randall.

Chapter Six

Daniel's Heart

Daniel King stood on the knoll behind his father's house. It was just before dawn. To the east, a dark row of trees marked the horizon. Long clouds drifted through the brightening sky. A golden glow grew around the tops of the trees, and the billows above were touched with a beautiful orange that faded into a dusky pink as it reached toward heaven. Above it all, the deep indigo of the dying night held time fixed in perfect suspension.

It was that mystical moment, just before the day begins, when all nature holds its breath, as though waiting for an unheard command from on high. Then the tiniest sliver of sun peeked over the eastern hills, and as the world exhaled, Daniel felt the soft brush of nature's breath against his face. Peace flooded over him. His heart was filled with a deep sense of connection to the land, and especially to this place.

The light gathered itself into golden shafts that revealed the green fields of Paradise below him. One by one, Daniel began to pick out the Amish farms of his

neighbors. There was the Beachey place with the finest
milk cows in Lancaster County. Up the road were the
Masts, and beyond them, the Nissleys and the Ottos—
carpenters and woodworkers that produced wonderful
handcrafted furniture.

Down the hill he could see the potato fields of the
Glick farm, and beyond that, the Keim's first alfalfa
cutting was a bright patch of green. In his mind Daniel
could see the names on the mailboxes that lined Leacock Road: Umble, Troyer, Swartzendruber, Raber, Pe-
tershwim, Shetler, Stoltzfus, Yoder, and Zook. Each
name was a patch in the quilt of the Amish community
that had lived and prospered here since 1720.

Daniel's eyes turned to the blue farmhouse a half-
mile away. It was the old Borntraeger place, now the
Hershberger farm. It, too, was part of the long con-
tinuum of Daniel's people in Pennsylvania, for Jenny
Hershberger was a Borntraeger, and her story reminded
Daniel of how *der kluge und liebende Gott* had held the
Plain people of Lancaster County to their inheritance.

*In a way, we are like the people of Israel, who have
an inheritance forever in their land. Gott promised it
to them and He always keeps His promise.*

Daniel sighed and kicked at a large stone that was
half-buried in the dirt. After a few nudges, the stone
broke loose and rolled away down the hill.

*That stone is Rachel. She wants to go rolling away,
and she will. She will fall into the river of the world and
be swept away and leave this place. And she will never
know the peace that is here.*

A small, black buggy rolled along Leacock toward
the Old Philadelphia Turnpike. A big, white gelding
with a flowing mane pulled it.

It's Tuesday and Andy Peterswhim is on his way to the market for his mother.

As Daniel watched the buggy disappear around the tree-shadowed bend in the road, he took comfort in the symmetry of his life. The seasons came and went, the crops were planted and harvested, the people were born, they lived, and they died. It was all part of a cycle that set his people apart, a cycle that only an uncluttered heart could see. It was timeless, stretching away into the past and moving forward into the future, like a great river that is always changing, ever-moving, catching the sun with a million different diamond-sparkle facets of its surface and yet somehow always the same, always there. For Daniel, that was the secret of the Plain Way. It was always there, seemingly fixed, yet when each day started, it was always a new journey, without any missteps to mar the way. If a man was accountable for his actions, to himself and to others, and if he walked in the light of God, there was grace for living and everything seemed to work together for the good.

With a deep sigh, Daniel turned and started down the hill. The path through the woods was as familiar to him as the walls of his room. He had been coming to the top of the knoll since he was a child. It was a castle keep where he could take refuge from the world and sort out his thoughts. Many times when they were children, he and Rachel had come here. But then Rachel had moved away, and it seemed as though a great piece of Daniel's life went with her. And later, when she returned and began to blossom into womanhood, her life separated them even more, and Daniel had to content himself with watching Rachel grow lovelier each day from afar.

He stopped and picked up a broken-off branch from the huge buckeye tree that stood a little below the crest of the ridge. There had been a storm and the ancient chestnut had shed many branches and limbs, and yet it still stood, unmoved from the place it had been growing for over one hundred years. To Daniel, it was a symbol of all that was permanent. It was under that tree that he and Rachel had pledged to be friends forever. He whisked the trail in front of him with the branch as he walked, and as he did, the old yearning rose inside. Rachel! Rachel!

Sie leben immer in meinem Herzen...always in my heart!

He struck the stick against a small bay tree, and the branch broke in his hand. His heart sank as he tried to come to grips with his feelings. She was an enigma to him. Daughter of an *Außenseiter* father and a half-Amish mother, Rachel had not lived a normal Amish life. Then her father, Jonathan, disappeared at sea. Everyone thought he was dead, and Rachel and Jenny went to Ohio to live. They were gone almost three years, and then suddenly one day, Rachel was back at the farm. But she was no longer the carefree child that had been Daniel's playmate. Tragic events had taken the lives of Jenny's parents in Ohio, and a deep sadness wrapped Rachel like a winter coat.

Daniel tried to reestablish their friendship, but Rachel was standoffish and quiet. Daniel knew somehow that Rachel was afraid of getting close to anyone. And then when her father had literally come back from the dead, Rachel grew even more distant. Jonathan had been an amnesia victim and he still struggled with physical and emotional issues that played havoc with his relationship with Rachel.

With nowhere else to place the blame for her sorrow and confusion, Rachel had come to blame being Amish as the root of it all. Now she looked elsewhere for her joy, and Daniel could see it in her eyes. Even when things seemed normal between them, it was as though she was looking through him, past life in Paradise, to a place that Daniel could hardly comprehend. When she began talking about going away to school, his heart ached. And yet Daniel could see the gift in her, a gift of healing and caring, and he knew that *Gott* had placed it within her. So Daniel's heart was torn—torn between wanting to be close to Rachel again and letting her go to fulfill her dream.

"Daniel! Daniel! Stop moping around and give me a hand here. *Wir vergeuden Tageslicht.* Time's a wasting!"

Daniel's reverie was broken as he came down the path and into the farmyard. His *daed* came out of the barn, leading a great black stallion. The smile in his eyes belied the gruff tone of his remark.

"Ja, Papa, ich komme."

Daniel stopped by the well pump. He hung his black hat on a nail and levered the red handle. A stream of icy spring water poured out, and he splashed his face. Then he quickly walked to his papa who handed him the halter rope. Black Dancer put his face down, and Daniel scratched behind the silky ears. The horse pushed his nose against Daniel's overall pocket.

"Looking for something, Dancer?"

Daniel pulled the apple out of his pocket and the horse took it from him in one bite.

Jonas King smiled at his son. "*Ja*, with you he acts like a pig, not a horse."

"He's a good boy, Papa."

The two Kings admired the beautiful animal. Jonas put his hand on Daniel's shoulder. "You look troubled, my son. Is it Rachel?"

"Yes, Papa. I am worried for her. She does not have peace in her heart. I see it in her eyes."

"Is it her trouble with Jonathan?"

"That's part of it, Papa, but there's more. Rachel is different. The things that happened to her have changed her. She does not see the world as we do. Instead, she sees it as a refuge, a place where she might escape from the hurt and the pain. Sometimes the things she says are from such a different point of view that it's as though she was never Amish. She takes no joy in the simple things. She is always looking away, out there somewhere."

The two men walked toward the pasture together with the horse following them. The early-morning sun warmed the air and Daniel's papa sighed and pulled a handkerchief out of his pocket. He wiped his face and then spoke again.

"Daniel, perhaps you need to let this girl go her own way. You are Amish to the heart of you. You love this land and the ways of our people. Rachel will never be happy here, I think, and if you were to marry her, she would bring you unhappiness. You should look for a good, plain Amish girl who will make a home for you and give you children. Hettie Troyer would welcome courtship from you. And there are others—beautiful, simple girls who love our ways as much as you do."

Daniel walked beside his father silently. There was

wisdom in his *daed's* words but no joy. He remembered how good Rachel had been with their mare.

If only she could see that everything she really wants is right here in Paradise.

"If only I could make Rachel see, Papa. She has a gift and she would be of great benefit to our people."

"*Ja, mein Sohn, Sie sind richtig*…you are right. Rachel would be an excellent veterinarian. But she has many crossroads before her, choices she must make, before she can see clearly enough to decide about the rest of her life. I am thinking that it is best to forget her and go on with your own life."

Daniel's heart felt like a great hand was squeezing it, and he couldn't breathe. He stopped and looked at his father. "But isn't there a way, Papa?"

Daniel's papa stopped and looked at his son. "I think that you love this girl more than you have told me."

Daniel looked back and then slowly nodded his head. His papa sighed.

"Then, the only thing you can do is to bathe this girl in prayer. If she is *das Mädchen, das Gott für Sie geplant hat*, then you must trust Him to work His will and way in her heart. Nonetheless, I am afraid there is much sorrow in all this. But I will pray with you and for you…and for Rachel."

"*Danki*, Papa."

But at that moment, Daniel knew only two things. He knew that Rachel *was* the girl God had for him. And he couldn't see how prayer would change anything.

Chapter Seven

Closing In

Sammy Bender looked through the crack in his door. The man in the hallway was medium height and powerfully built, with a sharp, hawk-like face set off by a short crew cut and black turtleneck under a brown, hound's-tooth wool jacket. The tan slacks were sharply pressed, and the black brogans bore a high-luster shine, military in its perfection.

"Whaddaya want?"

The hawk-faced man glanced down at a notebook and smiled. Somehow the smile made Sammy shiver.

"Sammy Bender?"

"Yeah."

"Formerly of Sing Sing prison?"

"I done my time…"

"Brother of Joseph Bender?"

Sammy didn't like the questions. "Say, what are you, a cop? I'm clean, see. I visit my PO every month."

Sammy started to close the door, but the man put his

shoe in the opening, reached into his pocket, and pulled out a crisp, one hundred dollar bill.

"I have no interest in you, personally, Mr. Bender. I only need some information that you might be carrying in that drug-addled brain. So if you let me in, perhaps I can help your determined quest to escape the cares of this world."

Sammy closed the door, released the chain latch, reached out, grabbed the money, and started to close the door. The next thing he knew, he was up against the wall in the hallway with a small revolver pressed against his face and a steel grip on his arm.

"Not a good way to begin a relationship, Sammy."

The man kept his grip while he put the gun back in its shoulder holster, and then he pushed Sammy down the hall.

In the front room, the man pointed to the ragged couch by the window. "Sit down, Sammy."

Sammy Bender sat. "Are you going to shoot me?"

"Why would I want to do that? Then I wouldn't be able to find out what I need to know." He smiled the same joyless smile. "Besides, it would make a mess in this elegant sitting room."

A ray of hope splintered the darkness in Sammy's brain. "So, what do you want?"

"I need to know about the woman and the little girl."

"The woman? What woman?"

"The woman, Rachel St. Clair, and her daughter, that lived with you in Manhattan."

"Oh, Rachel…" Sammy paused, thinking back. "I ain't seen Rachel since I seen Joe. And Joe's dead."

"Dead?" The man reached for his notebook. "How did that happen?"

"He died in a car crash in Ohio. The cop told me about it."

"The cop?"

"Well, he was a sheriff from Woozer or Weiser, I don't know."

"Wooster?"

"Yeah, that's it. Wooster."

"And what did he tell you about Joe?"

"When Joe and I robbed the bank, Joe drove the car. I got caught. Joe split. The sheriff told me Joe died in a wreck and he had Rachel's daughter, Jenny, with him. The sheriff was looking for Rachel."

The hawk-faced man pulled the hundred-dollar bill out of his pocket and laid it on the coffee table and then he pulled out two more and laid them beside the first in a perfectly even row. "I need more, Sammy."

Sammy looked at the money. "Okay, Rachel's dead, too."

"And how do you know that?"

"The sheriff went to my mom's house in Patterson. Joe had called her, all crazy because Rachel had over-dosed in Stroudsburg. There was a girl and a hippie with the sheriff."

Sammy went on, looking at the money. "The girl was Jenny."

That got the hawk-faced man's attention. "Jenny St. Clair is still alive?"

"Yeah, she was at my mom's house."

The man reached down and pushed one of the bills over to Sammy. "More, Sammy."

"Jenny went to Stroudsburg and found out that Rachel was really dead. She let my mom know."

The man reached down and pushed the second bill over. "And…"

It felt hot in the room. "Uh…"

"C'mon, Sammy, just a little more."

"Halverson! The sheriff's name was Halverson! And Jenny married the hippie. Jenny sent my mom a letter."

"And what was the hippie's name, Sammy?"

Sammy's brow furrowed. "That was a long time ago, pal."

The hawk-face man reached for the third bill and put it back in his pocket.

"Wait. Uh…the guy's name was Johnny or John. When my mom told me, I wasn't really paying attention."

"Good boy, Sammy."

The bill appeared magically on Sammy's side of the coffee table. Sammy picked up the money and felt the crispness of it. "Brand-new Franklins. This will keep me up for a week."

Sammy heard the door close and looked up. The hawk-faced man was gone.

"So Rachel St. Clair is dead. What about the girl?"

Augusta listened intently while the voice on the other end of the line replied to her question. Then she spoke again. "Jenny was alive in 1965. That's twenty-five years ago, Randall. Have you found her yet?"

Again, the voice spoke while Augusta listened. "Uh-huh, all right, Randall. Where are you now? Wooster? Why Wooster?"

Another long pause and then Augusta smiled. "Good work, Randall. Let me know when you find out more."

Augusta hung up the phone and turned to her grandson, Gerald. He was sitting on a couch in the sitting room at the St. Clair mansion. He tapped his fingers together nervously and then reached into his pocket and pulled out a pack of cigarettes.

Augusta waved her hand. "Not in here, Gerald. If you want to smoke those filthy things, do it outside."

Gerald frowned and put the cigarettes away. "So what did our spy have to say?"

"He's not a spy, he's a former Special Forces and CIA, exactly suited to our needs."

"Well?"

"All right, Gerald, here's where we stand. Rachel St. Clair, your great aunt, is dead. She overdosed on heroin in Stroudsburg, Pennsylvania, in 1950. The man she was with, Joe Bender, left her in a motel room and drove west with Jenny St. Clair. He was killed in a crash near Dalton, Ohio. Jenny survived and was adopted by an Amish couple in Apple Creek, Ohio. She was still alive as of 1965."

"How did Randall find all that out?"

"Gerald, you must never underestimate Randall. His intelligence-gathering capabilities are superb. He was able to gain access to police files in Stroudsburg. In them, he found that in 1965 Bobby Halverson, the sheriff of Wayne County, paid a visit to the department there. Jenny St. Clair, along with her adoptive father and another man, Jonathan Hershberger, accompanied him. They gave the police information that established Rachel St. Clair's identity. Randall is in Wooster following up on Halverson."

"Well, I wish he would hurry up. I'm getting tired of this whole game. I don't see why they won't just give me the money. I'm a St. Clair, too!"

Augusta looked at her grandson. He was such a beautiful boy, but so impatient. "Now, Gerald, don't get petulant. It's not going to be as easy to get our hands on the money as I thought. But I'm working on it."

Augusta stood up, walked over behind the couch and began to stroke Gerald's hair. "Haven't I always taken care of you, dearest? Just relax. Grandmother will handle everything."

Gerald turned to look at Augusta and then shrugged his shoulders and accepted the caresses.

The black BMW drove slowly up to the small house in Wooster, Ohio. Rose bushes grew along a white picket fence, and yellow forsythia blossomed on large bushes under the windows. An older man stood by the front porch watering some juniper bushes that grew on either side of the steps. The man was big and carried himself with a military bearing. He looked very tough, despite the years that had lined his face. Randall stopped the car and watched the man for a moment, assessing him. Then he climbed out and walked up to the fence. The old man glanced at Randall. "Mornin'. Can I help you with somethin'?"

Randall looked down at his notebook. "Ralph Halkovich?"

"Bull Halkovich. Nobody's called me Ralph since I broke my Aunt Daisy's window when I was ten."

"Okay, Bull. I'm looking for Bobby Halverson. The Sheriff's Department said you knew how to reach him."

"Uh-huh."

Bull went back to watering the bushes.

"I said I'm looking for Bobby Halverson."

Bull glanced up. "I heard you."

"Well, can you help me?"

Bull twisted the nozzle on the hose until the mist he was directing toward the junipers was cut off and then he laid the hose down. He walked over and looked down at Randall. "I don't go handing out Bobby's info to any Tom, Dick, or Harry in a fancy car with New York plates. Bobby's retired and he doesn't like people to come around, so you'll have to give me a real good reason to spill my guts."

Randall smiled and took a guess. "Semper Fi, Bull."

"You a Marine?"

"Yes, First Division, Vietnam, then Special Forces. How about you?"

"Nope, but I fought side by side with them in the Pacific."

"Wasn't Halverson a Marine?"

"Yep, won the silver star on Guadalcanal. He was a real tough customer…"

Bull's eyes narrowed. "Say, you trying to squeeze something outta me? How did you find out so much about Bobby?"

"Take it easy, Bull. In my line of business you have to do your homework. I represent a family that is looking for the granddaughter of Robert St. Clair. We understand that Bobby knows her and we'd like to contact him."

Bull put his hand to his chin and rubbed it contemplatively. Then he shrugged. "I don't know about any Robert St. Clair and I ain't giving you info on Bobby until I check with him. Gimme your card and I'll have him call you."

"I assure you that—"

"Gimme the card!"

Randall reached in his chest pocket. He felt the handle of his pistol and debated using a different tactic, but Bull was ahead of him.

"If you're thinkin' about pulling that popgun you got in your pocket, I wouldn't. I may be old but I'm still in army shape, and I could come over this fence and break your puny neck before you got it out. And besides, I'm too big to kill with that little .38. So leave that idea in the holster."

Randall's hand moved past the gun and pulled out a card. He handed it to Bull. "My number's right there. Have the sheriff call me."

"And who should I say you represent?"

"I represent Augusta St. Clair, Robert St. Clair's sister-in-law."

Bull looked down at the card. "Uh-huh."

Randall reached out a hand. "Nice to meet you, Bull."

Bull just stared at him with steely eyes, so Randall turned, went back to the car, climbed in, and pulled away. He drove to the end of the block and looked back. Bull was still staring after him. Then he turned and headed toward the house.

Randall smiled. "And now Bull goes in and calls Halverson. Army guys are so predictable."

He glanced at his watch and then headed back toward Pennsylvania.

Chapter Eight

An Open Door

The Paradise Post Office was right on the corner of Highway 30 and Leacock Road. Rachel parked her scooter by the phone booth and walked up the stairs and through the big glass door. Mrs. Shoemaker, the postmistress, waved at her and smiled.

"Yoo hoo, Rachel! It's here!"

Rachel glanced around to see if anybody heard. "Please, Mrs. Shoemaker, I don't want everybody to know."

"Whoops, I forgot."

Mrs. Shoemaker looked around furtively and then handed Rachel an official-looking envelope.

Rachel's heart leaped. An elegant logo was printed in the upper left corner, "Cornell University—Founded 1865." To the right were the words, "Cornell University College of Veterinary Medicine."

"Aren't you going to open it, dear?"

"I'm afraid to, Mrs. Shoemaker."

"Well, they can either say yes or no. So you might as well get it over with."

Rachel nodded in agreement. She had been waiting for six weeks for an answer from the admissions department and now here it was. Her hand shook as she undid the seal and pulled out the folded paper inside.

My Dear Miss Hershberger,

We received your application for admittance to the School of Veterinary Medicine. As you may know, our standards are very high and only a small percentage of applicants gain entrance to the school. What makes your case interesting is that we have never had an Amish applicant before. Normally, a person in your position, that is, one who has technically only completed the eighth grade, would not be considered for entrance, but your obvious passion for the field of animal husbandry, as detailed in your charming letter, convinced our committee to pursue this matter further. After careful review of your exceptional middle school transcript and the records from the community college where you ranked at the top of your class, we are willing to pursue your application further, with some conditions.

First, you will be required to take the Scholastic Assessment Test (SAT). You must score in the top ten percent in order to be eligible for consideration for entrance. You will also take the GED test to show us that your education has reached high school level or beyond. Once you have completed this testing, you need to come to Ithaca for a personal interview. Our final decision will be based on your performance in all of these areas.

As Dean of Admissions to the college, I must say that your letter was very interesting, and we were all quite impressed. If your skills can be shown to be as high as your desire, then your application may have a positive outcome. Please contact me personally if you have any questions. The conditions we have stipulated should be met by January. In the meantime, I wish you all the best in the pursuit of your dream.

Dr. Eloise Tillinghast
Dean of Admissions.
Cornell School of Veterinary Medicine

Mrs. Shoemaker leaned over the counter. "Well? What?"

Rachel folded the letter and put it into the envelope. Then she burst into tears. Mrs. Shoemaker came around the counter and took Rachel in her arms.

"Did they say no, Rachel?"

Rachel took a breath. "No, Ma'am. They…they will consider me if I can meet a few more requirements. If I do, they will give me an interview."

"So, that's good, right?"

"Yes and no, Mrs. Shoemaker. It's wonderful, but there's a big problem. I have to convince my folks to let me take the tests and travel to Ithaca for the interview if I pass. That won't happen. I don't know why I had my hopes up."

Mrs. Shoemaker put her arm around Rachel once more. "Is it your father, Rachel?"

"Yes, Ma'am. It's just that he's so strict. We fought

over me taking classes at the community college. This will put him over the edge."

"What about your mom?"

"I think she supports me in this, but she doesn't want to upset Papa. He's had some physical and emotional problems and…oh, I shouldn't be telling you all this."

Mrs. Shoemaker sighed. "It's okay, honey. You're a sweet girl, and you would make a fine vet. I won't say anything, but I will pray for you."

Rachel looked at the woman in surprise. "Are you a Christian, Mrs. Shoemaker?"

The postmistress chucked Rachel under the chin. "The Amish aren't the only ones around here that love God, sweetie."

Rachel blushed. "I… I'm sorry, I didn't mean it like that."

"There are all kinds of people in this big world. Now, you should head on home. You have things to work out, hard things. But, like I said, I'll be praying."

Rachel smiled through her tears. "Thank you, Mrs. Shoemaker; you are very kind."

Rachel peeked into the front room. A fire popped and crackled in the fireplace, and her *daed* was sitting in front of it, staring into the flames. Jenny sat in her rocking chair, sewing a torn pair of pants. From time to time, Jenny looked up at Jonathan and smiled, but he seemed lost in his thoughts. Rachel ducked back behind the doorframe, her heart racing, the letter from Cornell clutched in her hand.

I've got to say something, but I'm so afraid. Oh, Gott, why is everything so hard?

As Rachel turned to go back down the hall she felt

a soft hand on her shoulder. Her heart leaped into her throat, and she turned to see her mama.

"Rachel, what is it?"

Rachel stared at Jenny, and then took a deep breath.

"I… I have something… I mean… I…"

"What is it, Rachel? Are you in some sort of trouble?"

"No, Mama, it's just that I…"

Rachel's hands were trembling. Jenny took hold of them and looked deep into Rachel's eyes. She nodded toward the back and together they went down the hall into Rachel's room.

"What is it, Rachel?" Jenny asked softly.

Rachel looked at her mama and then handed her the letter. Jenny looked at the address on the outside and then back at Rachel. "What is this, *dochter*?"

"It's…it's… Oh, just read it, Mama."

Rachel sat down on the edge of her bed and put her face in her hands. Jenny opened the envelope, took out the letter, and read. When she finished, she sighed. Rachel looked up at her mama, hoping for a reaction that she could read, but Jenny's face remained stoic. Then Jenny sat down on the edge of the bed next to her. She put her arm around Rachel's shoulders and drew her close.

"What, Mama?"

Jenny drew a breath and held her that way for a long time. Finally, she spoke. "This is a hard thing, Rachel. My heart is torn for you. On the one hand, I am so proud of you and what you have become. You are so smart, and you make me so proud of you. But I am afraid that you have chosen a path that can only bring sorrow and strife to our family. Your papa, he…"

"He will say no."

"Perhaps if you let me speak to him first. You two make each other so angry." Jenny sighed. "It was not always so. Sometimes, I think it would have been better…"

But the thought remained unspoken. Jenny folded the letter and put it back in the envelope. "Also, there is more to this than just taking the tests and going to the interview, Rachel, even if we can get your papa's permission. There is your commitment to the Plain Way. It would not be easy to convince the elders that this is a good thing. They believe that higher education can promote ideas that are counter to Christian values, and rightly so. But they also believe that education is useful when it is for the good of the Amish community. The elders could decide that a good Amish vet would be of great value. So this is a matter that could be decided either way."

Jenny handed Rachel the letter. "Keep this and let me pray the matter through. I will see what *du leiber Gott* has to say. If I do not have a check in my spirit, I will speak to your papa. But I cannot promise anything. Will you abide by Jonathan's wishes in this matter if he says no?"

Rachel's insides twisted. "If Papa will give it a sincere consideration and give me a good reason why I should not do this, I will obey him. If he just says no, then I do not know what I will do."

Jenny sighed and reached down to stroke Rachel's face. "That is an honest answer, Rachel. *Wollen wir dem Herrn in dieser Sache vertrauen.* We don't want to trust ourselves so let's trust Gott."

Jenny left the room. Rachel remained sitting on the edge of her bed, staring down at the letter. Her head whirled with the possibilities. Acceptance into Cornell would mean that her dream of being a vet would be on its way to fulfillment. She knew she could handle the classes—that wasn't the problem. Handling her father was the greatest obstacle. Rachel's heart sank.

He will never, ever give his permission!

Rachel took down her long, auburn hair, went into the bathroom and washed her face and brushed her teeth. She came back to her room, got into her nightshirt, and slipped under the covers. But sleep did not come easily. Her mama's question kept running through her mind…

Will you abide by your father's wishes in this matter if he says no?

Will you abide by your father's wishes in this matter if he says no?

Rachel tossed and turned trying to get comfortable, but her mind kept racing. She knew what Jonathan's answer would be.

It's no use. No matter what Mama says Papa will never give in. He is too stubborn and besides, he is verrückt! *He's crazy! I wish he had never come back.*

A profound sense of guilt swept over Rachel as she thought about her father. She tried to remember the good days when she and Jonathan had been so close. Finally, her eyes closed and she drifted off.

But Rachel did not find peace, even in sleep. Strange images and thoughts began to play in her mind. Her papa, floating in the ocean, clinging to a piece of wreckage; her grandparents, Reuben and Jerusha Springer, lying dead in the front room of the little house in Apple Creek, Ohio; Jonathan returning home, not dressed as an Amish man but an *Englischer*.

Images of death and loss swept back and forth through her mind like the restless sea bringing flotsam and jetsam to the shore, only to drag it away again to be lost forever. Rachel groaned in her sleep. Finally, with a great effort of will, she broke free from the grip of the dream and jerked awake. She lay in her bed and felt the sweat on her arms and back.

Then she knew the answer.

If she wanted to fulfill her dreams she would have to leave, go far away and never look back. The tears began to fall, and then the quiet sobs shook her shoulders. The truth that she could not—would not—entertain, finally became clear.

No, I mustn't think that, I must not...

And then the words forced themselves from her lips, and she spoke into the darkness.

"I cannot stay Amish."

Chapter Nine

Phone Calls

Michel Duvigney tapped his fingers nervously on his mahogany desk. He got up and went to the antique carved oak Louis XIV Lion Head wine bar and got out the bottle of Le Voyage de Delamain Cognac. Then he reached for a small, hand-warming crystal glass and poured himself a drink. He set the bottle down and then picked it back up and added some more cognac to the glass.

He sighed. The cognac cost $8,000 a bottle and after today, he probably would not be able to afford it anymore.

The phone rang and Duvigney returned to the desk, warming the cognac in his hands. He put his nose down to savor the wonderful aroma, and then took a sip. The phone kept ringing. Finally, he picked up the receiver. "Well?"

The indistinct voice spoke a few words.

"All of it?"

Again, some words.

Duvigney put the phone back and then put his face in his hands. Ten minutes passed and then Michel Duvigney raised his head and sighed. He picked up the cognac and finished it. Then he punched the discreet intercom button on the silver inlaid panel on his desk.

"Yes, Mr. Duvigney?"

"Get me Randall."

Gordon Randall sat at a table looking out on the East River in Manhattan. The Brooklyn Bridge soared over his head and boats plied the calm waters. From his table he had a sweeping view of the New York skyline and the Statue of Liberty. This was Randall's favorite restaurant and he came often. A waiter approached. "There's a call for you, Mr. Randall. We'll transfer it to the phone booth for you."

Very few of Randall's clients would call him at this place, so he knew it was important.

"Fine, Peter. Tell the chef to hold off on the steak until I get back."

Randall pushed back from the table and walked to the private phone booth in the hallway. He slid the dark, mahogany door shut behind him, and picked up the phone.

"Randall speaking."

"Mr. Randall, Mr. M would like to speak to you."

"Fine, put him on."

Randall smiled. He knew that Mr. M was actually Michel Duvigney and that he was one of the elite financiers of New York City.

Really, these people must think I'm a muscle-bound cretin.

M came on the line. The man's sibilant voice always

reminded Randall of a King cobra. He'd seen plenty of those in Vietnam. When you heard a King cobra hiss, something bad was about to happen.

"Randall?"

"This is Randall."

"Good. I need to speak to you in person right away."

"Name the place, M."

"How fast can you get downtown?"

"Forty-five minutes with traffic."

"Good. Meet me at 145 Avenue of the Americas. It's a storefront. Just walk in and tell the clerk you're here to see me."

"I'll see you in forty-five minutes."

Randall headed toward the door. The waiter approached him.

"Are you leaving, Mr. Randall?"

"Yes, Peter. Something has come up."

Randall pulled a large bill from his pocket. "Sorry for the inconvenience, Peter. This should soothe the chef."

"Thank you, sir."

Peter picked up a phone by the front desk and spoke into it.

"Mr. Randall's car, please."

Randall smiled. "If my business doesn't take too long, I may come back and try for the steak again."

Randall walked out to the curb as his BMW pulled up. A kid in a white jacket got out and handed him the keys. Randall tipped him twenty dollars, got in, and headed for Manhattan.

It was midafternoon in Paradise, Pennsylvania. The old man sat on his porch and gazed off into the distance.

His thoughts wandered back to another time and place, a steaming jungle with the screams of men dying all around him. He was lying flat on his back and his hip felt like molten-hot steel stakes had been driven through it. A tall Marine with black hair stood over him, covered in blood, clutching a rifle in his hands. Japanese soldiers pressed up the trench, and the man was beating them back. Wounded and dying men lay all around, and the black-haired man was the only one standing. The Japanese kept coming...

"Reuben..."

The old man spoke the name and it slipped away on the breeze.

His thoughts fast-forwarded. He was in a hospital waiting room and the same man was being attacked again—this time by a lovely Amish woman. She was beating on Reuben's chest and calling him a fool. Reuben just stood there with horrible suffering distorting his face.

A tear came to the old man's eyes and he groaned. This time the golden retriever at his feet stirred and whined. The old man glanced down at the dog. The retriever whined again and stood up. He put his muzzle under the old man's hand and pushed his head against him.

"It's okay, pal. I'm all right."

The old man scratched the long ears. The dog responded by pushing his head harder against the man's hand. The old man reached for a pack of Camels on the table next to his chair. He took one, lit it, and took a deep drag. He looked down at the dog.

"Funny how those memories come back, isn't it boy?"

The dog wagged his tail, then lay back down at the old man's feet. The man took another deep and satisfying drag.

"You know, they say these things'll kill you, but they can't prove it by me."

The dog's tail thumped once on the porch as if to answer in the affirmative. The old man went back to his reverie. Another picture came into his mind. He was plowing through deep snow in a covered tractor, and Reuben was seated next to him. Outside the cab, the wind howled with a fiendish roar. Up ahead through the blinding sheets of white snow, the two men could see a small cabin. Then they were inside and the lovely woman was there again, but this time she had a little girl and Reuben was wrapping her in a blanket. Another fast-forward and the old man was standing in a nightclub with his arms around two people who were weeping and clinging to each other.

"It's been a long, strange journey, Rufus."

Another thump of the tail. The old man looked around. This time he saw the beautiful fields stretching out below his house and the trees by the small stream. The sweet melody of a songbird lifted on the air. Down the hill stood a blue farmhouse surrounded by a white picket fence. A man came out the front door. He was tall with longish, black hair under a straw hat. He wore a blue shirt tucked into denim pants and a medium-length beard obscured his face.

"No mustache, though," said the old man.

The dog looked up again. The man in the hat looked up the hill, saw the old man, and waved. The words floated up to him. "Hey, Bobby, how goes it today?"

The old man smiled and waved back. "Well, I'm still takin' nourishment, Jonathan."

"Good to hear, Bobby, good to hear."

Two women came out on the front porch. One was tall, with auburn hair and a lovely, but unsmiling face. The older woman was shorter and had golden red hair, touched with white. A few unruly curls spilled out from the white prayer *kappe*. She had her arm around the younger woman. They both looked up and waved.

Rachel and Jenny—my beautiful girls. Rachel sure doesn't look happy. It's been hard since Jonathan has been home—real hard.

Then a discordant sound broke the quiet. It was Bobby's phone ringing. Bobby got up and went into the house. The screen door banged shut behind him as he made his way to the kitchen.

"Halverson here."

"Sheriff?"

The deep gravelly voice was very familiar.

"Bull, is that you?"

"Yeah, Bobby, it's me."

"Well, well. What's up in Wooster that would engender a call to Paradise?"

"Well, something happened that I found a bit odd, and I felt like I needed to get in touch."

"What's up, Bull?"

"A guy came by my house—very clean-cut, military style, nice clothes. Said he was a former Marine and Special Forces guy and he looked it. He drove a BMW with New York plates and smoked-glass windows. He was looking for you."

"Why was he looking for me?"

"Well, actually he was looking for the heirs of Robert St. Clair, and he said you knew about that. I didn't tell him anything, especially when he told me who he was working for."

"And who was he working for, Bull?"

"Augusta St. Clair."

There was a moment's silence as Bobby pondered this bit of information.

"Wasn't Robert St. Clair Jenny's father? And didn't this St. Clair woman have a big part in Jenny's mother ending up strung out and dead?"

Bobby gave a low whistle. "Augusta St. Clair. I wonder how she got my name. And you're right, Bull. Robert St. Clair was Jenny's father and the son of one of the richest families on the planet. Augusta St. Clair is not someone that Jenny feels particularly good about. So, did this guy leave a card?"

"Yeah, I got it right here. Got a pencil?"

Bobby found a pencil stub and a scrap of paper. "Okay, go ahead."

"Gordon L. Randall. 2200 Park Avenue, New York. 718-533-5443."

Bobby held the phone between his chin and his shoulder and scribbled down the information. "Okay, Bull, got it."

"What do you think this is about, Bobby?"

"I'm not sure, Bull, but it can't be good. Augusta St. Clair is not a benevolent person. I'll need to talk to Jenny." Bobby paused then spoke again. "So, how are you doing, Bull?"

"Oh, I'm good, Bobby. I don't like retirement much, but I got my place in Wooster, and I got Timothy, my cat. I eat three squares a day and get my social security and my pension check every month. What about you?"

"I like it here in Pennsylvania. I got Jenny and Rachel and Jonathan, when he's having a good day."

"A good day?"

"Yeah, Bull. Jonathan's had a hard time since we found him. He's been home five years but he and Rachel don't get along, which is sad, because I know they love each other. But Jonathan's real erratic and Rachel is a very organized girl so it's hard between them."

"Ever think you'll get back to Wooster and Apple Creek, Bobby?"

"Yeah, I'd like to come see the old place, see you and some of the guys."

"Well, let me know when you're coming. We'll kill the fatted calf."

"Okay, Bull. I'll stay in touch."

Bobby hung up the phone. He looked at the piece of paper and shook his head. Then he went back outside and looked down the hill. Jenny was working in the vegetable garden and Jonathan and Rachel were nowhere to be seen. The dog got up and stood beside Bobby. Bobby reached down and stroked the dog's head and then sighed.

"Augusta St. Clair, Rufus. Now what in the world would she want with Jenny?"

He shook his head. Something was up. Bobby could smell it and it didn't smell good.

Chapter Ten

The Trail

Bobby Halverson studied the note in his hand. *Augusta St. Clair. Now there's a name out of the past.*

He put the scrap of paper in his pocket and went around the side of the blue house to the garden. Jenny was digging up a bed. She looked up and saw Bobby standing there. "Morning, Bobby. What brings you down the hill?"

Bobby laughed. "I can still walk a few hundred feet, Jenny."

"Give me a minute while I finish this, then we'll go inside for a cup of coffee."

At forty-three, Jenny Hershberger was almost as lovely as she had been when she was a girl back in Apple Creek. The red-gold hair still shone in the sun, and except for a few wrinkles around the eyes, the perfect face was nearly unlined. The only change that Bobby noticed beside the few strands of white in her hair was the deep sadness he sometimes saw behind Jenny's violet eyes. But given the events of the last several years and the death of her parents, that was understandable. She turned over the last few clumps of soil, wiped her hands on her apron, and beckoned him to follow her.

"Where are the rest of the Hershbergers today?"

Jenny pointed. Way out in the back fields, he could see Jonathan at work with a team of horses and a cultivator.

"Jonathan is weeding the potato rows and Rachel is at Daniel King's place. There's a new foal that needs looking after."

"Are Rachel and Jonathan doing better these days?"

"Does that question have anything to do with why you dropped by?"

"Kind of...but mostly just asking."

They went into the kitchen. Jenny fetched down two mugs while Bobby pulled up a chair at the table. Jenny poured the coffee. Then she sat across from Bobby and pushed the mug toward him. Bobby put his hands around it, feeling the warmth in his aching fingers. "I got a call from Bull yesterday."

"Bull Halkovich?"

"Yep, Bull Halkovich."

"And...?"

Bobby loved that about Jenny—no shillyshally, always cut to the chase. "Someone was asking questions about your mother."

"About Jerusha?"

"No, Jenny. They were looking for Rachel St. Clair or her daughter."

Jenny's eyes opened in surprise. "Who even knows about Mama Rachel?"

"Augusta St. Clair."

Shock passed over Jenny's face. The shock turned to puzzlement. "Why in the world would Augusta St. Clair be looking for me? Augusta St. Clair was the person behind my biological mother's death. And now she's looking for me? This can't be good."

Bobby nodded in agreement. "You're right about that. And after hearing Bull's description of the messenger, I don't have a good feeling either."

"Why, Bobby?"

"Well, the man who came to Bull's place, a Gordon Randall, was very professional. Marine, Special Forces, probably with his own private investigation company. He gave Bull just enough information to get Bull on the phone to me."

Jenny took a sip of her coffee. "Why can't we just ignore it? He doesn't know where you live."

"If he's the pro I think he is, he'll find me. Sooner or later, I'll be getting a knock on the door."

"What should I do?"

"Let me handle it, Jenny. I'll call and see what he wants. If Randall knows about me, he probably found Sammy Bender and 'interviewed' him. Or he's been out to Patterson to see Magdalena Bender. Eventually he will find out about your grandfather and this farm. He will find out that Rachel Borntraeger St. Clair's daughter is now Jenny Hershberger and that you're living here."

"Why do you think Augusta is looking for me?"

Bobby looked in his cup. The cream had made swirling patterns, dark brown like Guadalcanal mud...

"Bobby?"

"It must have to do with your grandfather Robert's

money. My guess is she's trying to get it but can't. If she could have, she wouldn't be looking for you."

"So, what does that mean for me?"

"It means that you need to let me do the talking. Don't speak to this Randall unless I'm with you. And don't sign anything. Knowing Augusta, if she's after money, she'll do anything to get it."

Gordon Randall pulled his black BMW into a parking garage across the street from the address Duvigney had given him. He drove to the top level and checked the rooftops across the street before he got out. It was a habit from his Special Forces' days.

Michel Duvigney or "Mr. M," had never asked for a face-to-face meeting, and Randall didn't feel good about it. All of Randall's clients were very wealthy or very crooked, most of them both. He had developed his clientele with the utmost care. He only took on those with impeccable financial references. Duvigney was one of those, as was Augusta St. Clair. Of the two, Duvigney was the one he could not read. Augusta St. Clair was an obvious gold-digging female who had clawed her way into a very wealthy family. Her agenda was patently obvious—get money and power. Duvigney, on the other hand, was like mist in a graveyard. Randall couldn't put his finger on what was bothering him, so he raised his antennae and stayed alert.

Randall went down to the ground floor and exited the garage. He crossed the street, pushed through the doors and walked in. Behind the large reception counter lounged a seedy-looking character with a mustache and a green fedora.

"Vat you vant?"

Randall noted that the man's accent was either Russian or Yugoslavian. "Randall. I'm here to see Mr. M."

The man got up and motioned Randall to follow him. They walked down a hallway to a green metal door that looked very new and very strong. Randall noticed the red flash of a tiny camera that was mounted above the door. His guide pressed a keypad. There was a click and the door swung open.

"Mr. M is vaiting for you."

Randall stepped through the door and continued down the hall until he came to an open elevator. Randall stepped in and the doors closed. He felt motion but there were no floor markers or buttons. The car stopped, the door opened, and he stepped into another short hallway with a door at the end. He walked to the door and knocked. A buzzer sounded and there was click He pulled the door open and stepped into a small room.

A thin, old man with white hair and sharp features sat behind a desk. The old man motioned to a chair across the desk from where he was sitting. Randall sat.

"So, Gordon, we meet at last."

Randall recognized the sibilant voice, and even face-to-face, it still put his teeth on edge. He also knew the protocol. "Mr. M, I presume?"

Duvigney smiled. "Yes."

Randall leaned forward. "Why the secrecy and why the rush…?"

Mr. M fidgeted for a moment and Randall sensed that the man was under a great deal of pressure.

"Gordon, some things have occurred that have accelerated the St. Clair woman's pursuit of the inheritance. I can't tell you more than that except to say that I need to impress you with the absolute necessity of finding the heir to the St. Clair fortune."

"Well, Mr. M, I think I understand the importance you place on this matter, so you will have to raise the stakes. The money you're offering doesn't seem like quite enough."

The old man stood up and shook his finger at Randall. "Why you…"

"Sit down, Michel."

Randall's voice was cold and quiet, but Michel Duvigney sat down like he had been shoved.

"That is your name, isn't it?"

Duvigney's mouth gaped open and then shut. Randall took the black notebook out of his pocket.

"Michel Duvigney, President of the Board of Trustees of Rosslyn Foundation, managers of the fortunes of the American branch of the St. Clair family."

Randall flipped over a couple of pages.

"The St. Clair family's lineage can be traced back to the Normandy area of France where they were known as the Sinclairs. The family is closely intertwined with the crowns of France, England, and Scotland. Throughout the last one thousand years, the St. Clairs have left an indelible mark in the history books. For that same one thousand years the Duvigneys have also played a role in this family as counselors, administrators and, might I add, assassins."

Randall put the pad back in his breast pocket. Duvigney looked like someone had struck him. Randall smiled. "Really, Michel, you don't think I would take on the mysterious 'Mr. M' without thoroughly vetting you? Now, let's get down to business. There's something amiss in the St. Clair kingdom or we wouldn't be meeting face-to-face, am I right?"

"How did you find out about me?"

"Your money bought you the best in the business. I do my homework and my sources are deep and impeccable. I know that you are the trustee for the American branch of the St. Clair Enterprises. I also know that the actual bulk of their fortune is almost limitless, but you personally are merely a middleman. So your need to bring this matter to a close involves something that may affect your position and perhaps your life. My guess is that you have made some unauthorized investments and have taken some big hits."

Duvigney slumped down in his chair. "What do you propose, Mr. Randall?"

"As I seem to have struck the nail on the head, I'm going to lay it out and you just nod in agreement. First of all, you have lost a great deal of money that does not belong to you."

Duvigney nodded.

"Second, if these losses are discovered, you will lose your position with its luxurious lifestyle and your masters might consider you expendable."

Duvigney nodded.

"Third, the only way this malfeasance can be discovered is if Augusta St. Clair puts in a legitimate claim for the inheritance."

Duvigney nodded.

Randall stood up.

"Where are you going?"

"I am close to locating Robert St. Clair's daughter. At that point, I will put a plan in motion that will eliminate the threat to you."

"You mean…"

Randall smiled again. "You needn't bother yourself with what I mean, Michel. Just get your checkbook ready. Now, please buzz the door."

Randall turned to go. "And one more thing, Michel. Don't think about taking any action against me. I am your only hope."

The door clicked open and Randall walked out.

Chapter Eleven

The Connection

Bobby Halverson watched the new black BMW come up the lane. He waved and the car pulled in behind Bobby's truck. The driver climbed out. He was exactly as Bull had described: clean-cut, well dressed, and very professional looking. The man was in good shape and would probably be a deadly opponent in a fight. He carried a leather briefcase and there was no telltale bulge under his coat.

Carries himself like a pro and considers us harmless enough to leave his gun in the car.

Bobby opened the gate and motioned the man inside. He walked up to Bobby and gave him the once-over.

"Sheriff Halverson?"

Bobby chuckled. "Ex-sheriff. I haven't been on active duty for almost ten years. Call me Bobby."

The two men shook hands and Bobby could feel strength in Gordon Randall's grip. Randall looked at Bobby in surprise at the return strength he felt from Bobby.

"Thanks for seeing me. Is Mrs. Hershberger joining us?"

"Yes, Mr. Randall, she's inside."

The two men walked into Bobby's bungalow. Jenny was sitting at the table. Bobby took the seat next to Jenny and motioned Randall into the chair across from them. Randall got right down to business.

"I'm here on behalf of Augusta St. Clair."

"Concerning?" Bobby asked.

"The estate of Robert St. Clair."

"And what does that have to do with Mrs. Hershberger?"

Randall shifted in his seat and looked at Jenny. "You are the daughter of Robert St. Clair—?"

Bobby smiled. "Mr. Randall, you can direct your statements to me."

Randall frowned. "I'm not exactly sure how you got in the middle of this, Bobby, but—"

Bobby interrupted him. "Since her parents' deaths, I have been Mrs. Hershberger's guardian and advocate. She is here to listen, too, but she is reluctant to make any comments."

Jenny looked at Bobby. "It's all right, Bobby. I just want to say one thing. Mr. Randall. I am not really interested in talking with the St. Clair family or their representatives. Please tell Bobby what you want, and we will consider it later."

Randall obviously did not like to be told how to conduct his business. He nodded to Jenny. "Fine, Mrs. Hershberger."

He turned his gaze back to Bobby.

"Mrs. Hershberger is the daughter of Robert St. Clair and Rachel Borntraeger St. Clair. The St. Clairs are

one of the wealthiest families in the world, and Robert
St. Clair was a principal heir to that fortune. When he
died in 1949, he left Rachel St. Clair a widow and Jennifer Constance St. Clair—Mrs. Hershberger—without
a father. In a normal process, Robert's fortune should
have passed to his wife. But the St. Clairs set up spe-
cific rules of inheritance several hundred years ago that
ensure the fortune will remain in the family's control."

"And just what does that mean?"

"Rachel St. Clair could not have inherited the fortune, but Mrs. Hershberger can, provided—"

"Provided what, Mr. Randall?"

"Provided she has the Key."

Bobby looked over at Jenny, who was staring at Randall with an expression on her face that Bobby had never
seen before. "And just what is the Key?"

Randall picked up the briefcase and put it on the
table. The latches made a sharp click, click.

Bobby winced.

*Like the bolt of my old M1903 being pulled back to
load in a shell just before the fight on Guadalcanal...*

"Sheriff?"

Bobby shook his head and refocused. "Sorry. What
about the Key?"

Randall laid a picture on the table. It was the illus-
tration of a knight. The man was wearing a loose gar-
ment that was pulled back to reveal a red, key-shaped
mark above his left breast.

"This is a print of a painting of Reynaud de Sinclair,
Mrs. Hershberger's ancestor, made around AD 1200.
That red mark is the Key, the St. Clair birthmark. Normally, it's found on the chest of the oldest son. This has
been true since the first St. Clair came to England with

William the Conqueror in 1066. The Key has always determined the heir."

"But Jenny is a woman, so how can she be of interest to you?"

"I'm getting to that. The daughter or granddaughter of a direct heir who dies can inherit, provided she meets two conditions: first, she must hold the Key. From time to time this birthmark has occurred in a female child. If she does hold the Key, then the estate is put into trust until she meets the second condition."

"And what is that condition, Mr. Randall?" asked Jenny.

Bobby started to speak, but saw the determined look on Jenny's face and held his peace.

Randall smiled. "The second condition is that the female inheritor with the Key shall find a suitable male St. Clair and marry him. This ensures that the fortune stays within the St. Clair family. In the case of discovering an adult heir such as Mrs. Hershberger, the woman has one year to fulfill the condition."

Randall looked at Jenny. Jenny stared back. "And if the heiress is married, Mr. Randall?"

"As I said, Mrs. Hershberger, the heiress must find a suitable male St. Clair and marry him within one year to inherit."

Bobby broke in. "And if the heiress is a baby and has the Key?"

Randall answered, still looking at Jenny. "In that case, the estate would be held in trust until the girl is eighteen, at which time the same condition concerning marriage applies."

Jenny pushed her chair back. "Well, Mr. Randall, you've made a trip for nothing. I do not hold the Key and if I did, I would not divorce Jonathan for all the money in the world. So you can tell Augusta St. Clair that she can sleep easy. I'll not be coming after her money. And why is all this coming up now?"

Randall twisted in his seat.

Bobby jumped in. "Well, Mr. Randall?"

"I'm not really at liberty to discuss Mrs. St. Clair's financial situation."

Bobby took a guess. "So, she's in trouble, financially, and she's looking for a way to get out."

Randall didn't answer, but Bobby could see that his random shot had struck home.

"Well, if you won't answer that, how about this? Augusta is a St. Clair. Why can't she inherit?"

"Very simple, Bobby. She is a St. Clair by marriage only."

"What about her children?"

"Augusta's husband died in the war. Her one son and his wife were killed in a ski accident in Switzerland over fifteen years ago. Her only living relative is her grandson, Gerald, and he does not hold the Key."

"So, as I guessed, Augusta is in a bind. I assume that this Gerald would be a suitable St. Clair heir if a daughter or granddaughter with the Key could be found?"

Randall didn't answer that one either. Instead, he took a different tack.

"I understand that you have a daughter, Mrs. Hershberger."

Jenny's face turned pale and she stood up.

"My daughter does not concern you. As I said, you've made a trip for nothing. Bobby will show you out."

Randall stood and shook Jenny's hand. She turned

and left by the kitchen door. Randall went out the front. When he got to his car, he stopped and looked around.

"Nice place you got here, Bobby."

"Yep. Thanks."

"If you have any other information, Mrs. St. Clair would be happy to make it worth your while to share it."

Bobby nodded but did not answer. Randall got the message.

"Well, thank you for your time."

Randall climbed in the car and headed back down the hill. Bobby walked back into the house. Jenny was standing in the kitchen. She was shaking and pale.

"Jenny, what is it?"

"The Key, Bobby. I lied to Randall. Rachel holds the Key."

Bobby's chin dropped. "What?"

"Rachel has the St. Clair birthmark."

Bobby sat down at the table. "Does Rachel know about this?"

"She knows she has a birthmark, but I never knew that there was any significance to it."

"Are you going to say anything to her?"

"Do you trust these people, Bobby?"

The question was almost a whisper.

"No, Jenny, I do not trust them. Augusta St. Clair is a cold, scheming woman who won't hesitate to protect her interests. Randall scares me. He's intelligent and highly trained. He's Augusta's tool and the extension of her wishes. I would not trust them with Rachel in any way."

Jenny sat down again and pulled her chair next to Bobby. Bobby put his arm around her.

"That's how I feel, too, Bobby. Rachel must never know."

* * *

Rachel trudged home from the King farm. The joy of working with the new foal had lifted her spirits for a while, but she had settled back into a gloomy mood. The soft scent of lilacs filled the air. Spring had burst upon Paradise but Rachel did not notice. Everything in her life was gray and flat. The offer from Cornell weighed heavy on her. She wanted to go but she knew she would have to leave her faith if she did.

I'm Amish and my papa will never say yes, and even if he did, the elders would never let me go. Oh, why was I born Amish? I can't stay here!

As she came to the lane, she was surprised to see a black automobile come slowly down. The man behind the wheel saw Rachel and pulled to a stop. The electric window rolled down and Rachel looked into a pair of steel-gray eyes. For some reason, she shivered. The man's smile made her feel creepy.

"Are you Rachel?"

Something about the man made Rachel's gut twist. "Yes…"

The man smiled again. "Don't worry. I'm a friend of the other side of your family."

"The other side?"

"You know that your mother was born a St. Clair, right?"

Rachel was suddenly afraid. "I knew that Mama's birth mother was named Rachel, but that's all. I was named after her."

Why am I telling him this?

The man pulled out a card. "My name is Gordon Randall and I work for your great-aunt, Augusta St.

Clair. She's trying to find out all she can about relatives on both sides of her family."

"Why is she so interested in her Amish relatives after all these years?"

Randall nodded, and though the air was warm, Rachel shivered again.

"Augusta is getting old. She has alienated many of her relatives. Now she wants to set things right before she dies."

That's a lie!

Randall leaned out the window and handed Rachel the card. "I'm sure she'd like to meet you. If you're interested, give me a call and I'll arrange it."

Randall rolled up the window, nodded, and drove off. Rachel felt sick. She waited until the car disappeared around the bend and then quickly turned back up the lane. She wrapped her arms around herself to keep from running.

Chapter Twelve

The Secret Revealed

Jenny Hershberger went up the stairs to her writing room. She opened the door and stood looking in. Against the outside wall under the large picture window stood a beautiful birchwood desk with an old Underwood typewriter sitting on it. Jenny went to the desk and ran her fingers over the smooth surface.

Papa! How I wish I could feel your strong arms around me...

Memories of her days in Apple Creek tried to push their way into her heart, tumbling over each other in a rush. She took a deep breath and turned away.

The walls of the room were lined with shelves filled with folders, books, and stacks of paper and notebooks. In the corner, stood an old cedar chest. Jenny went over and knelt down in front of it. She closed her eyes and lifted the lid. The smell of cedar mixed with her mama's lavender caressed her senses. It seemed that Jerusha was in the room with her. She opened her eyes and looked

down into the trunk. On the top were several packages
bound in brown paper and tied with string.

My books! Lord, will you ever let me publish these?

She set them aside, and then dug down into the trunk.
There were bits of material, scraps of batting, bolts of
cloth, extra material for repairs and small samples of
quilts that her mama had planned to make before she
died. At the bottom was the bundle Jenny was looking
for. It was large, wrapped in brown paper, and tied with
a string. Jenny took it out and opened it.

The Rose of Sharon, her mama's most beautiful quilt,
lay before her. The deep red silk that comprised the
magnificent rose centerpiece glowed softly in the afternoon light. The royal-blue silk behind it was set off
perfectly by the cream-colored backing. Jenny touched
the quilt. She could feel the soft double batting that had
kept her warm when her mama was fighting to keep
her alive in the heart of the worst storm in Ohio history.
Tears started in her eyes.

"Mama, oh, Mama. I miss you so. I wish that you were
here so I could talk to you. Oh, Mama, I need you now."

Jenny pulled the quilt up around her as she knelt.
She remembered the last time she had looked at the
quilt. She had been with Jerusha in Apple Creek, after
Jonathan had disappeared and everyone thought he was
dead. Jerusha brought out the quilt to comfort Jenny—
to show her the Springer family's story in the quilt's
design. There was the rose that was for Jenna, her sister
who had died; and the repaired edges that spoke of the
places in Jenny's life that had been restored. Jerusha's
words came back to her...

"The story of your life does not stop with Jonathan's
death, Jenny," her mama had said. "It goes on until it

is your time to go. You do not know which pieces you will discover tomorrow, but they are there, already determined by *die Vorkenntnisse des Gottes*. Now let me show you one more thing as a reminder."

Jerusha moved the quilt until the rose was under her hand. "Look! Do you see it?"

Jenny looked closer. There it was! Sewn into the center of the rose—a small, key-shaped piece of red silk so finely stitched that it was almost invisible.

"*Ja*, Jenny, a key. The Lord had me add it so that we would always remember—"

"That He is the key to our lives and without Him we cannot hope to comprehend what is happening to us and why?"

"Yes, Jenny, and if you put your life into His hands, He will guide your path and you will understand everything."

"I had forgotten about the key."

Jenny looked more closely at it.

"It is the strangest thing, Mama. Did you know that Rachel has a key-shaped birthmark right above her heart? It is almost the same color as the rose. Maybe *Gott* is still speaking to us through the quilt. Perhaps the journey is not over after all. We may be coming to a new beginning. That is a hopeful thought."

Jerusha had smiled at her then, and it warmed Jenny.

Now Jenny pulled the quilt closer, inhaling the fragrance of her mama.

The Key—how did mama know about the Key?

But today the Key did not give her hope, only fear.

Augusta St. Clair sat quietly in the sunroom of her Connecticut mansion. The view overlooked the formal garden and the lower lawn where there was a pool, a guesthouse, and tennis courts—out beyond that was the sea. Augusta could hear the cries of the gulls and the surf breaking on the shore. It reminded her of Martha's Vineyard—that summer with Jerod and... Robert...

The phone rang and Augusta was jolted out of her reverie. She went to the small table by the door and answered it.

"What?"

"Good morning, Augusta. I'm sure it's a nice day in Connecticut, no matter how you sound."

"Randall?"

"Yes, ma'am."

"Well?"

"I have good news and bad news. The good news; I located Jenny St. Clair. Her name is Hershberger now and she's married. She's Amish, like her mother."

"What's the bad news?"

"Jenny Hershberger does not hold the Key."

Augusta swore softly under her breath.

"Are there any other possibilities?"

"The Hershbergers have a daughter, but the daughter has no bearing on this situation. So it looks like Gerald will have to find a bride and produce an heir in order for you to get your hands on the money."

"I'll be dead by then, Randall."

"Well, as they say, Augusta, timing is everything."

The line went dead.

Ten minutes later, the phone in Michel Duvigney's office rang. Duvigney picked it up.

"Yes, what is it?"

"Randall here. I found the daughter of Robert St. Clair and she does not hold the Key. Looks like you won't be subject to an audit for at least twenty-one years—if Gerald produces an heir tomorrow. If he doesn't, the audit will be sometime after that."

"Good job, Randall. Your check is in the mail."

"And the bonus we spoke about?"

"You'll get your money, Randall. All of it."

"Good. We wouldn't want to see the information about your inappropriate activities involving the principal of the St. Clair trust in the hands of the wrong people, like the board of trustees."

"No, Randall, we wouldn't. Like I said, you'll get your money."

The line went dead. Michel Duvigney got up slowly, walked over to the wine bar and got out the de Delamain Cognac. He poured himself a glass. He picked up the phone and pressed a number. When someone answered, he spoke.

"Order me another bottle of the Le Voyage de Delamain Cognac, please."

He set the phone back in its receiver and sat down behind the desk. He felt much better. Lifting the glass in the air in a toast, Duvigney smiled. Things were looking up.

When Rachel came home, she stood in the hallway thinking about Gordon Randall—and the woman he represented.

Who is Augusta St. Clair? Why is she looking for us?

Rachel heard the sound of voices. It was her mama and papa, talking quietly in the front room. Rachel started to walk in when she heard something that made her stop and listen.

"...and he's looking for someone who holds the Key."

Jonathan's low voice answered Jenny. "What is 'the Key,' Jenny?"

"It's the St. Clair birthmark. It's a key-shaped red stain right above the heart. It is how the trustees of the St. Clair estate determine who inherits the fortune. My birth father, Robert St. Clair, had the St. Clair birthmark, the Key. When he died, all his money was put in trust until a new heir could be determined. Augusta must be having trouble laying her hands on the money or she wouldn't be sending out agents. There's something going on and it does not bode well for us, husband."

"And this Key—is it the same one that Rachel has?"

"It seems so, Jonathan. Randall showed me a picture of one of the St. Clairs. He had exactly the same birthmark above his heart."

"And the holder of the Key is the heir to the St. Clair fortune?"

Rachel's heart leaped. She couldn't believe what she was hearing.

"Yes, Jonathan, but there is a catch."

"What's that, Jenny?"

"Rachel would have to marry a St. Clair male to inherit, to keep the money in the family."

"How does that affect Rachel?"

"Augusta St. Clair has a grandson, Gerald. Randall hinted that Gerald would be a suitable choice."

"So, if Rachel married him, she would become wealthy?"

"Yes, Jonathan, very wealthy. And that is why we must not tell her."

As she stood listening to her parents, Rachel felt a great knot in her chest. She could not believe that her parents were conspiring to deceive her. This was her life they were deciding. She was about to open her mouth, but in that moment she felt the card in her hand. She walked back down the hallway and held it up in the light.

Gordon Randall
12 Plaza Way,
New York, NY 213-342-1200

Rachel felt hope rise up in her. This was her way out! She was the heiress to a vast fortune. She could claim it, and then she could do anything she wanted with her life. No more Papa yelling at her, no more elders telling her what she could do. She could pay her own way through school. It was like a miracle.

And yet, there was something very evil about Randall. But still… As the prospects began to churn in her mind something in Rachel's heart hardened. She would leave this Amish life and the hateful *Ordnung* that bound her with fetters of steel. She would escape from her papa's moods and rages. This was her way out. As she stood there in the hallway, a great battle began to rage in Rachel's soul. She thought of her mama and her home, all the things that she loved…and… Daniel.

Daniel? He's just a friend. I could never marry Daniel.

And yet there was something, like a light trying to force its way into a very dark place.

Daniel! He loves me. He loves me with all his heart. Daniel...

For just another moment she hesitated. And then Rachel shut the door of her heart and walked down the hall to her room, clutching Gordon Randall's card.

Chapter Thirteen

Who Am I?

Rachel sat on her bed for a long time, thinking. She had made her decision and she expected to feel release and joy. Instead, her heart was heavy, but right or wrong, she knew she must go on. She heard her mama calling her to dinner, but she did not answer. The gathering dusk shadowed the room and still she sat, thinking…staring.

After a while, there was a knock on the door.

"Rachel, are you coming to dinner?"

"I… I'm not hungry, Mama. I don't feel well, and I think I will just go to bed."

"Are you sure, my darling?"

"Yes, Mama."

Jenny walked away from the door. Rachel slipped out of her clothes and climbed into her bed. She lay there, feeling the softness of the sheets and the warmth of her quilt.

My bed… When I'm rich, I'll have a hundred beds to go in the big house I will buy.

And then, like a still, small voice…

For the love of money is the root of all evil: which while some coveted after, they have erred from the faith, and pierced themselves through with many sorrows.

Rachel sat up. The room was dark and still. She waited, holding her breath. Someone lingered in the room—at least it seemed like it. She had heard a voice. She spoke into the darkness.

"Who's there?"

No servant can serve two masters: for either he will hate the one, and love the other; or else he will hold to the one, and despise the other. Ye cannot serve God and mammon.

A chill went down Rachel's back. She knew who it was.

I don't want to listen. I've made up my mind. That's all there is to it, so don't try to convict me anymore. I don't need You.

The silence pressed down on her. She spoke into the darkness.

"I… I just want to live my own life. Can't You understand?"

But no answer came, only the mournful cooing of a dove in the oak tree outside her room.

When Rachel awoke, dawn's light was creeping through the window. A soft breeze swept in through the partly opened window, heralding another perfect morning in Paradise. Rachel lay still for a long moment, enjoying the soft scent of lilacs blooming in the yard outside. Then a little stab of pain touched her heart.

I need to talk to Mama.

Rachel got up and dressed. She slipped on her *kappe* and then looked in the mirror.

Maybe I won't be wearing these plain clothes much longer.

The thought pressed against her mind like a headache. She went down into the kitchen. Her mama was cleaning up some dishes. Jenny smiled as Rachel came in the room.

"*Gut mariye, dochter.* Are you feeling better?"

"*Gut mariye.* Yes, Mama. I'm fine."

Rachel stood silently watching her mama, the weight of her presence demanding a response. Finally, Jenny turned to her daughter.

"What is it, Rachel?"

"Is Papa here?"

"No, he is already out in the fields. Why?"

"Mama, I need to ask you some questions, but I don't want Papa listening in."

"We have some time, Rachel. Would you like some coffee?"

Rachel slipped into her chair.

"Yes, that would be nice."

Jenny poured two mugs.

"So, what is it you need to know, Rachel?"

Rachel blurted out her question.

"Who am I, Mama?"

Jenny paled. "What do you mean?"

"I want to know who I am, Mama. I heard you and Papa talking. You said that you would never tell me what you were talking about. It made me angry, and then sad that you would hide something from me."

Jenny looked at her daughter for a long time and then sighed.

"You are right, Rachel. It is not right for me to keep secrets from you. I am sorry."

"Will you tell me what you were talking about?"

Jenny poured a little cream into her coffee and stirred it. "We were talking about your grandfather."

"You mean *Grossdaadi* Reuben?"

"No, my birth father, Robert St. Clair."

"You have never told me anything about your birth parents except that you named me after Mama Rachel and that she married an *Englischer*."

"Yes. Rachel Borntraeger St. Clair. She was born here on this farm, just like you were. She grew up in Paradise and then she met Robert St. Clair and fell in love. She became pregnant out of wedlock and my *Grossdaadi* Borntraeger, who was a *Bisschop*, put her under the *meidung* because she would not give up Robert."

Rachel knew the answer to her next question, but she asked it anyway. "And who are the St. Clairs?"

"The St. Clairs are one of the wealthiest families in America. They live in New York."

Rachel pushed harder. "And why have I never known anything about them?"

Jenny stood up. "Come with me, Rachel, I want to show you something."

She led the way upstairs to her writing room. They went in and Jenny shut the door. Jenny went to the shelves and found a manila envelope. Inside it was a small blue book. Jenny opened it and showed it to Rachel. About half the pages were torn out.

"This was your *Grossmutter* Rachel's journal. It was given to me by the mother of the man who was responsible for Mama Rachel's death."

On the inside cover, someone had written something, but Rachel couldn't read it because it had been crossed out so thoroughly that it was illegible. Under that, written in neat cursive, was the name Rachel St. Clair. The handwriting was strong and smooth. Jenny turned to a dated entry. Rachel read it.

April 23, 1950.

Today I arrived in New York with Jenny. I got a room in a hotel. The room is tiny and smells of cigarettes. Jenny has been fussy. I know she misses Robert very much. Tomorrow I will go to see Robert's parents. They live on the Upper East Side. I hope they are as kind as Robert said. Surely they will love their granddaughter and want to help her. Robert, I miss you, too.

Rachel was puzzled. "What happened to Robert, Mama?"

"Robert was killed in an accident when I was three. That was why Mama Rachel went to New York. She couldn't go back to her family so she went to see if the St. Clairs would help."

Jenny pulled a stack of sheets out of the envelope. "These are pages that were torn out of the journal. When we were searching for my mother, we tracked her to the motel where she died. The police never identified the body so her belongings were in storage. There was a secret compartment in her suitcase and Jonathan found these. *Grossmutter* Rachel hid them to keep Augusta St. Clair from finding them."

"How did Rachel die, Mama?"

"She overdosed on heroin. The man she was with, Joe Bender, took me and left for California. He crashed his

car in Apple Creek and drowned when he fell through
the ice on a frozen pond. Mama Jerusha found me in
the wrecked car and saved me."

"Why would Mama Rachel want to hide the pages
from Augusta St. Clair?"

Jenny took the top sheet from the pile of pages and
read it aloud.

April 24, 1950.

*This morning I took the streetcar to see Robert's
parents. It was difficult, but I finally got to the
house. It's enormous! It sits right on a big park.
The streetcar man said the name of the park is
Central Park. My heart was pounding when I
went up to the door. There was a big knocker
so I knocked and after a while a young woman
came and answered the door. I told her who we
were and that I wanted to see Robert's parents.
She looked very surprised. She told me to wait
and closed the door. After a while another woman
came. She said her name was Augusta and asked
me what I wanted. When I told her, she smiled a
strange smile at me. I asked if I could see Robert's parents, but she was very suspicious. She
said that Robert's father had died shortly after
Robert's accident, and Robert's mother would
not see anyone. I told her about Jenny and she
laughed at me. She said that I was just another
fortune hunter who wanted to cash in. She told
me to go away and then she closed the door in my
face. I knocked again, but no one came. I went*

back to the hotel. Tomorrow I will take the proof and show her.

Jenny read on.

April 25, 1950.

Today I took the papers and went back to the house. A big man in a black suit answered the door. He told me that Miss Augusta had warned him that I would be coming back and he told me to go away. I begged him to let me see Robert's mother, but he said he would call the police. Then he closed the door. I knocked and knocked. After a while a car pulled up in front of the house and two men got out. They didn't say anything to me. They just put me in the car and took me back to the hotel. When I got out, they warned me that if I went back to the house I would be arrested and put in jail. Robert! Why did you leave me? I need you!

May 5, 1950.

For the last week I have been trying to call Robert's mother but they always hung up. Finally, they told me that if I ever called again, they knew where I was staying, and they would send the police and take my little girl away and put me in jail. My money is almost gone, and the man at the hotel told me I have one more day to pay him. God, why have you abandoned me in this horrible place? I wish I had listened to my daed. I miss them all so much, but I can never go home. What can I do?

May 6, 1950.

Today, when I went to get something to eat, someone came into my room, but the door was not broken and the windows were locked. Robert's papers were gone. I have the most important ones hidden, though, and they didn't find them. I think that the woman, Augusta, sent someone to make sure I couldn't prove anything. I had my diary in my purse so they didn't get it, but I'm going to take the pages about Robert out and hide them, too. Maybe I can find a way to see Robert's mother.

Jenny stopped for a moment. Rachel saw that her mama was crying.

"There is one more entry. Let me read it."

May 10, 1950.

I have been out on the streets since the two men came and put me out of the hotel. They said that Robert's mother sent them and they would take Jenny away forever if I didn't get out of New York. We've been sleeping under the stairs behind an apartment building. Today I met a man named Joe. He said he would let us stay in his apartment and that he would help me. I want to go home.

Jenny put down the stack of pages. "That's all there is. Shortly after that, Mama Rachel was with Joe Bender when he robbed a bank. The robbery failed but Joe and Rachel escaped. I was with them. On their way west, Rachel died. I have never told you this story because it is so terrible. I should have but I didn't think you needed to know it."

Rachel still couldn't quite wrap her mind around what she had heard. "So, this Augusta St. Clair…"

"Augusta St. Clair did everything she could to prevent Rachel from meeting Robert's mother. She sent the police to harass Rachel, and finally had her put out on the street. It was many years before I could bring myself to find grace for the things Augusta did. That's why I never told you about her."

Rachel reached in her pocket and pulled out the business card. "I met this man when he was leaving. Who is he?"

Jenny took the card. "He for Augusta St. Clair. Bobby warned me about him. He is a professionally trained killer and he means us no good. You must not contact him."

Rachel took a deep breath. "When were you going to tell me about the Key, Mama?"

Chapter Fourteen

Rachel's Choice

Rachel stared at her mama's face. The question lay between them like shards of broken glass. "You heard Papa and me talking, then?"

"Yes, Mama. You were talking about the Key. What did it mean?"

"The Key is a birthmark that the legitimate heir to the St. Clair fortune must have. It is key-shaped and red."

Rachel reached to her blouse and unbuttoned it. There above her breast, over her heart, was a key-shaped red birthmark. "Does it look like this, Mama?"

Jenny nodded. "I swear I did not know what that birthmark meant until the man named Randall came to see me. I didn't know, Rachel."

"But, what did he say about it?"

"Whoever has that birthmark is a legitimate heir to the St. Clair fortune. Your grandfather, Robert, had it but he was killed before he inherited. After Robert's father died, the money that would have gone to Robert was put into trust. Robert's father never accepted me as his granddaughter and he never told anyone about me. I think my grandfather St. Clair made my grandmother keep quiet about me, too, for social reasons. Augusta St. Clair never told the trustees about me. She let them believe that Robert died without an heir, hoping that the money would then go to her. As far as the trustees were concerned I never existed."

"Why is Augusta looking for you now?"

Jenny took a sip of coffee. Her hands were shaking and the coffee in her cup did a tiny dance before she set it down. "I'm not sure, Rachel. Something must have happened with the money. If her grandson had the birthmark, he would have inherited. Augusta probably tried to claim the money because she was married to Robert's brother but he died before Robert. The only reason a woman like her would start looking for legitimate heirs is because she needs me to get the money."

"But if I have the Key the money belongs to me, right?"

"There are certain conditions, Rachel."

"That I have to marry a suitable male St. Clair, right?"

"Yes, that's the condition. And Augusta's grandson is the obvious choice."

"But then I'd have the money, and I could live my life any way I wanted."

Jenny cringed. "Yes, but…but, Rachel. Think of what that would mean. You would marry an *Englischer*. You would go under the *meidung*. You would lose everything you have, your life, your family, me, your papa…"

"What it would mean, Mama, is that I could go to

college, I could become a vet, I could live my own life without a lot of rules and regulations. And without…"

Jenny's face was white. "Without what, Rachel?"

"Without a crazy man yelling at me, ordering me around, making my life a living hell."

Jenny stood up. Her face blanched and her body shook. "Rachel Hershberger! Your papa is not crazy; he is ill. He…he…"

Rachel stood up, too. Rachel pointed her finger at Jenny. "He's not sick; he's a bully. He just wants to control me. Sometimes I wish…"

"What do you wish, Rachel?" Jenny's voice was icy cold.

The words came tumbling out, like water rushing through a sudden break in a dam. "I wish he would have drowned in the ocean. I wish… I wish he really were dead!"

Jenny's mouth moved but no words came out. Rachel turned and rushed out of the room. She ran down the hall into her room and slammed the door behind her.

Rachel stood at the bank of phones outside the general store. She started to lift the receiver, but something held her back. Her mama's words rang in her head like sledgehammers on an anvil.

"This man works for Augusta St. Clair. He is a very bad man. Bobby warned me about him. He is a professionally trained killer and he means us no good. Whatever you do, you must not contact him."

Rachel stared at the phone in her hand.

What can I do? I should not call this man, but I need to know if what he said is true.

Then she had an idea. She dialed the zero.

"Operator, how may I help you?"

"Yes, operator, I need to be connected to information in New York City."

There was a pause and a click, and then another voice came on the line.

"New York information, how may I help you today?"

"I need the phone number of someone in New York City."

"Do you have a name, please?"

Rachel thought she heard someone calling her name. She looked around but she was alone.

"I need a name, ma'am."

Rachel swallowed hard. "Yes, I'm sorry. I need the number for Augusta St. Clair."

Augusta St. Clair sat at her desk, going over some papers. Randall's report had given her a severe case of indigestion. An open bottle of Tums and a glass of water sat in front of her. A buzzer sounded on the intercom.

"What is it, Eva?"

"There's a call for you, ma'am."

Augusta sighed.

"Eva, who is it? Surely you have a name?"

"Oh…yes, I do. It's a Rachel Hershberger."

"Rachel Hershberger? Who's that?"

"She says her grandmother was Rachel St. Clair."

Augusta's ears perked up.

"Rachel St. Clair?"

"She says she has the Key."

Augusta's heart skipped a beat.

"Let me speak to her."

There was a moment of silence, a click, and then Augusta heard the connection go live again.

"Hello, who is this?"

A soft, youngish-sounding voice answered.

"Mrs. St. Clair?"

"Yes, this is Augusta St. Clair. Who is this?"

There was a pause.

"This is Rachel Hershberger. My mother is Jenny Hershberger, but her birth name was Jennifer St. Clair. She is the daughter of Robert St. Clair and Rachel Borntraeger St. Clair."

Augusta took a breath.

"And why are you calling me?"

"A man—a Mr. Randall—came to our farm looking for the daughter of Robert St. Clair. He talked about the St. Clair fortune and the birthmark that proves who the heir is—the Key. I have that birthmark."

Augusta stood up from her chair. She kept her voice modulated to a low pitch as she began to walk back and forth behind the desk with the phone to her ear.

"Why didn't you just tell Mr. Randall?"

"I didn't know why he had come to our house. Then when my mama told me who he was, I didn't want to call him. There was something…nasty about him. I thought it might be better to just talk to you."

Augusta smiled. Randall definitely could be creepy. She probed deeper.

"Well, Rachel, how do I know you are who you say you are? Maybe you're just a girl with a blemish on your skin."

The voice on the other end flashed back at her. "That's how you treated my grandmother, isn't it? You just brushed her and my mama off and left them to die on the streets. Well, my mama didn't die. I think this isn't such a good idea, after all. I shouldn't have even called you."

The girl has spunk, like her grandmother...

"Wait, Rachel, don't hang up. I didn't mean to offend. But there is a great deal of money involved here, after all, and I need to be very sure of whom I'm dealing with. Now, let's just cool down and see how we can verify what you're saying. After all, if what you claim is true, you are my great-niece."

"As I said, Mrs. St. Clair—"

"Call me Augusta."

"As I said... Augusta, my *grossdaadi*, my grandfather, was Robert St. Clair. My mama showed me the marriage license and her birth certificate."

Augusta sat down in her chair.

"My men didn't find a marriage license. I mean..."

"That's right, your men didn't find it because it was hidden in the bottom of my *grosmutter's* suitcase. It's all in her journal: how you drove her away from Robert's parents, how you sent the police to harass her."

"Now listen, dear. I was only trying to protect my mother-in-law from further heartbreak. She had already lost two sons. There were many girls who claimed they had relationships with Robert or Jerod. What was I to do?"

The voice on the other end was firm and direct. "What you should have done was to meet with Rachel privately and see what she had to say. Then, if she had legitimate proof, you could have introduced her to her mother-in-law. If you had any grace in you at all—"

Augusta laughed. "I'm sorry, Rachel. I'm not laughing at you. It's just that in the world that I live in, there is not a lot of room for…for grace. So I am not a very gracious person."

"That is obvious from my *grossmutter's* journal."

"Point taken, my dear. Now, can we get beyond the unpleasantries and see what we can do about this?"

"What do you suggest?"

"I think we should meet so you can show me these documents. We would need to do a paternity test."

"Paternity test?"

"Yes, Rachel. I can have my personal physician—"

"I would prefer to have a neutral doctor do the test. I don't have a lot of faith in you…yet."

Augusta scowled, but her voice didn't show it. "That's fine, Rachel. Can you bring the documents?"

"Yes, I know where they are. I'll make copies to show you."

Augusta didn't like the initiative that Rachel was showing. "Well, I'd rather see the originals."

Rachel laughed. "Right. I may be Amish, but I'm not stupid. I would bring the documents and your man, Randall, would take them from me, maybe even kill me, and then my proof would be gone. No, we will do this my way. No matter how pleasant you sound, I do not trust you in the least. We will meet at a public place. I will show you the copies. Mr. Randall will not be there. I will give blood or whatever we need to take the test. I will show you the Key. And then you can decide what you want to do."

Augusta sat back down in her chair. She didn't like the way this was going. "You're pretty spunky for an Amish girl."

"I got it from my mama. And remember, you need

me. I don't need you. I'm sure there are others in the
St. Clair family that I can contact."

Augusta frowned again. The last thing she wanted
was for Rachel to see Duvigney.

"All right, Rachel. We'll do it your way. How can I
contact you?"

"You can't. I'm Amish, remember? We don't have
phones. I'll call you tomorrow at about this same time.
Have all the arrangements made."

The line went dead. Augusta stared at the receiver
in her hand and then plunged her finger down on the
intercom button. Eva answered.

"Yes, Mrs. St. Clair?"

"Get that grandson of mine down here immediately.
I need to talk to him right now!"

Rachel stood at the phone bank with the phone receiver still in her hand. She was shaking all over. The
phone call had been the hardest she had ever made.

*I'm glad she couldn't see me. She wouldn't have
thought I was so tough.*

Chapter Fifteen

The Meeting

Gerald St. Clair looked at his watch for the twentieth time. The two-hour trip from Manhattan had been extremely boring. It was always tedious traveling with his grandmother. She didn't let him smoke cigarettes or listen to the radio. And now she was dragging him out to a farm to meet…an Amish girl. Augusta had briefed him carefully, and he could just imagine how this Rachel would look—cow-like features, boots covered with mud and manure, and a stupid bonnet. He needed a drink badly.

"Grandmother, do we really have to go through with this?"

Augusta gave Gerald "the look" and Gerald glanced away.

"Gerald, look at me!"

Gerald tried to meet her steely gaze.

"Do you want to be poor?"

"No, Grandmother."

"All the privileges, the life of ease and comfort—do you want all that to disappear?"

Gerald sighed. "No, Grandmother."

Augusta pulled a compact from her purse. After another touch of lipstick, she snapped it shut. "Now I'm going to explain this one more time. This girl has the Key. That means she inherits everything except the pittance in my husband's trust fund and the house we live in. She gets the New York mansion and the Connecticut estate. When I say she gets everything, that means billions."

Gerald tried to counterattack. "When you say there's only a pittance, are you talking a few million, a few thousand, what?"

Augusta reached into her Louis Vuitton bag and found an official-looking document. She put on a pair of reading glasses, adjusted them on the end of her nose, and began to read. "The Trust of Jerod St. Clair—Current cash and bonds: $15,985,000. Expenditures 1989: $4,000,000. Income and interest 1989: $500,000. Net debit 1989: $3,500,000."

Gerald looked out the window and frowned. It was worse than he thought.

I really need a drink.

"So you see, darling Gerald, your trips to Europe, the gambling in Monaco, the women, the drugs and alcohol—your flamboyant lifestyle is grinding us right into the poor house. At this rate, we will be out of money in less than five years. And when it's gone, there's only the house. If we have to sell it, we will raise a few million, but that won't last. You would have to get a job."

Augusta chuckled but Gerald didn't think it was

funny. He thought about mentioning her penchant for Arabian horses, five thousand dollar bottles of wine, and trips to Paris, but he thought better of it. "But, this Rachel… I mean, do I really have to marry her?"

"Rachel Hershberger cannot inherit the estate unless she marries a male St. Clair within a certain time period. The St. Clairs put in that stipulation to ensure that the money would always remain in St. Clair hands. The only other option is for you to produce a male heir who would inherit when he turns twenty-one. Given that it would take you a minimum of nine months if you started today, and assuming that it would be a male, we would have to wait twenty-two years to get the money—if you survived that long working at a Dairy Queen."

Augusta returned to her magazine.

Rachel waited by the General Store in Paradise. She had copies of her grandmother's wedding license and her mama's birth certificate in an envelope. The St. Clairs were late. Rachel was so intent on looking for the car that she didn't hear the footsteps behind her.

"*Gut mariye*, Rachel."

Rachel's heart jumped. She turned to see Daniel King.

"Daniel, must you always come creeping up on me? You scared me."

A shadow crossed Daniel's face for just a moment, and then it passed. "A cat looking for a mouse creeps, Rachel. I was walking by. And judging by your face, I should keep on walking."

Daniel turned to go.

"Wait, Daniel. I'm sorry. It's just…it's just…"

"Just what?"

"I'm waiting for someone and I don't have time to…" She paused.

"To say hello to a friend?"

"Yes. I mean, no, I… Oh, Daniel, why do you always fluster me so?"

"Don't mean to, Rachel, but while we are here, can I ask when you will come to look at the foal again?"

Rachel felt a twinge of irritation.

Doesn't he know this is the most important day of my life? No, of course not.

"I don't have time to think about that, Daniel."

At that moment, a long black limousine pulled up in front of them. The door opened and a young man got out. He was dressed in charcoal slacks and a white pullover. He was very handsome with chiseled features and dark, wavy hair. His eyes settled on Rachel and a smile crossed his face. Rachel noticed that his eyes were taking in all of her.

"Rachel Hershberger?"

Rachel blushed under his frank perusal.

"Yes, I'm Rachel."

The man extended his hand and when she shook it, he held hers a little too tightly.

"I'm Gerald St. Clair. Very nice to meet you."

The intense blue eyes were focused on her face. Suddenly, Rachel felt very uncomfortable. She pulled her hand away and glanced at Daniel. He was looking at Gerald with a strange expression on his face.

"Gerald, this is my friend, Daniel King. Daniel, this is Gerald St. Clair, a…well, I suppose we are distant cousins."

Daniel extended his hand. "*Gut mariye*, Gerald."

"Excuse me?"

"It means good morning."

Gerald smiled. "Oh, oh sure. Good morning."

Ignoring Daniel's outstretched hand, he motioned toward the limo.

"Well, cuz, shall we go?"

Daniel looked at Rachel with a puzzled expression. Rachel felt very strange, almost like she was being torn in two.

"I have to go, Daniel. I will talk to you later."

"But, Rachel, who—?"

Rachel interrupted. "I'll tell you later. Now I must go."

Gerald took her arm and steered her toward the car. He glanced back at Daniel.

"Nice to meet you, Dennis."

"Daniel."

"Right, Daniel. Come on, Rachel. We have an appointment and we're running a little late."

Gerald opened the door, and they got in. The limousine pulled away from the curb. Rachel looked out the back window. Daniel King stood alone by the edge of the road, staring after her. Suddenly, Rachel had a very sick feeling.

Augusta St. Clair leaned forward in her chair as the doctor read from a thin binder.

"Although developed in the 1980s, polymerase chain reaction technique in DNA testing has only recently become the standard process for paternity testing."

Dr. Sanderson looked at Augusta over his glasses. The desk in front of him was empty of anything except the document he was perusing. The doctor continued reading. "PCR is a technique through which samples of

DNA fragments are copied and replicated many times until billions of copies are made. Additionally—"

Augusta broke in. "Yes, Doctor, I'm sure the science is very good. What I want to know is the probability factor for proving paternity."

The doctor went on. "As I was saying, because half of the child's DNA is inherited from the mother and half from the father, the child's DNA should match both biological parents. It will also prove that even distant cousins share the same common ancestor."

"To what degree, Doctor?"

"99.999 percent accuracy, Mrs. St. Clair."

"Good. What do we do to complete the procedure?"

"A buccal swab is all we need."

"A buccal swab, Doctor?"

"It's a way to collect DNA from the inside of a person's cheek. Gerald and Rachel simply need to let me swab them. Then we create DNA profiles which are compared to determine whether there is a genetic match."

"How long will it take?"

"We should have the results in about a week, Mrs. St. Clair."

"Good. And the birthmark?"

"It is a port-wine birthmark, which has been known to be hereditary in many cases. There is no evidence of tattooing or any artificial substances beneath the skin. I am quite sure that the birthmark is genuine."

Rachel was listening intently to the doctor. Augusta smiled to herself.

Come into my web, little fly...

Daniel King pulled his buggy up in front of his house and got out. His *maam* was out in front beating carpets.

Daniel unhitched the horse and began to lead him toward the barn.

"No greeting, son?"

Daniel looked up. "What? Oh, I'm sorry, Mama, I was thinking about something."

"Rachel?"

Daniel looked at his mother. He never could hide anything from her. "Yes, Mama. It is Rachel."

"Daniel, that girl is never going to love you like you love her. Her mind and heart are out in the world. She will never be an Amish wife."

Her words twisted in his heart like a knife. "You are right, Mama, but Rachel is in trouble."

"Rachel is always in trouble."

His *maam* turned back to the rug and began to beat it. Daniel led the horse to the barn and put some hay out for it. Then he walked out the back and took the path up the hill. He needed to think.

The afternoon sun warmed his back. The birds sang in the oak trees along the path, and the fresh air of Pennsylvania filled his senses. But Daniel's heart was heavy. He had seen something nasty in Gerald's face—lust and greed and wantonness—revealed in a way he had never seen before. It sickened him. Daniel did not know who these St. Clairs were, but they were not good people. And he knew Rachel would never find her dream with them.

Chapter Sixteen

The Breaking

Rachel sat at the restaurant table looking down at the filet mignon in front of her. Augusta leaned toward her.

"Rachel, dear, you've hardly eaten a bite."

Rachel pushed her plate away. "I'm sorry, Mrs. St. Clair."

"Augusta, dear. Call me Augusta."

"I'm sorry… Augusta. I just don't seem to have an appetite."

Augusta picked up her purse. "I'm going to powder my nose. Why don't you two get a little better acquainted?" She rose and walked away.

Gerald took a sip of his wine. "You must have a lot on your mind, Rachel, since it's almost been confirmed that you are a St. Clair and—"

"And I am the heiress? Well, when the DNA test comes back positive I will be."

Gerald let the remark pass. He gave Rachel another very appraising look and Rachel blushed. Gerald put his glass down with a repentant expression on his face. "I'm sorry, Rachel. Did I embarrass you?"

Rachel decided it was best to be honest with this man. "Yes, you did. I have never had anyone look at me the way you do, and it makes me feel…well, ashamed."

A strange look crossed Gerald's face. "I'm sorry. Most girls like to be looked at that way. I'm only staring because you're very beautiful."

"And you weren't expecting that, were you?"

"Since we're being blunt, no, I wasn't."

Rachel smiled for the first time. "What were you expecting?"

"You won't be angry?"

Rachel looked down. Gerald was so handsome and no one had called her beautiful in a long time. Except Daniel, of course. "Go ahead."

Gerald took a sip of his wine. "I had this picture in my mind of a large, shall we say, raw-boned girl, with calloused hands, laced-up boots covered with manure, and a hearty slap-on-the-back kind of attitude. You know, a farm girl."

Rachel laughed. "And I don't fit that picture?"

"Not in the least bit."

Rachel realized that her heart was beating rapidly in her chest. He was well-mannered, friendly, obviously intelligent, and very handsome. He had a perspective on the world that was entirely foreign, yet enticing.

Just then Augusta returned to the table. A waiter brought another bottle of wine. Augusta leaned over to Rachel. "Won't you have a small glass of wine with us, Rachel? It's a naïve domestic, but surprisingly good."

"I… I don't know. My parents never let me drink wine. Besides, I'm not twenty-one."

"Oh, just one won't hurt. After all, doesn't the Bible say, 'Thou dost cause the grass to grow for the cattle, and plants for man to cultivate, that he may bring forth food from the earth, and wine to gladden the heart of man?'"

Rachel looked at Augusta with surprise. "You know the Bible?"

"Well, of course, dear. I've been an Episcopalian all my life. I find great comfort in the Bible."

Rachel was confused. She had fully intended to despise these people. She blurted out a response. "If you think the Bible is so wonderful, why did you treat my grandmother the way you did?"

Augusta reached over and took Rachel's hand. "Rachel, when your grandmother came to New York, she was the fifth girl who claimed to have a relationship with Robert St. Clair. It was terribly upsetting to Robert's mother. How was I to know that she was married to Robert? She showed me no proof. Max was dead, so he couldn't confirm anything. He was so disappointed with Robert that he never showed us any pictures of your grandmother. He must have destroyed them. I was just protecting my mother-in-law."

Rachel wanted to pull away, but she held her hand still. "But you were so cruel to her. You put her out on the street and she died. You can't tell me that was just protecting my great-grandmother!"

Augusta glanced at Gerald who was looking down at his plate. "Yes, Rachel, you're right."

Augusta took a breath. "Here's the reality. Those of us with lots of money are constantly attracting grifters and phonies, investment bankers and attorneys. They're like parasites wanting to bite off a piece of what we have. They lie, cheat and steal to get what they want. In order to keep them away, you become like them. And when you do, you become hard and grasping. I don't like what I've become, but I am a product of my environment. Meeting you, if I had to do it over again, I would probably treat your grandmother differently. But that was then and this is now. I'm very sorry about what happened to Robert's wife, and I want to make it up to you. How can I do that?"

Rachel sat very still. Augusta's request had taken her by surprise. Then the smiling faces of the two people wore down her resistance. She picked up the empty glass in front of her. "I think you might start with a glass of that wine, Augusta."

Jenny Hershberger sat in the silent house with Jonathan. The room was dark except for the low light from a fire in the hearth. Jonathan stirred himself to put a few more logs on. Then he stood by the fireplace, leaning against the large stones that framed the opening. The day had been overcast and chilly, but for Jenny, the chill was in her heart.

"Where could she be, Jonathan?"

Jonathan rubbed the side of his head where the scar ran along his hairline, an unconscious habit since his injury.

"She's with them, and only trouble will come of it."

Jenny's heart was wrapped in a strange foreboding, tangible and oppressive. Around nine o'clock they heard a car coming up the driveway. The light from the headlamps cast strange shadows from the porch posts onto the walls of the room, like dark figures writhing in torment. Jenny heard a car door close and then the car retreated back down the lane. Soft footsteps came up the steps and across the porch. The screen door creaked as it swung open and then Rachel was standing in the doorway. Jenny's eyes met Rachel's and her heart sank. There was defiance there, and Jenny knew Rachel had made a decision.

"Rachel, where have you been? It's so late and we were worried."

"Mama, if Daniel came by, you know where I've been."

Rachel's words had a strange slur.

Jonathan stepped close to Rachel. "You've been drinking!"

"I had a glass of wine with my dinner, and a very good dinner it was. The St. Clairs took me to the nicest place I've ever been and…and I liked it."

Jenny got to her feet.

"The St. Clairs? Rachel, they… Augusta did terrible things to your *grossmutter*."

Rachel pulled off her shawl and hung it on the peg by the door. "There are always two sides to every story. Augusta told me what happened. She was very sorry. She was only protecting her mother-in-law."

Jonathan took Rachel by the shoulder. "She was only protecting her money, you little fool. Going off with those people and drinking! While you live in my house, you will not go with *Englischers* or—"

Rachel jerked her shoulder out of Jonathan's grasp. "Your house? Again, Papa, it's your house? Well, I have lived here longer than you. This is more my house than yours. Or is it Richard Sandbridge's house? You don't even know and neither do I."

The sound of the slap was like a cracking whip. Jonathan's hand rose again, but Jenny leaped forward and grabbed her husband's arm. "Jonathan! No!"

She felt the rigid arm relax and then it fell to his side. He looked at her helplessly.

Rachel stood holding her hand to her face. The red mark across her cheek flamed in the flickering light. Her words came like rifle bullets. "In the years to come, Papa, you will remember that it was you who closed the door."

Then she went down the hall to her room. The sound of the door slamming broke the night.

The sun was trying to force its way into overcast sky when Jenny arose. She wrapped her shawl tightly against the unseasonable chill and looked down at her sleeping husband. The scar from the terrible explosion so many years ago was very visible along his hairline. Jenny reached down and softly stroked the hair into place.

Oh, Jonathan. You've changed so much. Somewhere along this road you lost the part of you that loves life. It is so hard for you, and it is not anything you did. I wish I could do something, but only du leiber Gott *can heal your wounded heart.*

Jenny sighed and left the room. She looked at the crack under Rachel's door to see if her daughter was up, but there was no light and no sound coming from the room. She went upstairs to her study.

Ever since she had come back to Paradise, this room had been her refuge. She went to the pale birch desk, the desk her papa had made for her. Her hand caressed the smooth wood, sanded so beautifully that it felt soft to the touch. Jenny pulled out her chair and sat down.

She pushed the piles of papers and notes aside and laid her head on the table.

"Oh, Papa! How I wish you were here. I would wrap myself in your arms and listen to your wonderful voice telling me that everything would be all right. I need you, Papa."

Jenny remembered another sunrise, long ago, when she had been despairing of ever living again. That dawn had come creeping into her room like a mischievous child, softly kissing her awake with the delicate touch of a rose-colored morning. Jenny remembered the pale colors blushing in the fresh sky. She had risen and wrapped a shawl around her shoulders, just like she had this morning, and slipped outside.

The day was fresh and clean and warm, and the grass felt cool and damp against my bare feet. The plum trees were just sending forth their tiny, pink buds. A single wren twittered its call and stillness lay on the land.

Jenny rubbed the smooth surface of the desk. She could almost feel her papa's love emanating from the wood, the love that had sustained her and kept her all her life until the day...

Jenny didn't want to think about that other day, so she pushed her thoughts back to that morning, so long ago in Apple Creek. She remembered her papa coming out on the porch of their little house.

You were dressed for work and you were so handsome. The circle of your arms was like a fortress and a strong tower. I felt life coming back into me. It was as though I had been raised from the dead! Your words comforted me so.

Jenny put her head down on the desk and began to weep.

"Oh, Lord, where are You? I'm losing Rachel, and

I've never really gotten Jonathan back. I am so alone. Why won't You help me?"

And then a still, small voice that she had not heard for a long time spoke into her troubled spirit.

I never said there would not be hard times. I only said I would never leave you or forsake you.

Chapter Seventeen

Many Sorrows

Rachel looked up. Jenny stood in the doorway looking at the half-packed suitcase on the bed. Rachel saw the look on her mama's face, but she steeled herself against it.

"But where will you go, Rachel? How will you live?"

"I am about to become a billionaire, Mama. The St. Clairs have an apartment in New York, where I'll stay until Gerald and I are married. After that, we'll see what happens."

Rachel saw the pain on her mama's face.

"Please, Rachel, you must not do this thing. How can you even consider marriage? What about courtship? What about getting to know each other first?"

"Gerald is handsome, and he is attentive. As of now, we have a business arrangement, but who knows? I may come to love him. That would be an added bonus."

"He only cares about the money, Rachel!"

"Gerald thinks I'm beautiful, and he feels more for me than just friendship, but that is beside the point,

Mama. He is my ticket out. I want to become a veterinarian. Gerald has no problem with that. My money will pay for the best schools in the world, schools like the Royal Veterinary College. The St. Clairs have a house in London, and we could live there while I attend."

"But I thought you wanted to go to Cornell?"

"What does that matter now, Mama? Papa could have helped me financially. He made a lot of money when he was Richard Sandbridge. Now it's too late."

"Rachel, your papa gave most of that money away when he came back to the church. He wanted to forget everything that happened to him while he was gone."

Rachel turned back to her packing. "Another brilliant decision by Jonathan Hershberger, otherwise known as Richard Sandbridge."

"Rachel, why do you hate him so?"

Rachel felt her hands clenching as she stood with her back to her mama. Then the frustration of the last four years spilled out. "What do you expect, Mama? When he left us, it nearly killed me—"

"He did not leave us, Rachel. He couldn't help what happened."

"Mama, let me finish."

Jenny stopped and Rachel went on. "When he left us, everything changed. We went back to Ohio and you were so sad for so long. Everything was about you, your sorrow, your grief. What about my grief? You thought I was doing okay, but I was not. And you were so lost in your own pain that you had no time to really find out how I was feeling. At least I had *grossdaadi* and *grossmutter*, and they helped me for a while. Then they died and I was so afraid."

"Afraid?"

"Yes, Mama. I was afraid—afraid you would leave me, too. I used to wake up at night feeling like someone was standing on my chest. I just knew something was going to happen to you and then I would be completely alone. And then he came home and it did happen."

"What happened?"

"You left me, Mama."

"But how? I was right here all the time."

Rachel's voice rose. "No, Mama, you were not. Suddenly, we had a stranger in our house and everything was about him. Poor Jonathan, he's not well. Poor Jonathan, he shouldn't be disturbed. You never had time for me anymore and I hated that. It was like I was a stranger, standing out on the porch and looking into this house where all this love used to be, but I was out in the cold and you both were inside."

As she spoke, Rachel stepped closer to her mama until she was standing in front of Jenny, shaking like a leaf in a storm. "You left me, Mama! You may have been here physically, but you were gone. Gone taking care of a poor fool who couldn't even remember his name most of the time. He certainly didn't remember me. And all he could do was shove rules down my throat. I got to the point where I hated the rules."

Rachel took her mother by the arms and looked right into her eyes. "Don't you understand, Mama? I hate being Amish. God has opened a door for me to leave. And I'm going."

Rachel went to the closet and pulled down some more things.

"Rachel, this is not God."

"Who is it then, the devil?"

"But the people you will be with, the man you are marrying—"

Rachel flung the clothes on the bed. "You don't know what you're talking about! You haven't even taken the time to meet them, to talk to them."

"But they are *Englisch*, Rachel."

Rachel pointed her finger at Jenny. "And so are you, Mama. You're a St. Clair, too, and the St. Clair side of you has always fought against being Amish."

"No, Rachel. I have always loved being Amish."

"Have you, Mama? You write books, and get your column published in the paper and meet people from outside the church, while everyone looks the other way. Everyone says that an Amish girl can't become a vet. Well, what about an Amish girl who becomes a famous writer? The truth is that writing is the way you escape from everything Amish. Where do you go when you lock yourself in your room and write? You go away, Mama. For you to oppose me is so hypocritical!"

Rachel turned back to her suitcase. She stared down and then slammed it shut. "I don't know why I'm packing anything. I certainly won't be wearing these clothes anymore!"

Just then, there was a knock. The bedroom door opened and Jonathan's face peeked around.

"Hey, I heard yelling. Why can't we all just mellow out here?"

Rachel's stomach twisted. How she hated that voice! She didn't even look at Jonathan. "Good morning, Richard."

Jenny jerked as if she had been slapped.

Rachel re-opened the suitcase and put in a few more things. "Don't worry, Richard, everything's 'cool' in here. Jenny and I were just having a chat. I'm leaving, you know."

Jonathan looked confused. "Where are you going?"

"I'm getting married, and I am moving to New York."

Jonathan's face brightened. "Oh, that's great. Who's the lucky guy?"

Jenny took Jonathan by the arm. Tears poured down her face. "Come, Jonathan. You need to lie down."

"But, uh…but Rachel's getting married. Aren't we invited?"

Jenny turned. The stricken look on her mama's face was almost too much for Rachel, but she pushed her regret aside. "The wedding is a private affair, Richard, but when I'm settled, I'll get in touch."

Jonathan looked at Rachel. "Well, that's fine, just fine. The guy who's getting you is sure lucky."

Jenny began to pull Jonathan out of the room. "Come, Jonathan. You must rest."

Jonathan followed. Jenny closed the door behind them. Rachel heard Jonathan's feet shuffling down the hall. Then she heard his voice. It seemed far away, lost and lonely.

"Jenny?"

"Yes, Jonathan?"

"Jenny, where's Rachel? Where's my Rachel? I've looked and looked and I can't find her."

Rachel began to sob, quietly. She walked to the door and put her hand on the knob, but she couldn't turn it. She stood there, desperately wanting to fling the door open and run after her parents, but she didn't. Her hand slipped from the knob as tears streamed down her face.

She spoke quietly into the empty space her parents had left behind them.

"I'm here, Papa, I'm here. Come and get me, Papa. I need you."

But there was no answer.

Jenny sat in the rocking chair at the foot of the bed. All the shades were pulled, and the room was dark. Jonathan had been asleep for six hours, lying on his back like a dead man. Rachel's words careened around Jenny's thoughts like billiard balls.

"...what about an Amish girl who becomes a famous writer? Writing is the way you escape from everything Amish. Where do you go when you lock yourself in your room and write? You go away, Mama. For you to oppose me is so hypocritical."

"Lord, Rachel is right. I've used my writing to escape—from grief and sorrow, from hardship, from... from Jonathan, and yes, even from being Amish. I left her to fend for herself while I hid in my room. And now it is too late. Rachel *fühlt sich verlassen*, she feels desolate, and so she is making a terrible decision. Oh, Lord, you must make her see."

Jonathan groaned on the bed. His voice sounded weak in the darkness. "Jenny, who are you talking to?"

"I was praying, Jonathan."

"What about?"

"Rachel is leaving us."

Jenny could hear the bed creak as Jonathan twisted around. "Leaving? Where is she going?"

Jenny put her face in her hands and began to cry quietly. "She met with the St. Clairs. She has been certi-

fied as the true heir to the St. Clair fortune, and she is
going to marry Gerald St. Clair."

"What! The *Ordnung* strictly prohibits Amish girls
from marrying outside our faith…"

Something snapped inside Jenny's heart. She stood
up and went to the side of the bed. She could see Jonathan's face in the dim light. It was twisted in anger and
he was struggling to get up. Jenny pushed him down
and stood over him. "*Ordnung! Ordnung!* You have
crushed our girl beneath the weight of laws that none
of us can keep. What has happened to you, Jonathan?
You used to understand. The *Ordnung* cannot save us,
only Jesus Christ can. You have forgotten about grace.
We are children of grace, Jonathan, not of the law."

"But, Jenny, the *Ordnung* is what keeps us from the
things of the world."

"And what about love? Love for your family, for your
only daughter. Love that would keep her warm and
safe while she grew up and began to make real decisions for her own life. Times have changed, Jonathan.
You could have helped Rachel. You have some of your
royalty money left. You could have gone to the elders
and helped them to see that an Amish veterinarian who
understood our ways would be a great blessing to our
community. You could have paid her way, guiding her
and standing beside her. But instead, you beat her and
broke her with the law."

Jonathan trembled. "I only wanted to protect her
from the world. I—"

"But you never knew her. You never asked her what
she wanted. And I have been your accomplice. Rachel
was right in what she said to me. I left her. I put all my
focus on you and my writing and I left her alone in the

dark with her fear and her grief. She didn't need to be judged. She needed her papa and her mama. And we were gone, just as surely as if we had both been on that boat that blew up out on the ocean. And now she's gone…"

Jenny's heart broke and she sank to her knees. Great, gasping sobs tore from deep within her. Jonathan stared at his wife. He stretched a trembling hand toward her and touched her shoulder. Jenny twisted away.

"You have forgotten your first love, Jonathan. You have put your trust in the law but the law can't heal you. Only Jesus can heal your mind and your heart."

"But, Jenny, I need you."

"No, Jonathan, you need the Lord. You need to seek Him with all your heart. He is the God who will heal you. I can't do it anymore."

Jonathan stood up. "I'll stop her. I'll make her understand."

He went to the door and opened it. He started down the hall toward Rachel's room. Jenny lifted herself from the floor and screamed after him.

"You fool! Don't you understand? Rachel is gone and we have driven her away."

Jonathan stumbled down the hall toward Rachel's room.

"Rachel? Rachel, where are you?"

Jenny's scream cut through the air between them like a knife.

"She's gone! Don't you understand, you poor, sick fool! Our daughter is gone!"

And then Jonathan stood there helplessly while the sound of Jenny's sobs echoed through the dark and empty house.

* * *

Rachel stood beside Gerald, clad in a simple white dress. A touch of makeup highlighted her perfect features, and her auburn hair was swept into a cascade of curls—she was lovely, but her face was set like stone.

Gerald kept glancing over at her. Soft music from the organist filled the chapel. Candles and flowers decorated the altar in front of them, and Augusta stood beside them, dressed in a dark, expensive suit. The Episcopal Bishop continued reading from the wedding service, but Rachel didn't hear him. Her thoughts were far away, in a little blue house on a farm in Paradise, Pennsylvania.

Oh, Mama, Papa, what am I doing?

"Do you, Rachel, take this man, Gerald, to be your lawfully wedded husband, to have and to hold, for richer, for poorer, in sickness and in health, until death do you part?"

Augusta's soft voice interrupted Rachel's thoughts. "Rachel?"

Rachel looked at Gerald and Augusta. She wanted to scream "no," and run. Run down the aisle, out of the church, and back to her home. But she didn't. She felt the words forming in her mind and then she heard herself speaking them as if from far away. She closed her eyes.

"I do."

Chapter Eighteen

A Two-Edged Sword

Daniel King hated days like this. The cold, blustery wind drove like nails through his coat. Icy rain slapped his face, and the gray clouds scudding overhead matched his mood. He pulled his coat tighter around him as his horse hauled the black buggy along the highway. An occasional car swept by, splashing water against the wheels and up on the floor. The red warning triangle was very visible on the back of Daniel's rig, but there were still some *Englischers* who took a perverse pleasure in coming as close as they could, especially on days like this.

Daniel had not paid attention to the overcast sky before he set out, and now he was paying the price. He was miserable and wet. Finally, he saw the sign for Old Leacock Road through the rain and turned off the highway. He touched his shirt pocket, felt the letter, and wondered why Rachel had sent it to him.

Rachel had left Paradise without even a goodbye. Then today, a letter had arrived. It was short and seemed chatty, but Daniel could read between the lines. Underneath the bravado, something was wrong. His thoughts churned as he drove into the teeth of the wind. Finally, he saw the turnoff to his farm, and he gratefully guided the horse into their lane. He drove to the barn and turned inside. Water dripped off the brim of his hat as he unhitched his horse. He grabbed a towel off a rack, and dried the animal. Then he sat down on a bale of hay and pulled the letter out of his pocket. The envelope was postmarked Greenwich, Connecticut. He pulled the letter out and read it again.

Dear Daniel,

I hope this letter finds you well and happy. I am sorry I didn't say goodbye to you. Everything happened so quickly, but you are my best friend and I should have taken time to see you. Please forgive me.

Right now, Gerald and I are staying in Greenwich, Connecticut, with Augusta. It's a wonderful place, and the horses, oh, Daniel! You would love the horses. They are the finest money can buy. Augusta loves horses, so at least we have that in common.

As for my inheritance, there is a slight delay in receiving the money, so I have to wait to apply to vet school until the spring. Mr. Duvigney, the administrator of my grandfather's estate, says there are quite a few technicalities involved in transferring such an enormous sum of money into our accounts. Augusta is not too happy about that.

As for married life, Gerald and I basically have a business deal, so the romance part of it seems to be on hold for now. We do not see things the same way, but I am hoping that once we know each other better, we can resolve our differences amicably. The main thing that troubles me is that even though they go to the Episcopal Church, I'm not sure Gerald even believes in God, and that troubles me. I have not been the most faithful adherent either, but I know that Gott is real, even though He seems far away.

Daniel, please don't worry. I am doing what I wanted to do and that's a good thing, I guess. When I get started at vet school I will feel better about everything, but I do get lonely for my folks and I miss our friendship. I hope this letter doesn't get you in trouble, since I am under the meidung, but I would love to hear from you sometime.

Anyway, look after my mama and Jonathan, too.

Rachel

Daniel sighed and shook his head. He spoke out loud. "So, you don't see things the same way as a spoiled, rich *Englischer*? I wonder why!"

The horse snorted at his outburst, and Daniel looked around to see if anyone else had been listening. Rachel was right. When she married Gerald St. Clair, she was put under the *bann*, and he was forbidden to communicate with her. Daniel knew that his parents would be displeased if they saw the letter.

There was a loose board in the wall at the back of the stall, and he slipped the letter in behind it. Then he left the barn and went into the house. He looked around to make sure nobody was downstairs, and then he went into the room his father used for an office and got an envelope, a piece of paper, and a pencil. He went back out to the barn, sat down, and began to write.

Dear Rachel,

*I got your letter and you are right. I should not
communicate with you. But you are my friend, and
you sound very lonely. I know you well, Rachel,
and I can read between the lines. In your haste to
distance yourself from Jonathan, you have made
a choice that is not what you expected.*

*But that part is done. What I care about is you
and your life. I will always be your friend, and
if you need anything at all, please let me know.*

Daniel
P.S. I miss you, too.

He stared at the last words. He wanted to say how
much he loved her, but she was married, and he could
not bring himself to write the words. He lowered his
head and was silent. A tear dropped from his eye and
he wiped it away. He prayed silently.

*Lord, please be with Rachel. Protect her and guard
her. Set your mighty angels round about her and keep
her safe.* Danki. *Amen.*

Daniel put the letter in the envelope and wrote Rachel's address on the front and hid it. He felt like someone had shoved a sharpened fence post through his heart.
He could wipe away the tears from his eyes, but he could
do nothing about the deep pain twisting him inside.

Two weeks later, Daniel was hanging around outside
the post office. Several Amish folk had come and gone,
and he was waiting until he could go in unobserved.
Rachel had sent the first letter to Daniel in care of Mrs.

Shoemaker, the postmistress, so Daniel wouldn't get in trouble. So he was expecting another letter to arrive in the same fashion.

Finally, the coast was clear and he went inside. Mrs. Shoemaker motioned for him to come to the counter. She whispered in a conspiratorial way.

"Daniel, I have something for you from Connecticut. I hope it's from Rachel. It's too bad you kids can't just talk to each other. I never understood this shunning nonsense."

Mrs. Shoemaker saw the hurt in Daniel's eyes and stopped.

"No offense, Daniel. I'm sure your customs serve their purpose, after all."

She pulled out a small manila envelope, and handed it to Daniel. The postmark was from the same town in Connecticut, but the return said Augusta St. Clair, not Rachel.

Daniel tore open the envelope. Inside, he found two items. One was the letter he had written to Rachel. The letter was unopened. Daniel unfolded the sheet of paper that was with it. It was heavy linen stationery with the St. Clair family crest on the top above Augusta St. Clair's name. The message was to the point.

Dear Mr. King,

I am writing on behalf of my granddaughter-in-law, Rachel St. Clair. She wishes me to inform you that she wants nothing further to do with you or her old life. She requests that you cease annoying her and that you not communicate with her

*in any way. If you persist in your efforts, we will
be forced to seek injunctive action.*

*Yours Truly,
Augusta St. Clair*

Daniel's heart sank. Something didn't feel right. He
looked up. Mrs. Shoemaker was making strange pointing motions with her eyebrows. Then he felt a large
hand rest on his shoulder.

"What's this?"

Startled, Daniel looked around. His father stood behind him, looking at the two letters in Daniel's hands.
Mrs. Shoemaker suddenly remembered something she
had to do in the back room and disappeared.

"Can I see that?" his papa asked.

Reluctantly, Daniel handed over the letter from Augusta. His father read it and then sighed.

"And the other?"

Daniel pulled away. "It is personal, Papa."

"Also, *das ist persönlich?* From Rachel?"

Daniel trembled under his father's stern gaze. "*Nein*,
Papa. It is a letter I wrote to her."

Mr. King motioned Daniel to follow him and walked
outside. He put his arm around Daniel's shoulders.
"Walk with me, son."

They walked down the steps. The King's buggy
was standing next to the phone booth at the side of the
building. Daniel's mother was waiting in the buggy,
and she started to speak as they passed. But Daniel's
papa motioned to her and kept walking. The fallen
leaves crunched under Daniel's feet, and the crunch-
ing sounded like bones breaking. The stark, bare limbs

of the trees stood up like withered arms reaching out for a last bit of life from a cheerless sky. They walked a few blocks before Mr. King spoke. "You know that Rachel is under the *meidung*, the *bann*?"

"*Ja*, Papa."

"And you know that it is forbidden to communicate with her?"

"*Ja*, Papa."

Mr. King stopped and turned to his son. "Daniel, you are a good son. You are strong and faithful, yet you are also kind and gentle. You have never given me any reason to be other than very proud of you. The *Ordnung* may seem strict and without grace. It may seem to you that we are keeping rules by the letter of the law and not the spirit. And yet I know that the *Ordnung* is good. They have been written to protect our faith and our people and to keep us pure and undefiled from a world that is walking with the devil."

"I know that, Papa—"

Daniel's father went on. "I will not say anything about this. I trust you and know that except for your deep love for this girl, you would never have broken our rules."

Daniel dropped his eyes. The pain in his heart was almost more than he could bear.

"But I also know that if you continue on this path, it will only bring you great sorrow."

Daniel looked at his papa. "*Daed*, Rachel is in trouble. Something's wrong. She sent me a letter a few weeks ago, and I could tell she was troubled."

"Of course she is troubled. *Sie wird gestört.* She disobeyed her father and mother; she married outside her faith; she is bound by enormous wealth. Son, you cannot serve *Gott* and mammon, too. Her conscience is tearing at her."

"But, *Daed!* She needs my help."

Mr. King held up the letter from Augusta. "Daniel! You are so bound up by this girl that you cannot see the truth. This is not a letter from"—he glanced down at the signature—"from Augusta St. Clair. It is a letter from *du lieber Gott*. He is telling you to stop, to give her up, to get on with your life. Don't you understand?"

There was a long silence. Finally, Daniel spoke.

"*Ja*, Papa. I understand."

But he did not understand at all.

It was late in the day. Daniel sat on a stump among the trees on the top of the knoll. He was looking east. It had turned cold, and a flurry of snow had fallen. But then the clouds had cleared and now the setting sun cast long shadows toward the east. The remains of the brief storm scudded east on a brisk breeze and the trees above him rustled and shook. Daniel pulled his coat closer around him and then stood up and stamped his feet to get the circulation going.

That cold front is moving east. It will be snowing in Connecticut tonight.

He was stiff from the cold, but his thoughts were not on the temperature. Rachel was in trouble. Daniel could feel it in his whole being. Finally, he slipped to his knees, bowed his head and began seeking the Lord in prayer.

Lieber Gott im Himmel, *I have to do something. Rachel needs me. Those people that she went with, they are bad.* Helfen Sie mir, Herrn, *show me how to help her.*

And then, as clearly as if a voice had spoken, Daniel knew what he had to do.

Chapter Nineteen

Surrender

A month after their wedding, Gerald and Rachel flew to Italy. Rachel resisted going on a long trip with a man she hardly knew, but Augusta finally prevailed by suggesting that they needed to keep up appearances for the sake of their position in society. She made light of their "business" relationship as she helped Rachel pack. "My dear, you'll love the Amalfi Coast. Oh, it's my favorite place in Europe—the Bay of Naples and Mt. Vesuvius."

Rachel was pleasantly surprised at Gerald's treatment of her as they traveled. After a few days she actually began to like him. He was solicitous and charming. He wined and dined her, and, as a surprise, took her on a boat trip to Capri.

When they sailed out onto the deep blue bay, Rachel was swept away by the beauty of her surroundings and by Gerald's attentive ways. She was drawn to him, infatuated with his good looks and intelligent conversation, and slowly she was pulled into the vortex of a new kind of life—a life that held endless possibilities, fueled by an unlimited supply of money.

Capri was beyond her wildest dreams. As they sailed into the port, Rachel saw the great spur of rock towering above the sea. An ancient villa perched like an eagle's nest at the top of the cliff, high above the sparkling waters. The stunning view stole Rachel's breath away, and she looked at Gerald in amazement.

"That's our hotel, Rachel, the Caesar Augustus. I've booked two suites, the best in the hotel."

As they climbed into the small launch that was to take them into shore, Gerald took Rachel's arm to steady her. The touch of his hand was intoxicating, and a strange thrill ran through her. She smiled at him and he took her hand. Rachel blushed and turned her eyes away.

Is this what falling in love is? If it is I... I like it.

She pressed against him as the launch cut through water that spread like glass beneath the brilliant Mediterranean sun. His arm crept around her bare shoulders, and he pulled her close against him. She hid her burning face against his shoulder. New and surprising feelings flashed through her.

This is just a business arrangement. I don't love him...or do I?

A chauffeur waited beside a limousine at the dock and they waited while the driver loaded their luggage. Then they drove up a cobbled, winding street to the hotel. Gerald climbed out and held the door for Rachel. A beautiful little town spread out before them. "You can walk a few hundred feet and be in Anacapri. We can go tomorrow. Then we can take a boat around to Grotta Azzurra. It's a cave under the cliff that you cruise through—the bluest water in the world. And Roman emperors had villas on this island. There's a lot of history here."

Gerald's boyish enthusiasm amused Rachel. As they walked into the lobby, the concierge looked up and smiled. "Welcome back, Signor Gerald. And who is this lovely lady?"

Gerald took Rachel by the arm. "Hello, Adriano. It's good to be back. And this is my brand new wife, Rachel."

A big smile broke over Adriano's face. He came around his desk and extended his hand.

"Buongiorno, signora St. Clair. Matrimoni e vescovati sono destinati dal cielo."

Rachel looked to Gerald for a translation. Gerald laughed. "He said marriages are made in heaven. I hope that's true for us."

Adriano looked puzzled but Gerald smiled. "Just a little joke, Adriano. Now, what about our rooms?"

Adriano glanced down at the register. "You have reserved two suites, Signor Gerald?"

Gerald spoke to Adriano in Italian. *"La signora St. Clair proviene da un...un upbringing molto severo ed è molto timida. Vorrei dare a lei come molta...ah...privacy possibile fino a quando lei è più abituata a me."*

Adriano smiled and bowed. *"Sì,* Signor Gerald. I understand perfectly."

Rachel leaned close to Gerald. "What did you say to him?"

Gerald whispered back. "The truth. I told him you were very shy and I wanted to give you as much privacy as possible."

Adriano rang a small bell and a bellboy appeared

magically. Adriano handed two sets of keys to the young man. *"Si prega di prendere la signora St. Clair a Cesare Master Suite e il signor St. Clair a Capri."*

The bellboy nodded and went looking for their luggage. Adriano smiled. "He will return in a moment and take you to your rooms. Again, *signora* St. Clair, welcome to Capri. *Congratulazioni e possono avete figli maschi!"*

Gerald leaned over and whispered in her ear. "It's a traditional Italian wedding blessing. He says he hopes you have male children."

Rachel turned beet-red while the two men laughed. The bellboy returned with their luggage and led them to their rooms. At the door of her suite, Rachel turned to Gerald. "Thank you for getting me my own room. It is awkward, I know, but I appreciate it and hope you understand."

Gerald took her hand and bowed over it. Then he kissed it. "Think nothing of it, Rachel. I want you to be comfortable and happy." He paused… "My greatest hope is that when we sort through the…strangeness of this arrangement, you might come to have feelings for me as I am…as I am beginning to have for you."

Rachel felt something like an electric shock and the heat came into her face again. He looked into her eyes for a long moment. Then he let go of her hand and nodded to the bellboy. "It's a beautiful suite, Rachel. Get unpacked and then meet me at the pool and we'll go for a swim before lunch. You won't believe the view."

Rachel gathered her emotions together. "That sounds fine. I'll see you there shortly."

Gerald went off down the corridor. The young man opened the door, and motioned for her to enter. Rachel stepped into the room and stopped, amazed. It was the most beautiful room she had ever seen. The walls were pristine white and beautiful matching drapes hung in the arches that soared above the doorways. The parquet floors shone with a luminous glow and the accents were gorgeous red and gray. The furniture was dark wood and there were lamps of gleaming brass. Rachel walked into the room. The young man came in behind her and set her luggage down. He turned to go. Rachel reached for her purse, but the young man smiled. *"No, la signora St. Clair. Il signor Gerald mi ha già dato un suggerimento."*

He smiled at her puzzled look and tried again in English. "Mr. Gerald. He already tip."

Rachel nodded as the young man left. She turned back to the room. It was spectacular. Circular in shape, it had huge arches all around. A glass door opened out onto a terrace. White curtains framed the arches like clouds, and through them, Rachel could see the afternoon sun blazing off the beautiful Bay of Naples, ricocheting off tiny, breeze-borne waves like a million bright candles.

She toured each room. The immaculate bathroom walls shone with white tile trimmed in blue, and the sinks were jade-green marble. Above the sinks a bronze-framed mirror reflected the sea that was visible through the enormous window behind her.

The master bedroom lay beyond an archway draped with diaphanous curtains. Rachel stepped through the archway. The material drifted against her skin like caressing fingers. She looked down at the huge bed. Strange feelings rushed through her, and for a moment she couldn't catch her breath. She felt the softness of the mattress, the touch of the magnificent coverlet. An image began to take shape in her mind. Gerald with her, in this room…

She returned to the living room, picked up her suitcase and went back into the bedroom. There was a stand by the window, and she put her suitcase there and opened it. She sorted through the clothes that Augusta helped her buy until she found the swimsuit. It was a simple one-piece, modest but lovely.

Rachel undressed and put on the suit. There were white terrycloth robes hanging in the bathroom closet, so she found one that fit her, and put it on. Then she grabbed a towel from the cupboard and headed for the door. As she passed the bedroom, she stepped back through the sheer curtains. As she stood looking down at the bed, the images came again. They were vivid and passionate; Gerald and her, alone in the room, as husband and wife. She tried to push them away, and then suddenly her heart was pounding wildly.

What is happening to me? I've never had such thoughts.

She backed away from the bed, took a deep breath, and then turned and almost ran from the room.

The rest of the day was like a dream. They went swimming in the infinite horizon pool on the edge of the terrace. When Rachel was in the water, it was as though she were floating above the world. The sea stretched away to the horizon, where an island rose out of the low-lying white clouds. It seemed to be suspended magically above the water. Gerald swam up next to her. "That's Ischia. It's one of the Phlegrean Islands. It's beautiful, isn't it?"

Then she felt his arms slip around her. She had never

felt the touch of a man's skin so intimately before. He turned her face to his. "But not as beautiful as you, Rachel."

And then his lips found hers, and she felt herself being drawn into his very being. They stayed there in the warm water, and it was as though she were looking down at another girl from high above. And then suddenly, it was so intense that she couldn't breathe and she broke away.

"What, Rachel? Didn't you like it?"

She reached out and took his hand. "Yes, Gerald, I like it. It's just that I never…"

He put his finger to her lips. "It's all right, I understand. Come on, let's have lunch."

He turned and swam to the edge of the pool and pulled himself out. The muscles in his back and arms rippled as he did, and Rachel followed slowly, feeling alone without him.

Later that night, they sat on the terrace looking out over the bay as the full moon stood high above the Tyrrhenian Sea. The summer night was perfectly still, the surface of the water was smooth as glass, and the moonlight made a silver path on the sea. Gerald sipped his wine and then reached for Rachel's hand.

Rachel was stunning in a white, off-the-shoulder summer dress. Her long, dark auburn hair was pinned softly at the nape of her neck, and her violet eyes drank in Gerald's face. She was being swept away, and yet part of her was still saying no. Something inside her was clinging to the last bit of her old life, like someone holding desperately to a tiny bit of rock while the flood rages all around them. Warning bells blared in her heart, but a heat was rising in her that engulfed and silenced them.

Gerald stood and drew her to him. They walked to the edge of the terrace and lingered in the shadows. Gerald's lips found hers again and suddenly she was responding to him with her whole being. They stood in the embrace for what seemed forever, and then Gerald whispered in her ear.

"Shall we go back to your room, Mrs. St. Clair?"

She hesitated. The strangest sensation washed over her—like a tornado tearing through her ordered little world, stripping away everything familiar and loved. She closed her eyes to steady herself, and saw a man. But it wasn't Gerald. It was Daniel! He was standing on top of their knoll, under the tree where they had pledged their friendship and love so long ago. Daniel was looking east, and she knew that he was troubled. In that moment, she felt as though everything about her life was wrong. She wanted to cry out, to stop the folly sweeping her away in a white-hot flame. A thought came to her like a life preserver tossed to a drowning woman caught in a maelstrom.

Daniel, Daniel...come save me!

She wanted to scream it, but before she could say the words, burning lips pressed against hers. She opened her eyes but it wasn't Daniel that held her, it was Gerald—her husband.

She almost pulled away, but then the strange, unfamiliar heat began to course through her body again. Before she could stop herself, she was clinging to Gerald, pulling him close, and kissing him back with such passion that he was the one who pulled away in surprise.

He stared at her, and then he smiled in anticipation

and his eyes asked the question again. Rachel nodded. The old world was swept away as though it had never been. Gerald took her hand. Rachel let go, opened her heart, and followed him into the darkness.

Part Two

The Prison

Too often, we make a prison of our dreams.

The Prison—
From The Journals of Jenny Hershberger

Chapter Twenty

The Lie

Rachel sat propped up in her bed in her private suite in the St. Clair mansion outside Greenwich, Connecticut. The first November storm had blown through during the night and dumped four inches of snow, and the grounds of the estate had been transformed into a wonderland. The black wrought-iron benches that lined the path leading down to the ocean stood in stark relief against the soft, white blanket that covered the ground.

But Rachel could not see the beauty. Instead, she saw bare trees that rose like silent sentinels in a frozen world, naked branches raised in supplication as though imploring an unseen God for succor.

Like my heart.

A soft knock on the door roused her from her reverie.

"Mrs. St. Clair?"

"Come in, Monique."

Rachel's French maid came in with a small tray bearing her morning coffee in a solid silver pot. A picture came into her mind of her papa pouring strong, black coffee out of the old aluminum coffee pot into big ceramic mugs and singing softly to himself. Her papa had a wonderful voice. He used to come into her room when she was a little girl, before the "gone" time. He would tuck her in and give her a good night kiss. Then she would take hold of the little finger of his strong hand and hold it tightly.

"Sing for me, Papa."

She recalled Jonathan's smile and his strength as he lifted her for a moment with his finger and then let her back down. Then his rich baritone filled the room as he sang. "*Loben wir ihn von ganzem Herzen! Denn er allein ist würdig.* Let us praise Him with all our hearts! For He alone is worthy…"

How she loved the *Loblied*, the old praise song. Jonathan would sing it slowly and melodiously and she would feel herself beginning to slip into sleep. She would lift her tiny arms to him. "Now sing the other one, Papa. Mama's special song."

Jonathan would wrap his arms around her and whisper in her ear. "All right, my darling girl, but just for you, because I love you as much as I love your mama."

Tonight, I whisper in your ear, I always want you near, tonight.

Tonight, I sing this song of love, You're the one I'm dreaming of.

Tonight…

And Rachel would drift off to sleep, in the safest place that ever was—deep inside her papa's love.

"Mrs. St. Clair, your coffee?"

Rachel jolted back from her daydream. The girl was still standing next to her bed, holding the tray.

"Oh, I'm sorry, Monique. You can put it here, and please, call me Rachel."

"Yes, Miss Rachel. Mr. Gerald wants to know if you are coming down for breakfast."

Rachel's heart twisted within her as she thought of Gerald. Gerald St. Clair, handsome, charming, beguiling, spoiled, petulant. Why had she rushed into marriage with him?

The money, of course.

"Tell Mr. Gerald that I won't be down this morning. I'm not feeling well."

Monique nodded. "Shall I have the cook prepare you some soft-boiled eggs and toast?"

"Yes, that would be nice."

Monique took the tray and left. Rachel roused herself and sat on the edge of the bed. She picked up her coffee, but before she could sip it, the strong smell twisted her stomach. She got up quickly and went into the bathroom. She knelt down by the toilet and threw up. She had been sick every morning for two weeks. At first, she thought she had the flu. But now she knew what was happening. She sat on the edge of the huge tub and put her face in her hands.

Why wasn't I more careful?

And then the tears began to fall as she remembered Capri.

When Rachel awakened Gerald was gone. In his place in the bed lay a single red rose and a note.

Rachel,

Thank you for last night. It was truly delightful!

*I've gone back to my room to change. The rose
is the first of many. Please meet me for breakfast
around ten and then we'll see the sights.*

Gerald

She folded the note and set it on the nightstand. Then
she lay back and stared at the ceiling. She wanted to
feel like a new bride should feel—fulfilled and joyous.
But instead, she felt only emptiness.

But it was all so wonderful last night. Why am I feeling like this?

She picked up the rose and smelled it, but it wasn't
very fragrant. She closed her eyes and tried to imagine
the night before, but the only image that came into her
mind was the old chestnut tree on top of the knoll behind Daniel King's house. Her eyes opened in surprise
and she stared at the ceiling again.

*Why am I thinking of Daniel? I should be thinking
of Gerald.*

She didn't feel like she had the night before. The fire
that had burned so fiercely in her body had dwindled
down to ashes. As she lay there, she couldn't quite put
her finger on what she was feeling. And then she understood.

Regret! I regret what happened.

Remorse swept over Rachel like a huge, dark wall
of floodwater and she turned over and buried her face
in the pillow. And then great sobs began to wrack her.
She lay there for a long time, wrestling with the enormity of what had happened. She had given herself to
a stranger. That precious gift she had saved all her life
for the man God had for her had been tossed away in a

moment of wine-induced desire. She felt violated and stupid and...

I feel like a prostitute. I sold myself for money!

Rachel finally stopped weeping and got up. She went into the bathroom and stared at herself in the mirror. Her eyes were red and swollen and there was no joy in her face. Her head hurt from the effects of the wine and her body ached. She thought of Gerald waiting for her downstairs and a wave of revulsion swept over her.

She turned on the shower and stepped in. The ice-cold water shocked her and cleared her head. She waited for a few minutes before she turned on the hot water. She stood under the water for a long time, but it did not make her feel clean.

Instead, she felt shame so intense that she had to lean against the wall to keep from falling. Finally she roused herself and stepped out. A breeze from the sea floated in through the window but it wasn't refreshing. It chilled her, and she shivered.

I'm so sorry, Lord. Please forgive me.

But there was no answer to her plea. She dried off and then went into the bedroom to dress. The rumpled bed, which had seemed so inviting last night, now gaped at her like an open mouth.

I have decked my bed with coverings of tapestry, with carved works, with fine linen of Egypt. I have perfumed my bed with myrrh, aloes, and cinnamon.

But my house is the way to hell, going down to the chambers of death.

She sat down and put her head in her hands. She wanted to pray, to throw herself on God's mercy—anything to take away the feelings—but the words wouldn't come. Rachel hadn't talked to God in a long time.

After she got dressed, she made her way to the dining room. In the lobby, she saw Adriano behind his desk. On a sudden impulse, she went over. The concierge was going over some paperwork that was spread out on his desk. He looked up and smiled at Rachel.

"*Buongiorno*, signora St. Clair. How are you this morning?"

Rachel got right to the point. "Adriano, you obviously know Mr. St. Clair very well. Has he been here before?"

The concierge looked uncomfortable. He hesitated for a moment and then answered. *"Si, signora. Il signor Gerald è stato quello di farci visita diverse volte negli ultimi anni."*

Rachel stared at him. Adriano shifted to English.

"Ah, excuse me. You do not speak our language. Yes, Mr. Gerald has been to visit us often over the years."

"And did he bring women with him?"

Adriano spread his hands in a helpless gesture. Rachel stepped closer and spoke in low tones. "Adriano, Mr. Gerald is not paying for this trip. I am, and I need you to answer some questions for me."

Adriano swallowed hard and nodded.

"Has Mr. Gerald brought women here before?"

Adriano hesitated and then spoke. "Mr. Gerald comes twice a year. He started coming about five years ago when he was still in college."

"And the women?"

"Mr. Gerald always brings a woman—always beautiful, but always a different one."

Adriano hesitated and then went on. "You are the most beautiful of them all. When he introduced you as his wife, I was so happy to see that *si era sistemato e sposato*, ah, that he had finally *mettere la testa a posto*, how you say, was not so wild anymore, eh? Please don't say I have spoken to you, signora."

Rachel tried to stay as calm as possible. "Thank you, Adriano. You have been most helpful. I will not betray you to Mr. St. Clair."

Rachel could see the appreciation in the man's eyes. When she went into the restaurant, she could see Gerald sitting at a corner table. He was wearing white shorts, a blue shirt, and tennis shoes with a sweater draped around his shoulders. He was already sipping a glass of wine. Rachel walked up to the table. When he saw her, he stood up and smiled. "Good morning, Mrs. St. Clair."

He reached for her but she stepped back. "Gerald, I want to go home."

A blank look came over his face. "Home?"

"Yes, I want to go home."

"You mean back to Amalfi? But what about last night?"

Rachel raised her hand in a dismissive gesture. "Last night was a mistake that I…deeply regret. I let you use wine and moonlight and this place to seduce me, and I am profoundly ashamed. And I don't want to go back to the mainland. I want to go back to America—today!"

A strange look twisted Gerald's face, and then it was as if Rachel were seeing him for the first time.

"A mistake? No one ever called a night with Gerald St. Clair a mistake before."

His arrogance infuriated Rachel. "By 'no one,' I assume you mean the many women you have brought here. I must have been quite dull for you—a virgin who doesn't know the ropes in the bedroom."

Gerald's face clouded. "Well, you weren't exactly a professional—"

Rachel reached over and slapped him hard across the face. Gerald's hand clenched into a fist, and he lifted it to strike her. The other patrons were staring at them. Gerald quickly put his hand behind his back. He spoke in a low voice.

"You are fortunate that there are people around, otherwise I would—"

"What? Beat me up and leave me here? I think I'm seeing you for the first time. I don't know why I let you touch me."

His face became a stone mask.

"I'm Gerald St. Clair. Nobody slaps me."

Rachel put her finger on his chest and jabbed. Her voice was low and cold. "The name Gerald St. Clair only means something now because I married you. Otherwise you would have squandered what meager money you have left and then you would be Gerald Nobody. I may be a simple country girl, but I'm not stupid. Augusta would never have come looking for me if you people weren't in trouble financially."

Gerald's face paled under her onslaught.

Rachel bored in. "Let me explain this to you. The money belongs to me and I say how it is dispersed. If you want to continue living your degenerate lifestyle, that's up to you, but I've got my own plans. I'm going to school. Now get your things. We are leaving."

Gerald looked at her helplessly. "But Grandmother always arranges everything…"

Rachel almost laughed. The man was nothing but a lecherous little mama's boy. "All right, Gerald. I'll take care of it. You just run along and pack your bag."

Gerald gave her a look of pure hatred. "You'll regret this you...you..."

Rachel smiled sadly. "If you want to say 'whore,' go ahead. Because after last night, that's what I am."

Chapter Twenty-One

Deep Darkness

"What do you mean by 'financial technicalities,' Michel?"

Augusta St. Clair sat, fuming in her chair, listening to Michel Duvigney on her speakerphone.

"You must realize, Ms. St. Clair, that transferring the interest income from two hundred billion dollars into your accounts takes a great deal of time. This whole business has taken us by surprise. We never imagined that Robert had an heir, and you are directly responsible for that omission."

Augusta was not pleased at the answer. "Wait a minute, Michel. When I met Rachel's grandmother, I assumed that she was just another gold-digger after the money. How was I to know that she was really Robert's wife?"

Duvigney remained silent.

"And another thing. I thought that the money was held in trust."

Duvigney sighed. "The money is held in trust, yes, that is correct, Ms. St. Clair."

Augusta glanced at Eva, her secretary. Eva scribbled something on a pad and handed Augusta the note.

Don't get angry, Madam. You know what the doctor said.

Augusta waved Eva away and asked another question. "If the money is in a trust, why don't you just make me a trustee and let us control our own money."

Another sigh.

"The trust does not work that way, Ms. St. Clair. The principal is not transferrable. You cannot spend the inheritance; you can only receive the benefits from it. It was set up that way to keep the principal safe from profligate heirs. And there are others who benefit from the principal. There are several lines in the St. Clair family, and all true St. Clairs benefit from the fortune.

"There are cousins, and others, like yourself, who are widows of lesser heirs. And there are orphaned children who are receiving money from the smaller trusts. Robert St. Clair's inheritance is only a portion of the St. Clair fortune. Granted, it is the largest portion, but there is much more to this than just handing over a few bank accounts and some properties. Oh, no, Ms. St. Clair, we will not be making you a trustee. Rachel St. Clair is the heir, and she is the person with whom I should be having this conversation."

Augusta pressed on. "And how does my grandson figure in all this?"

"If you wish an analogy that may help you understand, I will give you one. Rachel St. Clair is the heir. She fulfilled her obligations by marrying your grandson and taking the St. Clair name. Now all of her heirs will be St. Clairs and the fortune remains in the family. As for your grandson, Gerald St. Clair is like Prince Phillip of England. He is married to the Queen, but he is not the King. He is the Prince Consort. Like Phillip, Gerald has an extraordinary income but he does not have any authority. Like Elizabeth, Rachel holds the power. And like Elizabeth, if Rachel dies, the power will not pass to her husband, but to her son. At this point, that is Gerald's situation."

"What if Rachel should die?"

"The estate passes to the eldest child, or to any one of her children with the Key."

"And if she dies and there are no children?"

"Then Gerald St. Clair receives the income from the bulk of the St. Clair inheritance in his own name. However, if Rachel and Gerald do have children and if they divorce, then Rachel continues as the recipient of the income and passes it to her children, who would be considered legitimate St. Clairs. Gerald would receive an allowance, but he would be out of the picture."

Augusta stood up and began pacing. "Michel, the operative word here is recipient. That implies receiving and Rachel has received nothing. When is that going to change?"

"I have started that process and Rachel should be receiving the first check within a week. It will be drawn from the proceeds of some of the investments that I have transferred into Rachel's name."

"And how much will that amount be?"

"Again, Ms. St. Clair, I should be having this conversation with Rachel."

"Rachel has given me power of attorney to act on her behalf."

There was a pause, and Augusta could tell that she had been put on hold. Then Duvigney's voice came back on the line. "If you will send me those authorizations, I will make a note in Rachel's file stating that you are a representative on her behalf."

"I sent them last week, Michel. Why do I get the feeling that you are stalling me?"

"I assure you, Mrs. St. Clair, that I am facilitating this process—"

Augusta interrupted him. "I may not be on your level, Michel, but I have many friends. I do not like to be trifled with. Rachel has authorized me to set up a joint account for her and Gerald, as well as an individual account for her. She wants part of the money placed in the joint account for the management of the estate and for Gerald's allowance. The rest will go into her private account. I would suggest that the first installments be put into those accounts as quickly as possible. I hope my friends don't have to intervene. Do I make myself clear?"

"Very clear, Augusta, but there is no need to pursue this matter. I have already sent a substantial check."

"And what do you consider to be substantial?"

"Around four million dollars."

"That's better. And I want an update next week as to the final resolution of the estate. Goodbye."

Augusta punched the speakerphone button. She turned to Eva. "Get Gerald down here, immediately. And call Randall."

The calls had come in, just a few seconds apart. Randall's new caller ID showed Duvigney's phone number on the readout. Then Augusta's number popped up. He picked up the receiver.

"Talk to me, Michel."

There was a short pause. Randall knew Duvigney was trying to figure out how he knew who the caller was.

"Randall, I've got a problem."

"I know. Augusta is pressuring you to come up with the money. And, unfortunately, you don't have it available at this moment, due to your unwise investments. Am I right?"

There was another pause. Randall knew he was keeping Duvigney off-balance.

"The money is not gone, Randall. The principal of the estate is untouchable. It is held in several extremely stable, income-producing instruments, and the heirs enjoy the fruit of those investments. You are, however, correct in assuming that my firm made some unwise decisions and depleted the interest balance accounts for Robert St. Clair's portion of the inheritance. It will take some time for those funds to replenish themselves. In the meantime, I am keeping the St. Clair woman at bay by selling off some of my personal investments. But I cannot have her continue to pressure me. It would not be in the best interest of my firm if I had to open my records. Perhaps you might come up with a way to make the whole matter simply…disappear?"

"Well, well, Michel! I sense a bit of desperation here. I understand what you are proposing, and it is not as simple as you think. The St. Clairs move in powerful circles. You will need to give me some time to come up with a solution."

Just then, a subtle click on the line let Randall know that the other call was waiting.

"Hold on, Michel. I'll be right back."

Randall clicked over. "Gordon Randall Security."

"Mr. Randall, this is Eva Swanson, Augusta St. Clair wishes to speak with you."

"I will get right back to her. I'm on another call."

"Thank you, Mr. Randall."

Randall moved back to Duvigney's call. "It seems that Augusta might be having some problems, too, Michel. Let me call her. Once I know what she's up to, I may have an answer to your dilemma."

"Very well, Randall, but don't keep me waiting."

"Not at all. Oh, and did I say that these kind of covert actions are very expensive?"

"How did I know that you were going to tell me that?"

"It's the nature of the beast. I'll call you."

Randall was amused. First Duvigney and then Augusta. Both of them needed his help quickly. That meant more money in his bank account. Duvigney was obviously worried. The old thief had probably been dipping into Robert St. Clair's estate for years.

And why not? There had been no known heirs when Robert St. Clair died. Only when Augusta had started pressing Duvigney did the truth about Rachel Borntraeger St. Clair and her daughter, Jenny, come out.

Randall chuckled. Who could have guessed that a little Amish girl in a small Pennsylvania town would prove to be the heir to the great St. Clair fortune? Certainly not Duvigney!

Randall glanced down at the tape recorder to make sure the recording light was still on. Then he called Augusta.

Gerald St. Clair sat stiffly in the chair across from his grandmother. Augusta could tell he was dying for a smoke, so she kept him waiting while she looked over some documents. Finally, Gerald spoke up. "Do we have some kind of a problem, Grandmother?"

Augusta looked up. Gerald was a true St. Clair. Devilishly handsome, a graduate of the finest Ivy League prep school and college, accomplished tennis player, notorious womanizer, and altogether a totally nonproductive, worthless, human being. Augusta sighed. She wished that Gerald were more like Robert.

Robert St. Clair... The most beautiful man I ever met and the only one of the family with any gumption at all. What a team we would have made...

Yes, Robert had been the St. Clair worth catching, and she had made it very clear to him just how much she wanted to be with him. But he had spurned her. He fell in love with that Amish girl and married her. It was a bitter memory, for she had loved Robert passionately. And she could see Robert in Rachel. The same determination, the same passion...

"Grandmother?"

The apple doesn't fall far from the tree.

Augusta smiled patronizingly at Gerald. With all his faults, she needed him. He was her only link to the St. Clair fortune. "Yes, dear, we do have a problem. I spoke with Duvigney."

Gerald repositioned himself in the chair. "Well, what's the good news?"

"The good news is that he is sending us a check for four million dollars."

Gerald scowled. "Only four million? We'll go through that in a few months. Where's the big bucks? You promised me billions if I married Rachel."

Augusta sat on the arm of her grandson's chair. She

stroked his hair gently and gave him a kiss on the cheek. "There, there, darling. Your grandmother will come through for you. But there is a bit of a problem."

Gerald twisted away from Augusta's caresses. "And what might that be?"

"It seems that even though you are married to Rachel, you don't really have any claim on the money as long as Rachel is alive. As Duvigney put it, she is the queen, but you are not the king."

Gerald reached toward his coat pocket for a smoke, but saw the warning in his grandmother's eyes. "And if she dies?"

"Then you are the heir, but only if Rachel has no children. Have you fulfilled your…your husbandly duties yet?"

A strange look that Augusta could not read came over Gerald's face, and then he shrugged and smirked. "Grandmother, you're blushing. Of course I have."

"Then you must stop those activities immediately. Rachel must not get pregnant. That would jeopardize our standing."

Gerald spread his hands. "Right now we're not sharing a bed. Rachel and I had a little tiff in Capri. She's a little distant right now, but I can win her over."

Augusta sighed. "I don't think you will work it out, and the truth is, I don't want you to work it out."

"What do you mean, Grandmother?"

"Sometimes you can be very slow, Gerald. Rachel told me that she will be submitting her application to veterinary school right away. With her money, I'm sure they will accept her. She will be moving to Ithaca in the spring. That means that you will be living on an allowance, which will not be enough to support us in the manner to which we are accustomed."

Gerald swore under his breath.

"It's probably for the best, Gerald. Go to your other women if you must fulfill your needs—but no more with Rachel. If you want to get the money, there must never be any children."

Augusta lowered her voice. "So you see, we have a problem. Rachel must never leave here. I have shared our dilemma with Randall and he has assured me that he will find a solution."

Gerald's mouth dropped open and he stared at Augusta. Then he shuddered. "Grandmother, you really are wicked, aren't you?"

Augusta turned to her grandson. "Yes, Gerald, I am very wicked. You can't even imagine how wicked I am. Always remember that."

Chapter Twenty-Two

The Guardian

Willy Oxendine sat looking out the front windows of the Old Greenwich Station in Greenwich, Connecticut. Most days his job as Station Master was fairly dull and so when the MTA afternoon train pulled in, he always played a little game as he watched the passengers get off. He tried to imagine where they were coming from, what they did for a living, and where they were headed. Of course, most of the passengers were from Greenwich and Old Greenwich, so that was why one passenger in particular caught his attention right away.

Hmmm. There's one that's not from around here...

The young man got off the train, turned up the collar of his pea coat, and looked around at the crowd of commuters. The icy wind tugged at the coat, and Willy watched the young man button it even tighter around his neck. Then the stranger headed toward the station, his heavy duffle bag leaving a trail of icy shards through the crusted snow. The young man pushed through the lobby door. He stomped his feet and slapped himself with his arms to get the circulation going again.

Black watch cap, pea coat, duffle bag...maybe he's a sailor? Nope, doesn't have the swing in his walk.

The young man's face sported a two-day growth of blond beard. He walked straight over to the counter. "Excuse me, sir, but do you know of any folks who need an experienced stable hand?"

Willy gave him the once-over.

Ah-ha! Farm boy—lookit them hands. Seen a lot of hard work and that coat fits tight around them big shoulders. A hay-bucker if I ever seen one.

The stranger's face registered in a good way—clean, honest, what ya see is what ya get kinda face, and Willy smiled. "Well, son, are you really good with horses? We got a lot of rich people that buy horses and don't know a dang thing about 'em."

"Yes, sir, I am very good with horses. Been around them all my life."

"You got any references? These folks are picky."

The young man hesitated and his face fell. "Well, sir, I didn't think to bring any when I left home. I... I left in a hurry. But all I need is a chance to show somebody what I can do. I'm a hard worker and I'm dependable."

Willy stared hard at the honest face and right away he trusted it. "Okay, I'll take your word. Just so happens that Benny Peterson is looking for another hand out at the St. Clair place."

A strange look crossed the young man's face. "St. Clair? I've heard of them. Very wealthy, aren't they?"

"That's right, son, very wealthy and very snooty. Young Gerald St. Clair just got married and his wife is a real looker. They're all there right now. Gerald and his bride and that tarantula of a grandmother."

The old man picked up a pen and wrote something on a piece of paper. "Here's the address. 21445 Field Point Circle. Go around to the tradesman's entrance and ask for Benny. Tell him Willy sent you. What's your name?"

The young man hesitated. "Dan... David. It's David Kaufman."

The old man smiled and pointed across the street. "Okay, Dan David. Well, off you go. The place is out at the end of Field Point Circle, right on the ocean—about a thirty-minute drive. There's a taxi stand right over there. It's only five bucks to get to St. Clair's. You got any money?"

The young man nodded. "Sure, I got some money..."

"But not a lot, right, kid?"

The young man grinned and shook his head.

The old man reached in his pocket and pulled out a twenty-dollar bill. "This will get you out there and tide you over until you get paid."

"I can't take that, sir..."

"The name's Willy, and you can take it. I'm bettin' you'll get the job and then you can pay me back. You know where I am."

The young man stuck out his hand and the two men shook. Willy pressed the money into the young man's hand.

"It's very kind of you, Willy. I'll pay you back soon."

Willy looked back down at his paperwork. "I know you will, son. Now get goin' or somebody else will get that job."

Daniel walked through the delivery gate at the St. Clair mansion. A man shoveling snow directed him to the stables. In a few minutes, Daniel stood by the stable door, looking around at the magnificent estate. Off to the right, a huge stone house stood under sweeping elm trees. Snow covered the meticulously tended grounds surrounding the house. Daniel looked in the wide front doors of the white wooden barn. The long hallway inside ran the length of the building, and there must have been fifty stalls. Daniel could hear horses nickering and the occasional whistle of a stallion.

Just then, a thin, wiry man walked briskly around the corner of the barn. He saw Daniel and stopped. "Wadda ya doin' here, buddy. Lost or somethin'?"

"I'm looking for Benny Peterson. Willy sent me. He said Benny was looking for some help."

The man looked at Daniel and then turned away. "Nah, we don't need any help. Willy is always sending me charity cases."

Daniel stepped forward. "But he said you were looking for help. You are Benny, aren't you?"

Just then there was a loud crash from inside the stable. Someone shouted. Daniel and Benny ran inside. They saw someone lying on the ground trying to hold onto the reins of a kicking, bucking horse and screaming for help. Benny pulled up short and grabbed Daniel. "Criminey, it's Diablo. I told Johnnie not to mess with him. That stallion is crazy."

Benny shouted at the man on the floor. "Johnnie! Don't try to hold him! Just get up out of there."

Then, before Benny could stop him, Daniel ran forward and grabbed the reins. He began to speak quietly to the excited animal as it reared up again. The man on the floor scooted away, leaving Daniel alone with the big stallion. Still speaking softly, Daniel inched closer to the horse. The animal began to calm, and soon he stood still. Then Daniel reached out slowly and put his hand on the stallion's face. The big horse snorted and then nickered. He stood still while Daniel began to rub his face and behind his ears, all the while talking in a quiet voice. In a moment, the huge animal was completely quiet.

Daniel looked at Benny. "Where do you want him?"

Benny's mouth hung open. He pointed to an empty stall. Daniel led the now quiet stallion inside and then closed the stall door and latched it. The big horse put his head out and Daniel stroked his face some more. Benny walked up. "Say, kid, where'd ya learn to do that?"

Daniel grinned. "I grew up on a farm. Been around horses all my life."

Benny put his hand to his chin. "What else do you know about horses?"

Daniel shrugged. "Like I said, I've been around them all my life. Anything that has to do with horses, I can do."

He turned to go. Benny quickly took him by the arm. "Hey, where ya goin', kid?"

"You said you didn't need anyone, so I better get back to town and see if anyone else is looking for help. I need a job."

Benny put his arm around Daniel's shoulder. "Now don't get all excited, buddy. How did I know you were some kinda horse whisperer? I actually could use another hand, and if Willy liked you then you're okay with me."

Daniel laughed. "He liked me well enough to loan me twenty dollars until I get paid."

Benny slapped Daniel on the back. "Okay, kid, you

got the job. If Willy will part with a twenty, you must
be all right. Get your gear and follow me. What did you
say your name was?"

"I didn't, but it's David—David Kaufman."

"Okay, Davey-boy. We'll get you settled in and then
you can get to work."

Daniel breathed a silent prayer.

Danki, mein gnädiger Gott.

Then Daniel thought he heard a soft voice answer
back.

You are welcome, Daniel.

Rachel sat at her desk, writing. She sighed and stopped.
Then she crumpled up the paper, threw it in the waste-
basket and started again. Finally she put her head down
on her arms.

*How can I tell Mama what has happened to me? I'm
so ashamed. And besides, I'm shunned. They won't even
open the letter.*

The room seemed oppressive and close. Rachel's
stomach churned.

I need to get out and get some air...

She slipped on some jeans, a sweater, and a warm
jacket. She wrapped a woolen scarf around her neck and
pulled on a pair of warm, fur-lined boots. She went out
through the French doors, onto the veranda. The sun
shone wanly through the clouds that filled a gray sky.
Random flakes of snow were drifting down, carried in
the grasp of a brisk breeze, and the cold air slapped at
her face like dead hands.

She walked along the path that led toward the tennis courts. A few leaves that had long passed beyond
the flaming colors of fall were still clinging like dried

pieces of skin to the branches of the trees. Away beyond the stables she could see someone working one of the horses in the exercise ring. For a moment she considered going over to the stables, but thought better of it. She wanted to be alone.

She headed for the old caretaker's cottage out in the woods on the back part of the grounds. It had a wood stove and comfy old couches—much more to her taste than the overdone mansion. As she came to the trees that lined the entrance to the overgrown path, she saw a set of footprints in the snow. They were headed in the direction of the cottage.

I wonder who else knows about this place.

The last rays of the afternoon sun filtered through the trees, and the light in the woods grew dim. As she followed the footprints, she saw another trail of footprints come in from a side path. She saw the cottage ahead through the trees. Light shone in one of the windows.

A sudden caution gripped her and she stopped, wondering whether she should turn and go back to her rooms. But something pressed her on and she walked up to the window and peeked in. A movement caught her eye. Someone was coming out of the back bedroom. She ducked down behind a juniper bush. She stayed that way for a moment and then peeked up again. A man stood with his back to the window, looking toward the bedroom door. She couldn't see his face but she knew it was Gerald.

Gerald said something to someone in the bedroom. Then she heard another voice—a woman's voice. She watched in dismay as the woman walked out of the bedroom, dressed only in her underwear. The woman stopped in front of Gerald and stood seductively for a moment before pulling a sweater on. It was Monique!

Then the maid walked up to Gerald and put her arms around his neck. His hands began to run over her body familiarly, and suddenly Rachel wanted to throw up. Gerald and Monique began kissing. They kissed for a long time and then Gerald pulled away, said something, and headed for the door. She bent down and picked up a pair of jeans from the floor by the bedroom door. The front door latch clicked and Rachel had just enough time to duck behind the bushes before Gerald came out.

From her hiding place she watched him as he glanced around and then headed off through the woods toward the mansion. Rachel peeked back in the window. Monique finished dressing. She had a satisfied smile on her face as she pulled on her coat and scarf.

Rachel couldn't stand it any longer. She turned and ran into the woods. She ran and ran. Branches whipped at her face and the trees loomed up, reaching for her as she ran and ran. Suddenly, her foot caught on an unseen root and she sprawled, face-first, in the snow. She lay there for a moment and then she threw up. Uncontrollable retching wracked her body. Finally, the convulsions stopped and she got up. The woods were dark and silent. The cold reached into her and she began to shake.

"Oh, God, oh, God, what have I done? Help me, please, help me. I need you so much!"

She felt weak and leaned against a tree. Then, softly and quietly, the words came.

I will never leave you nor forsake you.

Chapter Twenty-Three

Double Cross

The black BMW drove up a private driveway behind the St. Clair mansion. The snow creaked beneath the tires, violating the perfectly still morning. The car eased to a stop and Gordon Randall stepped out. He took in his immediate surroundings, instinctively looking for anyone hidden among the trees. Satisfied, he lifted his briefcase from the seat, and walked briskly down a narrow path to a small door set in an alcove in the side of the house. He noted the surveillance camera. One of the wires attached to the back was hanging loose and Randall smiled.

Amateurs!

He knocked twice. Augusta St. Clair opened the door. Her smile reminded Randall of a crocodile about to pull a wildebeest off the bank of an African river.

"Well, a personal greeting. I must be moving up the food chain."

Augusta's smile disappeared. "I thought it best to meet you myself, since our business is so…personal. Please come in, Gordon."

Augusta led the way down a windowless hallway to a dark wood door. She opened it and ushered Randall in. As the heavy door clicked shut behind them, Randall felt a slight change in air pressure. Augusta went around the large oak desk and sat down. The room was paneled in dark wood with heavy beams crisscrossing the ceiling, and there was a small fire blazing in an iron-grated hearth.

"The window behind me is triple-pane glass and the door is hermetically sealed. The room is completely soundproof, so we can say whatever needs to be said."

Randall squeezed the handle of his briefcase and then set it on the floor next to his chair. He took out a small notepad and a pen. "So, how may I be of service, Augusta?"

"This is a very delicate situation, Gordon. After you located Robert St. Clair's heir and we established that she had the Key and was the heiress, we were able to work out an arrangement with her."

"Yes, Rachel married your grandson and that allowed you to inherit the money."

Augusta nodded. "Yes, she did marry Gerald. The protocols dictated that any female heir who is not a St. Clair must marry an eligible St. Clair male. Gerald was that male. But your other assumption is wrong. Gerald does not have access to the money. His new wife is in control of where and how the money is dispersed. Of course, I have been able to act as her advisor on several matters but for the most part, she controls everything. And since this was originally Robert's mansion, she is now the owner. If she ever divorces Gerald, we will receive a pittance while she takes this house, the town house in New York City, and the bulk of the income from the estate."

Randall nodded and made a note. "I'm sure it's infuriating for you to have to go begging to Rachel for every little thing. And isn't it true that if Rachel has children, Gerald is even further out of the picture?"

Augusta nodded again. "Yes, and she has proven to be strong-willed, intelligent, and an independent thinker."

"In other words, she is not the simple little Amish girl you thought she was, and you cannot manipulate her or control what she does with the money."

"You are as perceptive as ever, Gordon. We have already clashed, and she is discovering what kind of a person Gerald really is. I think she regrets marrying him. I wouldn't be surprised if she decides to move out of here soon. So our dear Rachel has become a burdensome stone, as the Bible says."

"And you need to take that burdensome stone from around your neck, am I correct?"

"You are correct."

Randall looked at his notes. "So, instead of being your tool, Rachel has become an impediment to your plans to get the St. Clair fortune, and you wish me to devise a solution that will remove the impediment… permanently?"

"Yes, Gordon, that is correct."

Randall closed the notepad. "Very simple problem, very simple solution—almost traditional in these cases. Arsenic poisoning. Small doses added to her food and in two to ten days she's gone."

Augusta scowled. "But, Gordon, won't people get suspicious?"

"You forget, Augusta, I cover all the bases."

Randall reached into his pocket and pulled out a piece of paper. "This is from the *New York Times*." He began to read:

U.S. Health Agency Declares Flu Epidemic

The Centers for Disease Control declared yesterday that a nationwide influenza epidemic exists and that it is the most widespread outbreak of the disease since 1984–85.

The flu, predominantly a strain called A-Shanghai, has been identified in every part of the country, and major outbreaks have been found in 35 states, epidemiologists at the centers say. Since reporting began, there have been 130 deaths attributed to the A-Shanghai flu nationwide.

"We're in an epidemic," said Dr. Walter Benson, a specialist in viral diseases in New York City.

"So you see, Augusta, it's simple. Rachel comes down with what looks like a flu bug, and five days later, she dies of A-Shanghai flu. Your doctor certifies the cause of death and nobody is the wiser. You do own a doctor, don't you?"

"Yes, Gordon, I 'own' a doctor. And what about her family? Won't they ask for an autopsy?"

"No. Most Amish families will refuse to solicit an autopsy. Her parents will wish to have her body returned home as soon as possible to prepare it for burial. They perform the interment themselves. In three days she's buried and gone.

"As far as the means of death, arsenic has a somewhat sweet taste and a small amount can be added to food or drink without the victim noticing a thing. It's available commercially as rat poison, so you could keep it here without suspicion. A very simple scenario: Rachel catches the flu after a trip to the city, and within ten days, your problem is solved."

Augusta looked hard at Randall. "And what part do you play in all this, Gordon?"

"What part do I play?"

"Yes. You see, I have no one here who has…shall we say, the professional expertise to handle this situation. I will need you to manage it for me."

Randall frowned. "I am available for this kind of operation, but the fee is extremely high. If you can meet my price, I'll come back in two days."

Randall wrote a number on a page in his notebook, tore off the page, and passed it across the desk.

Augusta's eyes widened. "One hundred thousand dollars!" She swallowed and then nodded.

Randall made another note in his book. "I will need a deposit today—half of the amount now, the rest when Rachel is dead. You can tell your staff that you have had a few threatening calls, and you brought in a security expert. Set me up somewhere out of the way. I'll be bringing a few of my special ops guys to put up a security shield so I'll need a place for them also. I'm going to clamp a tight lid on this place, so order a week's worth of supplies out here. Anything else?"

"Gerald will help you."

"Gerald?"

"Yes. If my grandson is so eager to be a billionaire, he can get his hands dirty. He's not too happy with his wife at the moment. All you need to do is 'train' him. I want his fingerprints all over this…operation. Do you understand?"

Randall stood and picked up his briefcase. He shook his head and laughed. "Forgive me for underestimating you, Augusta. You cover all the bases, don't you?"

"Yes, Randall, I cover all the bases. You and your men can use the old caretaker cottage at the back of the estate. Follow this driveway about a quarter of a mile. You'll see an unused road on the right. Turn in there and the cottage is straight ahead. There is a bunkroom and it's heated. Bring your own supplies. I don't want anyone to know you are there. Oh, there's one more thing."

Augusta held out her hand. "Leave the notebook with me, Gordon. I don't want any incriminating evidence hanging around that might cause me embarrassment in the future."

Randall smiled. "If we're partners, shouldn't we trust each other?"

Augusta reached in her desk and pulled out her checkbook. She wrote out a check, tore it off, and held it up. "It's not that I don't trust you, Gordon. It's just that I don't *really* trust you. I'll trade you this check for that notebook."

Randall shrugged, took the check, and handed over the small book. Augusta stood up and led him to the door.

"Down the hall to the right and out the door you came in. I'll see you in two days."

Randall nodded and left. As he walked down the hall, he squeezed the handle of his briefcase again. He felt the recording device inside vibrate and click off. Randall smiled to himself. He went out the door, climbed into his car, and drove away.

* * *

Rachel awoke the morning after she had seen Gerald with Monique. She lay in her bed for a long time, wondering what to do. Finally, a thought came to her.

I haven't prayed in a long time.

She slipped off her bed onto her knees. She felt strange and disconnected and awkward, but there was no one else to talk to. She bowed her head and tried to pray, but for some reason, the words would not come. And then she remembered a scripture her mother kept on a little hand-stitched plaque on the kitchen wall in their home in Paradise.

If we confess our sins, He is faithful and just to forgive us our sins, and to cleanse us from all unrighteousness.

Another picture came into her mind. She was five years old and she was sitting on the grass under the old apple tree in their back yard. Her papa was sitting next to her and they were both munching the crispy last bites of an apple. Her papa's arm was around her and they were enjoying the bright sun of an Indian summer day. The trees were clothed in a riot of fall colors; orange, red, yellow, golden. White, fluffy clouds sailed the azure sky above. Rachel turned to her papa.

"Papa, what are the *Ordnung*? I hear the other kids talking about them and they sound scary."

Jonathan pulled his girl closer. "Ah, the *Ordnung*. Well, my darling girl, the *Ordnung* are very special to the Amish people. We live differently than most of the other people in the world because we want to separate ourselves from the things of life that hurt us. So we have the *Ordnung* to guide us when something happens and we need help to know what to do. I guess the best way to think of them is that the *Ordnung* are a way to have boundaries and guidelines to help us behave the way God wants us to."

Rachel remembered being puzzled. "What are bounaries, Papa?"

"Boundaries, little one." He pointed to one of their fields. "Do you see the sheep, Rachel?"

Rachel nodded.

"Well, the sheep need to stay in that field because they belong to us. If they got into someone else's field, they might eat their garden or wreck something. So what keeps our sheep in our field?"

"The fence, Papa."

"That's right, Rachel, the fence. The fence is a boundary. It keeps the sheep where they belong. The Bible says that we are God's sheep. Now, God does not put us in a field and put a fence that we can see around us, but He does give us His Word and when we read the Bible, we learn how God wants us to behave and in that way, He sets a fence around our hearts. If we go outside that fence, we end up somewhere that God knows we do not belong."

"Is the Bible the *Ordnung*, Papa?"

"No, little one. The *Ordnung* are not written down. Over the years, the men who lead our church have read the Bible and then they have decided on a way to behave that the church follows by learning it from those who go before, like *grossdaadis* and *grosmutters*."

Rachel pondered that for a moment. "Then, when we stay inside the boundaries, does that make God like us better?"

Jonathan laughed. "So many questions, my curious one! No, Rachel, keeping the rules does not make

God like us better. What makes God so very happy is when we let His Son, Jesus, come into our hearts. The boundaries, the *Ordnung*, are like a signpost that tells us the right way to go. But they don't get us to where we are going. We need Jesus to do that for us. Let me explain…"

And so, for the first time in her life, Rachel heard the wonderful story of salvation from her beloved papa as they sat in the grass eating apples. And when Jonathan was finished, Rachel took his hand and looked up at him shyly.

"Papa, I want Jesus to live in my heart and help me to be good always."

And then her beloved *daed* held Rachel in his arms and helped her to pray the prayer of salvation.

And then came the "gone" years when her papa disappeared and they thought he was dead. Then he came home, but somehow he wasn't really her papa anymore. And he didn't talk about Jesus so much, but he mostly talked about the *Ordnung* and how Rachel was not keeping the *Ordnung* the right way. So Rachel forgot about the boundaries and the Savior who had been in her heart since that day so long ago. And she began to live her life for herself.

And now she was kneeling beside a strange bed in a strange house, married to a man that hated God, and she was pregnant with his child. She laid her head in her arms and began to weep. And she called on the name of her Savior, and for the first time in many years, she felt the sweet presence of the Lamb of God. As she opened her heart and told Him all of her troubles, something inside her started to thaw.

Then, like the frozen streams of the Northland that

feel the warmth of the spring sun, throw off the steel grip of winter and break free of the ice that holds them motionless and still, the river of life slowly began to make its way through her broken heart, and Rachel felt the love of her Lord and the soft touch of His nail-scarred hand.

Chapter Twenty-Four

The Plot

Rachel didn't know how long she knelt beside the bed. Her legs were stiff and her back ached, but, for the first time in years, her mind was at peace. As for Gerald and Monique, she knew what she had to do. She went to the bathroom, dressed, and washed her face but did not put on any makeup. When she was finished, she went back into the bedroom and dialed the kitchen. Collins, Augusta's butler, answered.

"Yes, Ms. Rachel."

"Collins, send Monique to my room."

"She'll be right up, ma'am."

In a few minutes there was a knock. "Come in, Monique."

The maid peeked in. "You are up early, madam. Can I get you something?"

Rachel pointed to a chair. "Sit down, Monique."

The girl sank into the chair across from Rachel.

"Monique, I am very angry with you."

Monique squirmed in her chair. "But why, madam?"

Rachel sighed.

What has happened to me? I used to live a peaceful life on a farm...

"I know about you and Gerald. I was at the cottage and saw you after you...well, after you were...together."

Monique turned pale. She started to say something, and Rachel stopped her.

"There is nothing to say, Monique. I understand why you could be led astray by Mr. Gerald's persuasive ways, but you didn't have to..."

Rachel felt her face burning with embarrassment. "I want you to leave this house. Today!"

Tears welled up in Monique's eyes. "But madam, I have no place to go."

In spite of her anger and shame, Rachel's heart went out to the girl. She hated Gerald for what he had done. "Monique, this is for your own good. Gerald will only use you and then throw you away. You need to leave immediately. Collins will drive you into town. I will arrange for a hotel room until you find work."

Monique gave Rachel a haughty look. "But Mr. Gerald, he will be so angry. He loves me."

Monique stood up and pointed a finger at Rachel.

"Maybe you are the one who should leave. Mr. Gerald says you are very mean to him and will not do what a wife should do. He will divorce you and marry me. He loves me, not you. I will be his wife and make him happy."

Monique stood there with a smug look on her face.

Rachel put her face in her hands. Then she looked up. "Monique, you're a foolish, gullible girl. Gerald doesn't love you and he never will. And there is something that Gerald obviously did not explain to you. He has no money. The money is all mine. This house belongs to me, the house in New York belongs to me—it's all mine, Monique. If Mr. Gerald divorces me and marries you, he will have nothing."

Monique drew herself up. "That is a lie! Gerald is rich, he told me—"

"Monique! Listen to me! Gerald has some money from his trust, but he will run out in a few years. He told you he was rich to get you into his bed. Gerald will never divorce me because I am his ticket to the lifestyle he loves."

Rachel was trembling. "Monique, I want you out of this house in an hour. It may be true that I am not a good wife, but that does not give you an excuse. Once you're gone, you might keep seeing Gerald, but you won't do it under this roof. Now go!"

The girl marched toward the door. Before she left she turned to Rachel. There was a challenge in her eyes. "We will see what Mr. Gerald says when he hears you are sending me away."

Monique flounced out of the room. Rachel sank back down in her chair. The room was spinning.

This can't be happening to me...

After a long time, Rachel called Gerald's room. His patronizing voice grated on her like a carrot on a metal scraper.

"Well, good morning, Rachel. How's my darling wife?"

Rachel got right to the point. "Gerald, I know all about you and Monique."

There was indifference in his answer. "So I heard. She came tearing in here crying. It was most upsetting. I will have to take a Valium to settle down."

"You don't sound too upset, Gerald."

Gerald laughed. "Actually, you did me a big favor in kicking her out. Monique was getting a little…clingy."

Rachel could hardly believe what she was hearing. "But, Gerald, you made promises to her…"

"Oh, those. Sometimes you have to stretch things a bit to get what you want."

"But that poor girl thinks you are in love with her. You used her, like you used me, just to satisfy your own lust."

Rachel blinked back her tears. She felt trapped. Gerald's voice was hard, grinding into her.

"Don't play so high and mighty, Rachel. You didn't have to marry me, but you did. You didn't have to sleep with me, but you did. You could have stayed a good girl and passed on the whole deal. You could have lived out your life in Paradise, but you wanted the money, so we made a bargain. You lusted after the money the same way I lusted after Monique. There's really no difference between you and me, now is there?"

Rage rose inside Rachel; rage at Gerald's indifference, rage at her own foolishness. Suddenly, she was screaming at him over the phone. "You are right. I'm no better than you, but I'm going to do something about it. Gerald, I'm divorcing you and I'm going home. I'm not going to raise my baby in this horrible place!"

There was a gasp of surprise from the other end of the line. "Your what?"

"My baby! I'm pregnant. It happened that night in Capri."

Rachel began sobbing. "I thought you loved me, but you just wanted sex. I feel like a prostitute. My mama and papa were right. The world is a horrible place."

There was a long silence and then Gerald spoke. "Calm down, Rachel. Give me a minute…"

Rachel heard Gerald take a deep breath.

"This is a bit of a mind blow. This changes everything. After all, it's my child, too. Can we talk about this when we calm down a bit? I don't really want you to divorce me. You might not believe this, but I do have feelings for you. Maybe I can change."

Rachel was caught off-guard. It was the first honest thing she had ever heard him say. She didn't trust Gerald, but he was right about the baby.

"All right, Gerald, we can talk, but don't expect much to change. I don't trust you."

Gerald's voice was soothing and contrite.

"I totally understand, Rachel. Give it a day or two and then let's talk this over."

Augusta was in the barn, looking over her Arabian horses when Gerald caught up with her.

"Grandmother, I have to talk with you…privately!"

Augusta could tell her grandson was upset. She handed the reins of her stallion over to the young man who was helping her. She waved her hand imperiously.

"Take this horse back to his stall and make sure he's fed and watered."

The young, bearded man nodded in the affirmative. "Yes, Mrs. St. Clair, right away."

"I haven't seen you around here before? What's your name?"

"I'm David, ma'am. David Kaufman. Benny hired me a few days ago."

Augusta scrutinized the bearded face. The young

man looked familiar but she could not place him. "Well, if Benny hired you, you must be good with horses."

"Yes, ma'am, I am."

Gerald stood there, fuming. Augusta loved letting him know who was in charge. She turned to him. "Now, dear, what is it that's troubling you?"

"Not here, Grandmother. Someone might hear us."

He pulled her into an empty stall and lowered his voice. "Grandmother, Rachel says she is divorcing me."

Augusta scowled. "What precipitated this hasty action on her part, Gerald?"

Gerald twisted his hands awkwardly. "She...she caught me messing around with Monique. She's pretty upset."

Augusta raised her hand in a dismissive gesture. "It's not something we need to worry about."

"Grandmother, that's not all. Rachel is pregnant!"

"What?"

Augusta stared at Gerald. Despite the cold, he was sweating.

"Rachel is pregnant."

Augusta looked at Gerald for a long moment and then slapped him, hard. The sound of her hand was like a whip crack. "You stupid fool! I told you to leave her alone."

Gerald rubbed his face. "When you told me that, it was already too late. She got pregnant in Capri."

Augusta stared at Gerald as he cowered before her.

He really is a pitiful human being. If I could do this without him, I'd have Randall take care of him, too.

She sighed and put her arm around Gerald's shoulders. "You are very fortunate to have someone watching over your interests."

"What do you mean, Grandmother?"

"I have anticipated this situation and taken steps to remedy it."

Gerald pulled away. "Remedy? How can you remedy this? She wants to divorce me."

Augusta opened the stall door and looked up and down the hallway. The barn was quiet, except for the cooing of the pigeons huddled in the rafters. She turned back to Gerald.

"Gordon Randall and I have worked out a solution to our problem. He is coming for a brief stay. During that time you are going to be his assistant in facilitating the demise of your obstinate wife."

"Assistant?"

Augusta's voice was like icy daggers ripping at him. "Yes, assistant, you helpless little pipsqueak. You keep pushing me to get the money. Well, there's only one way to get it. You're going to poison your wife and we're going to say she got a very virulent form of A-Shanghai flu. Dr. Schumacher will certify the cause of death, we'll ship her back to Pennsylvania, and you will be the heir."

"But, what about the baby?"

"Collateral damage. Can't be helped."

Gerald looked about the room as if trying to see a way to escape. "Look, Grandmother, I don't think I can go through with this."

"And why not?"

"Something's changed. For the first time I've found a girl who is real, and pure, and honest. And now she's having my baby. I can't hurt her. I... I love Rachel."

Augusta's hand lashed out again and Gerald withered under the blow.

"Now you listen to me, you weak little boy. If I didn't need you I would have figured out a way to take care of you years ago, and you wouldn't be the first St. Clair I've dealt with."

Gerald went pale. "What do you mean, I wouldn't be the first one?"

"That, my dear grandson, is none of your business. I want you to understand something. Your life is worth nothing and you are standing on very shaky ground. I want that money and I want it now. That means Rachel has to go. If you mess this up, I will see you dead before you touch another dime of St. Clair money."

Gerald tried to take a stand. "You won't kill me, Grandmother, you need me. You can't get the money without me."

Augusta laughed out loud. "You're a fool, Gerald. The difference between you and me is that I see the whole picture, and I plan for the future. You just live from day to day. Do you really think that I don't have other options—that I have put all my eggs in the untrustworthy basket named Gerald St. Clair?"

She laughed again. "If you think that, you really are a fool. Now, if you want to live, you'll not say another word. And tomorrow you and Randall will begin the treatment that will resolve our dilemma. Do you understand me?"

Gerald's face was white. Augusta patted him on the face, but it was still a slap. "Gerald, my foolish, foolish boy. You need to understand how far your grandmother will go to achieve her purposes."

He capitulated. "Yes, Grandmother."

Augusta smiled sweetly. She patted his face again. This time it was a caress. "That's better, dear. You just trust your devoted grandmother, and you will be well taken care of."

She took Gerald by the arm. Together they walked out of the stall, down the hallway and out through the big doors.

The barn was silent for a few minutes, and then the door of the tack room next to the empty stall creaked open. Daniel peeked out, slipped out of the room and walked quickly through the barn and out the back door.

Chapter Twenty-Five

The Key

Jenny Hershberger stood at the window of the little blue farmhouse in Paradise, Pennsylvania. Outside, gray clouds scudded across the sky, signaling the coming of another storm. The chill wind had piled the snow from the last nor'easter high along the fences that marked the lane leading out to Old Leacock Road. Bare, brown trees painted with white frost lined the lane. Pennsylvania lay in winter's icy grip, but for Jenny, the winter was in her heart.

The sound of someone tramping onto the porch drew her away from her vigil. Bobby Halverson was out on the porch stomping the snow off his boots. His old dog, Rufus, whined and fussed, anxious to get out of the cold. Jenny opened the door and motioned them both in. Rufus trotted past Jenny and headed straight to the fireplace where he lay down as close to the burning logs as he could. Jenny looked up at her old friend. Bobby reached out, and then Jenny was inside the circle of his arms, weeping.

Bobby patted her awkwardly on the back until her sobs stopped. Jenny pulled a handkerchief from her pocket and wiped her eyes. She smiled at Bobby. "Sorry, Uncle Bobby. I'm still pretty *umkippen* over Rachel. Come in and sit down. I'll get some coffee."

From the kitchen, Jenny saw Bobby sit in a chair close to the fire. He held out his hands to the warmth. Rufus whined again. Bobby patted him on the head. "Yes, boy, it is cold. Our old bones can feel it today, can't they?"

Rufus put his head up for more rubbing as Jenny returned with two mugs of steaming coffee.

"Sugar and cream, just like you like it, Bobby."

Bobby took the proffered mug and spoon and stirred the coffee. Jenny sat down on the couch, and the two sat there for a while, sipping the hot brew.

"Where's Jonathan today?"

Jenny sighed. "He's lying down. He got another migraine." There were a few moments of silence, and then Jenny spoke again. "Bobby, what am I going to do?"

"Have you heard from our girl?"

Jenny sipped her coffee as she stared into the fire. "We heard from Rachel right after she got married. Gerald was taking her to Europe. Her letter sounded cheerful enough, but I know my daughter. Underneath the excitement, there was uncertainty. She was realizing what a mess she has made of her life. Jonathan was glad to get the letter, but the next day, he sent it back with a note reminding Rachel that she was under the *bann*. We haven't heard from her since."

Jenny got up and went to the window. She looked out on the snow-covered yard. The past few months had taken their toll. She could see herself reflected in the glass, and there were new wrinkles.

I'm aging every day. My hair has gray strands.

"I feel old, Bobby. And I can't get anything done. I just stand here at the window, hoping I will see Rachel trudging down the lane. It's a good thing it's winter and everything is on hold. If I'm like this in the spring, this farm will fall to pieces."

"What about Daniel King?"

"No one has heard from him. His *daed* came by after Daniel left. They had an argument over Rachel, and he thought Daniel might be here. Rachel sent Daniel a letter and Daniel responded. He's loved Rachel since they were little, so he isn't about to let the *meidung* keep him from looking after her. Jonas tried to get Daniel to forget Rachel, but Daniel loves her too much. Daniel was very worried about Rachel. He packed up his clothes and left. I think he followed her to New York."

Jenny set down her cup. "What has happened to my life? It used to be so peaceful here. The three of us were together on the land. We were always happy and Rachel loved her papa so much. I felt every day that *du leiber Gott* was walking with us, guiding us, and leading us. Then Jonathan disappeared and when he came home, everything was different. It just seems that the Lord is so very far away. I don't know what to do."

Jenny's voice trailed off and silence filled the room.

Bobby put down his coffee. "That doesn't sound like the Jenny Hershberger I know."

Jenny looked up in surprise.

"The Jenny Hershberger I know has never quit, or whined, or complained. She takes the good with the bad and finds a way to overcome all obstacles. And for an old agnostic like me, the one bright spot in my own search for meaning in life has been watching my Jenny standing strong in her God. You've changed, Jenny. You stopped trusting God when Jonathan came home and started doing everything on your own. I don't know much about how God works, but what I do know, I learned from your dad and mom and you and Jonathan. Don't you think you should ask Him what to do instead of coming to a broken-down old Marine who can only shrug his shoulders when you ask?"

Jenny sat with her mouth open, staring at Bobby. He smiled and reached over to pat her arm. "Didn't expect that, did you? I'm just saying that it seems like you've given up on life. Why, I remember that when hard times came, the first place your mama, Jerusha, went was to her knees. I think that you might have gotten away from the source of your own strength."

Jenny sat for a long time. "Uncle Bobby, I didn't know you knew so much about our faith. You've always said that it was good for us, but you weren't interested."

Bobby ran a hand through his thinning hair and took a sip before he answered. "Look, Jenny. I never said I wasn't interested—I'm just kinda slow. But I have learned this. You can't hang around Christians for the better part of your life without something rubbing off. I'm in my eighties now, and when you get to be my age, you are closer to the end than the beginning. You can't wait to be a deathbed penitent, because you never know when you might come face-to-face with your own mortality. I thought I learned that in World War II, but somehow I forgot."

"Uncle Bobby, you sound like you have made some kind of decision."

"Well, we will talk about that later. Right now, I want to know what you are going to do to get yourself out of this funk."

Jenny stood up. "You are right, Uncle Bobby. *Sie schlagen den Nagel auf dem Kopf.*"

Bobby smiled. "So I hit the nail on the head, eh?"

"And you've picked up a little German along the way, also?"

"Some."

Jenny went and knelt by Bobby's chair and put her arms out. He reached out and put his arms around her.

"You are right, Uncle Bobby. I've forgotten about prayer. I've been so focused on keeping everything organized that I forgot I'm not in charge. The Lord showed me that a long time ago when I was trapped in that cave waiting for my papa to come for me."

A voice behind them spoke. "I was there, too, Jenny."

Jenny turned.

Jonathan was standing in the doorway. "I remember how it all happened. God kept showing Himself to me through miracle after miracle. The way I came to Apple Creek and met you, the way we rescued you from the gang that was chasing me, the way we found your birth mother; those were the things that opened my eyes to the truth that I needed Jesus in my life."

Jonathan came around the couch to face Jenny. "I haven't been a good husband or a good father for a long time, Jenny. I've been using my injury as an excuse to withdraw from you and Rachel. Now Rachel's gone because of me. Before I met Jesus, we used to laugh at Christians and tell them to stop beating us with their Bibles but that is exactly what I've been doing to Rachel. The *Ordnung* does not save us. I used to know that, but I forgot. I need your help, wife, to remember."

Jenny took Jonathan in her arms. Her heart went out to the gentle man who had suffered so much.

Jonathan looked into Jenny's eyes. "I want to share something the Lord showed me today when I was reading."

He went into the bedroom and came back with his Bible. He motioned Jenny to the couch and sat beside her. He opened the Bible and read: "Proverbs 12:25 says, 'Anxiety in the heart of man causes depression, but a good word makes it glad.'"

Then he turned to another section and read again: "Philippians 4:6-7 says, 'Be anxious for nothing, but in everything by prayer and supplication, with thanksgiving, let your requests be made known to God; and the peace of God, which surpasses all understanding, will guard your hearts and minds through Christ Jesus.'"

Jenny looked wonderingly at her husband as the Word sank into her heart.

Jonathan put the Bible down and took Jenny's hands. "I've been acting like some kind of a religious zealot. I've been spouting the rules with no place for grace in my heart. I have forgotten the way *Gott* has worked in our lives to restore our family. I have been depressed and I didn't know why. And then I read these verses and it became clear. I'm anxious—anxious about everything. I'm afraid that I'm going to lose my mind or have a stroke or worse. And that has been making me depressed. And then I get *verrückt*, crazy and cranky and…oh, Jenny, I've been miserable to live with."

Tears welled in Jenny's eyes. She reached out and softly touched the cherished face.

"But then I read the last part: '…a good word makes the heart glad.' And then I remembered Philippians: 'Be anxious for nothing…' The Bible tells us, commands us, not to be anxious."

Jenny went on for him, quoting the beloved verse. "'…in everything by prayer and supplication, with thanksgiving, let your requests be made known to God; and the peace of God, which surpasses all understanding, will guard your hearts and minds through Christ Jesus.'"

Jonathan nodded. "Yes, Jenny, don't you see? We haven't been praying and it's my fault. I'm the head of this house. I need to lead you in prayer. And we need to make our needs known to God, with thanksgiving. And then we will have the peace that we need."

Jenny sat in amazement, looking from Bobby to Jonathan. And then, in a moment of understanding, she knew that God was working in her life once again. Another favorite scripture came to her mind. She spoke it softly. "'I will enter His gates with thanksgiving in my heart; I will come into His courts with praise.'"

Jonathan looked up. "Yes, Jenny, that's it. He's given us the key all along. He wants us to come into His presence and He has shown us the way. Prayer, thanksgiving, and praise will lead us right into His throne. Oh, Jenny, I'm so sorry."

Suddenly Bobby laughed out loud. "Hallelujah!"

Jenny and Jonathan stared at him.

"I feel like I'm in a revival meeting. It hasn't been like this in this house for a long time."

As Jenny sat there in the glow of what God was doing, a picture came to her mind. It was the second time she had remembered the Key, the one her mama had sewn almost prophetically into the Rose of Sharon quilt.

"… You do not know which pieces of your life you will discover tomorrow, but they are there, determined by *die Vorkenntnisse des Gottes*. He has already planned them. Now let me show you one more thing as a reminder."

Jerusha moved the quilt until the rose was under her hand.

"Look! Do you see it?"

Jenny looked, and there it was! Sewn into the center of the rose—the small, key-shaped piece of red silk so finely stitched that it was almost invisible. Jerusha smiled. "The Lord had me add it to the quilt so that we would always remember…"

"That He is the Key to our lives, Mama, and without Him we cannot hope to comprehend what is happening to us and why…"

And then Jenny remembered what she had said to Jerusha.

"Perhaps the journey is not over after all, Mama. In fact, we may be coming to a new beginning. That is a hopeful thought."

Jenny's heart leaped. The Key, she had forgotten the Key. And then Jenny knew that God was not finished with their family, and that in a moment of great love, He had once again touched their family with his great wisdom and power. And for the first time, she understood why *Gott* had put the Key into their lives. She slipped to her knees beside the couch.

"Lead us in prayer, husband."

Bobby started to get up. Jenny put her hand on Bobby's arm. "Please stay, Bobby. We need you to agree with us. You love Rachel as much as we do."

Bobby nodded and sank back down in the chair.

And so Jonathan began to pour forth their needs before a loving God, praying for his wife, praying for Rachel, praying for Daniel. And as their hearts softened and melted before Him, the gentle presence of the Holy Spirit filled the room and their hearts drifted out to that place where tears and laughter become one in the presence of the Master and giver of life. And hope began to rise within Jenny's heart; and a faith that somehow, someday, everything would be restored.

Chapter Twenty-Six

Pressure

"Michel, where is the money?"

The question was not posed in conciliatory tones. Finally, Duvigney spoke, the sibilance in his voice very pronounced. "I am growing weary of your incessant badgering, Augusta."

"And I am growing weary of your incessant evasions, Michel. My granddaughter-in-law should be receiving an immense income every month. So far we have received a pittance. Now, I'll speak slowly so you can understand me. Where...is...the...money?"

"You should have received one million dollars on Monday."

Augusta laughed. "One million? That's a drop in the bucket. Rachel should have received ninety million just from the interest that has accrued since her grandfather died. And the ongoing income should be two million a month. Gerald and Rachel have been married since July. It's now the middle of November. So the way I see it, we should have received around one hundred million dollars. Where is it?"

"You must give me some more time. As I told you, it is not easy to move such a large amount of money—"

"Michel, you're lying. There is something fishy going on here, and I intend to get to the bottom of it."

Duvigney began to protest. "Now, Augusta, I assure you…"

Augusta wanted to grab Duvigney by his scrawny neck. But she couldn't so she took a breath and then throttled her tone down from furious to threatening. "Do you know what I think, Michel? I think you've been spending the money. I think you and your friends thought that Robert St. Clair was the last of his line, that there would never be an heir with the Key and that his portion of the inheritance was sitting in a dead account. So you helped yourselves. What you took out would certainly build back up in the fifty years you had to play with before another heir was assigned. But you got greedy and spent too much—so much that an audit would be very embarrassing. But you didn't worry. After all, you're an old man. Six more years and then twenty-one years before anyone can claim the money. Why, you'd be long gone. And then out of nowhere, a little country bumpkin shows up with the proper DNA and, to make matters worse, she has the Key. And now you have to come up with money you don't have. That's what I think, Michel."

Augusta thought she heard a choking sound, and then Duvigney retorted. "Those are preposterous allegations. As I was about to say, I am making the final arrangements right now to resolve this whole matter."

"Michel, do you know Parker Salisbury?"

"The United States Attorney for New York? Why, yes, I know him."

"You will get to know him even better because you will be hearing from him a lot in the near future."

"I have no reason to see Mr. Salisbury—"

"Oh, but you will, Michel, you will. Parker is an old friend of mine. He would be happy to do me a favor."

Duvigney laughed but there was no humor in it. "You must have something on him."

"Nothing very important, just some rather explicit photos. But the point is that if I ask him, which I will if we don't have ten million in Rachel's bank account tomorrow, he will be more than happy to launch an investigation into this whole affair. Do you get my point?"

"I understand, Augusta. You will have the money tomorrow."

"That's better. And the same investigation will begin if I don't have the bulk of the accrued interest from Robert's trust within thirty days."

Duvigney gasped. "I can't come up with ninety million dollars in thirty days."

"Michel, I would suggest you call in some favors. Otherwise, you will become the focus of an anti-corruption campaign led by a very earnest United States Attorney who is dying to make a national name for himself. Can't you just see the St. Clair name plastered all over the grocery store news racks? Parker would love that, but I know you and your friends would not. Therefore, if you don't want to trade your thousand-dollar suits for prison orange, I would start making some phone calls. Do you understand?"

A brief silence and then the click of the connection being broken was Augusta's answer.

* * *

"Randall, if you are going to help me out of this situation, you must do something now. The St. Clair woman is pressuring me, and I can't come up with the money she's demanding."

Michel Duvigney's whining voice was music to Gordon Randall's ears. He listened but his mind was already churning.

This is all working out as if it had been scripted.

He interrupted Duvigney. "Michel, I want you to relax. Things are moving along much more smoothly than you know."

"What do you mean?"

"I mean that I am going to be staying at the St. Clair mansion, and I will deal with all of the matters at the same time. The girl, Gerald, and Augusta will all be taken care of within the week."

"And how do you plan to do that?"

"That's not your concern, Michel. However, you can be assured that within seven days, your problems will be over…that is, if you meet my fee requirements."

"And just how much is this going to cost me?"

"One million dollars."

Randall heard Duvigney suck his breath through his teeth and then cough.

"That's absolute piracy, Randall. I'll need some time…"

Randall took off the gloves. "Michel, don't play games with me. Augusta St. Clair is putting the pressure on you for millions of dollars that you don't have. I can make that pressure go away, this week. Which way do you want to go? Try to find the millions, or write me a check for the pittance I'm asking. Or should I bow out and let you find someone else? Of course, that would take some time, and by then the investigation would be under way."

"Investigation?"

"Michel, you called me. You want the St. Clair problem to go away today. What this telephone call means is that Augusta has come at least as far along the trail of the missing money as I have. She knows you're stalling and she's guessed that you have misappropriated the funds. So she threatened you, probably with a criminal investigation. Am I right so far?"

"Go on, Randall."

"You know what would happen if someone started poking around in Robert St. Clair's financial affairs. They would turn over a few rocks and there you would be, blinking in the light like an evil little salamander. Oh, no, Michel, you don't want Augusta to take one more step down that path. So just write the check now and send over it to my favorite restaurant. You know where it is. I'll be having lunch there at one o'clock. That's in one hour. If your guy doesn't show up, I will assume you have decided to go elsewhere for help."

The sibilant voice was noticeably shaken. "Now, Randall, don't be hasty. My man will be there with the money."

"Very sensible, Michel. Once I have the check, you can be certain that your worries are over."

"Thank you, Randall. I won't forget this."

The line went dead. Randall chuckled and turned off the recorder. "I won't forget it either, Michel, not one word."

Daniel sat on the bed in the hired hands' quarters behind the barn. His heart was pounding. He had heard

Gerald and Augusta talking in the barn, but he had not been able to hear everything that was said. He did know two things. Rachel was pregnant and the St. Clairs were planning something evil. Augusta had mentioned the name Randall, but Daniel did not know who he was. He slipped to his knees beside the bed.

"*Lieber Vater im Himmel*, I come to you for help today. Rachel is in trouble and I'm not sure what to do. Please show me what I must do to help her."

Daniel knelt there for a long time, and then, like fresh drops of rain on a green field, the words came into his heart.

Have not I commanded thee? Be strong and of a good courage; be not afraid, neither be thou dismayed: for the LORD thy God is with thee whithersoever thou goest.

And then again…

…the people that know their God shall be strong, and do exploits.

And one more…

Get up! Go out to the training pen!

The command was so resounding that Daniel literally jerked to his feet. He grabbed his coat and cap and went out the door. The sun had just set and the last few beams of light barely penetrated the gray overcast sky. Snow was piled up around the fences and along the houses. A chill wind blew steadily from the east, and there was a tang of sea air. Daniel started to walk faster.

Slowly, be cautious…

The command pulled Daniel up short. He looked around to find who was speaking, but there was no one. Carefully he made his way around to the training pen. The enclosure was empty and the ring was a foot deep in snow. The trees and shrubs pressed in close around the fence, and Daniel made his way carefully along the far side.

"What do You want me to do, Lord?"

Wait! Watch!

Daniel stood there in the growing dark, wondering just what he was doing. Then he heard the sound of a car coming down the gravel road that ran behind the barn. He ducked down behind the fence and watched through the boards. An SUV appeared. It was headed out toward the back of the property, going slowly through the snow. The windows were smoked and Daniel could not see inside. It passed him and continued down the road. He made his way through the bushes along the road. Ahead, he could see the lights of the vehicle. Then he saw it turning off the gravel road into the trees.

They're going to the old caretaker's cottage...

He followed the road until he could see the cottage. The SUV was parked in front and four men were climbing out. One of the men gave the others some directions, and they opened the back, took out two large trunks, and carried them inside. Then one of the men drove the van to the back of the cottage and covered it with a camouflage tarp. Then he returned and went inside. As he passed Daniel's hiding place, his jacket flapped open and Daniel saw that the stranger was wearing a pistol in a shoulder holster.

Something terrible is happening, and Rachel is in the middle of it. I've got to get her out of here!

Chapter Twenty-Seven

Discoveries

The St. Clair mansion stood silent, a great dark hulk looming out of the surrounding blackness. The fitful wind blew an occasional drift of snow off the roof to fall in whispered whiteness down the walls like softly floating waterfalls. A slim crescent moon attempted to cast its light on the pale landscape below, but more ragged clouds began to blot out the night sky. A few icy flakes drifted out of the indigo heavens. The piled snow creaked softly under the feet of the man approaching the back door of the mansion. Gordon Randall was on a mission.

When Randall reached the entryway, he pulled out the key Augusta had given him and opened the door. Then he crept quietly down to Augusta's office. He pulled a small black kit from his pocket, took out a stiff piece of wire, and worked it into the door lock. In another few seconds, he was inside the room. He went to the window and pulled the curtains closed. Then he clicked on a flashlight and looked around. The room was organized and neat; the desk, a model of efficiency with every pen in place, and the furniture was spotless. Randall shook his head.

This will be easy. Augusta thinks she's on top of everything, but she's so easy to read. A person this neat is obsessive. They never do the unexpected. So the safe...

Randall walked to the bookshelf behind the desk and began to run his fingers under the shelves until he felt the button, there was a click and the bookshelf slid sideways.

...is right here. And it's an old walk-in Yale! Really, Augusta...

Randall reached into the kit and pulled out a small stethoscope. He slipped it on, placed the diaphragm on the front of the safe and began to turn the dial until he heard the tumbler fall, and then to the left and then back to the right. The safe lock clicked, and the door moved slightly under his hand. He twirled the wheel, pulled the door open, and stepped inside.

He looked for a light switch, found it on the wall and switched it on. There were drawers on the back wall and shelves with documents in folders to the sides. Randall pulled a few drawers out of the wall. They were filled with jewelry and gold coins. He pushed them back in and continued searching.

After a few minutes he found a large drawer that was locked.

A safe inside a safe. There must be something important in this one.

Randall looked through his toolkit and found a strangely curved pick. He inserted it into the lock and manipulated it until he heard the click. He opened the drawer and began to leaf through the contents. There

were several notebooks, what looked like a diary with
a lock on it, a stack of pictures and several letters still
in their envelopes. He took the pile and set it on a desk
in the corner. He picked up the stack of pictures. They
were old Kodak prints that had been hand colorized.

The first one had three people at the beach, two
men and a woman. He looked at the woman for a minute. She was young and beautiful, a real knockout in a
one-piece bathing suit. Suddenly, he realized that the
woman was Augusta. She was standing between the two
men. One was well over six feet and had flaming red
hair. The other was slightly shorter and had dark brown
hair. The two men had remarkably similar features—
strong prominent chins, broad foreheads, both very
handsome—obviously related. They were grouped together with Augusta in the middle and the men's arms
around her. Augusta was staring up at the red-haired
man. Her gaze betrayed the fact that she cared for him,
but he was looking straight at the camera. The name,
Robert, was written under his picture. The other man
was staring at Augusta. Randall turned the picture over.

*Robert and Jerod St. Clair, and me—August 1944—
Martha's Vineyard.*

Randall looked at the other pictures. All of them
were of Augusta, and most had Jerod and Robert with
her. They were in nightclubs or at theaters or in a cozy-
looking apartment. Randall scratched his head.

*This girl knew how to play the game. She meets a
rich kid, gets him hooked, and the next thing you know,
she's making the high society rounds and renting a
place in uptown Manhattan. I can just imagine how
she played this poor sucker.*

The last picture was dated February 15, 1945. There

were two people in the picture, Jerod and Augusta. Jerod was in an Army aviator's uniform and he had his arm around Augusta. They were at a train station. Augusta wore a warm-looking coat and she was turned sideways to the camera. The coat did not hide the slight bump in her tummy. Randall knew what it was.

Jerod's baby...

He picked up the letters. They were held together with a rubber band. Randall slipped off the band and scanned through them. One letter caught his attention. It was a letter addressed to Augusta but there were two letters inside. Randall pulled them out. The first one was from Augusta to Robert. It was dated December 15, 1944.

> *My Dearest Robert,*
>
> *It's been a month since you left for Lancaster, and I haven't heard a word from you. I am writing because there is something I must tell you, Robert. I am six weeks pregnant with your child and I am so happy. I know it is yours because, believe it or not, I have never been with Jerod, only you. I want to be with you always. I know we can work it out with Jerod, he will understand that we are truly in love and won't stand in our way. He's a good kid. Please come home.*
>
> *Yours forever,*
> *Augusta.*

Randall stared down at the letter.

Not Jerod's baby, Robert's baby! My, my, this is getting very interesting!

Randall unfolded the second letter. At one time it had been crumpled and torn in two, then carefully smoothed out and taped back together. There were small, discolored spots on it.

Tear stains!

The letter was dated December 23, 1944. It was from Lancaster, Pennsylvania. Randall read on.

Augusta,

I received your letter and I need to say a few things in response. Augusta, our night together was a huge mistake on my part. I was drunk and if you are honest you will admit that you made yourself very available that night. I never would have done such a terrible thing to my brother if I had been in my right mind. He loves you with all his heart. I have done him a terrible wrong.

I don't believe your claim that you have never been with Jerod. He is totally in love with you and has hinted many times that the two of you had more than just a friendship. So it is difficult for me to believe that I am the father of your child. Therefore I cannot marry you because I do not love you.

I'm very sorry,

Robert

Randall stared down at the letters.

Not the Christmas present Augusta expected, I'll wager.

The story was almost too incredible to believe. Jenny

Hershberger and Gerald's father were siblings. They had different mothers, but Robert St. Clair was their father. That meant that Rachel and Gerald were half-first cousins.

Randall put down the letters and picked up the diary. Another twist with the lock pick and the book lay open. The flyleaf had the name: Francine Bosnan at the top. And then below that, another name: Augusta Moukhransky. Shoved in between the flyleaf and the first page were several pictures. They were of Robert St. Clair and a beautiful, dark-haired girl. A small baby was in Robert's arms. Randall turned the top picture over.

Dad, this is Rachel, my wife, and your grand-daughter, Jenny. Rachel is such a wonderful wife and mother and Jenny is a delightful little girl. I know you'd love them if you would just meet them. Won't you relent and let us come see you?

Robert had signed the note. Randall shook his head. *So Augusta already knew who Rachel and Jenny were when they came to the house in 1950. She lied to me!*

He leafed through more pages. The first part was filled with girlish ramblings about finding a wealthy, handsome husband and leaving the Bronx and then, several pages in, there was an entry titled, "The Big Day". Francine was leaving the Bronx, moving to New York and changing her name so she would be able to meet the right people. She had chosen the name Augusta Moukhransky.

Randall smiled.

Smart girl! Moukhransky is the name of a branch of the Russian imperial family. Her background couldn't be investigated because the Bolsheviks killed all the Romanovs. She did her homework and arrived in New York with an exotic name, a mysterious family background, and a beautiful face. She probably took the town by storm.

Indeed, she had, as the diary soon revealed. Within a month after arriving, she met Jerod St. Clair at a USO dance in Manhattan in 1944 and began dating him. Randall read the entry.

July 15, 1944

USO Dance at the Stage Door Canteen. The Andrews Sisters were performing. I met a charming young man, Jerod St. Clair, and he was very attentive. He's very, very rich. I guess I don't have to look much further.

Several more entries detailed a whirlwind romance with Jerod St. Clair. Augusta was not in love with Jerod, but she certainly appreciated his money and the idea of marriage to the young man was intriguing to her.

And then Randall read an entry that was underlined in red.

August 15, 1944

Jerod has invited me to his family's vacation compound at Martha's Vineyard!!!! This is the most exciting thing that has happened to me, ever! I'm

*sure Jerod is going to propose. We are leaving
tomorrow. I have so much to pack.*

Followed by a very interesting entry two days later...

August 17, 1944

*Yesterday, we took the train to Boston and then
the Cape Flyer out to Woods Hole. From there we
rode the ferry to Martha's Vineyard. And then the
most amazing thing happened. When we arrived,
Jerod's older brother, Robert, was waiting for us.
Robert is wonderful!!! He's taller than Jerod and
has the handsomest face I have ever seen. As soon
as I saw him, my heart started pounding. I guess
I fell in love with Robert at first sight. Jerod is
going to propose, but Robert, oh, Robert! I have
to be with him. What am I going to do? Jerod is
madly in love with me. If I don't play my cards
right, I could lose both of them and be back where
I started. But I won't back down. I'll just put Jerod
off until I know where I stand with Robert. One of
the St. Clair boys is going to marry me. I'd prefer
Robert, but I'll take Jerod in a pinch.*

Augusta's plan of seduction unfolded in the pages.
Randall smiled as he read of Augusta's conquest.

October 22, 1944

*Last night I was with Robert. We were all sup-
posed to go out to dinner, but Jerod got sick, so
he made Robert take me to the Stork Club anyway.*

*After dinner I invited Robert up to my apartment
for a drink. After some really good champagne,
I turned on the charm and Robert couldn't resist
me. It was wonderful! But it didn't work out exactly the way I planned.*

There was much more to the entry, but Randall
closed the book and pushed the knob on his wristwatch.
The dim glow showed him the time.

*My, how time flies when you're having fun! I'll get
to this later but now I've got to finish up and get out
of here!*

Randall pulled a tiny camera out of his pocket, laid
the diary down on the table, and quickly began taking
pictures of all the pages. When he had photographed everything, he scanned through the notebooks. He photographed anything that looked interesting. At one point,
he came across a list of negotiable securities that were
held at a local bank.

Nice! Over a million dollars' worth!

He snapped a picture of the list. Then he carefully put
everything back in the order he had taken it out, closed
the drawer, and locked it. After looking around to see
that everything was in order, he turned off the light, left
the vault, and locked the safe. He checked everything
to make sure it was back in place, opened the curtains
in the office, and exited the room.

He slipped down the hallway, out the door, and went
back down the path. As he walked, he patted the camera in his pocket.

I've got you, Augusta. I've really got you now.

Chapter Twenty-Eight

The Diary

Back in his room, Randall opened the camera and re-moved the memory card. He put it into the player and began to go through the material he had photographed.

Digital cameras! Who would have believed it—you have to hand it to those Japanese...

Randall flipped to the entry about Robert and Augusta. He began reading where he had left off. After a while, he whistled softly. The story read like a television soap opera.

Augusta, Augusta! So you had to fall back to plan B, after all...

October 22, 1944

Last night I was with Robert...but it didn't work out exactly the way I planned...

Augusta stirred. The bed was warm and she pulled the covers up around her shoulders. From outside her window, the sound of brazen taxi horns and buses grinding their gears filtered up from 5th Avenue.

Augusta listened to the sounds of the city. Then she turned in the bed, but there was no one beside her. The place where Robert had slept was empty. Augusta raised herself up on her elbow and looked around. Bright sunlight streamed in the open window blinds. Augusta stretched like a cat and lay back down. Memories and images from the night before flooded her mind.

Robert! Oh, Robert!

"Robert?"

There was no answer. Augusta called out a little louder.

"Robert?"

Silence. Augusta got up, grabbed her silken robe and slipped it on. She remembered the look on Robert's face when she had taken it off the night before.

You liked what you saw, didn't you, Robert...

She went out into the living room. There was nobody there. She went to the front door, opened it, and looked up and down the hallway. The *New York Times* was in front of her door. She picked it up. The headline blared at her.

MACARTHUR IN PHILIPPINES! HUGE YANK ARMY SWARMS ASHORE, CAPTURES CAPITAL OF LEYTE ISLE!

Augusta went back inside. She dropped the paper on the coffee table. Where was Robert?

"Robert?"

She walked into the small kitchenette. Robert was gone! She glanced down and saw a note lying on the kitchen table.

Augusta,

*I am very remorseful about what happened last
night. I've betrayed my brother. I am leaving for
Pennsylvania today. It will be a good thing. I want
to be as far away from you as I can. You are a
beautiful woman, and hard to resist, but I have
made up my mind that last night will never happen again.*

Robert

Augusta crumpled up the note and hurled it against
the kitchen wall.

"That's what you think, Robert St. Clair!"

December 24, 1944

It was the day before Christmas. Outside her window snow was filling the streets with a soft whiteness
that matched the season. Christmas music came from
the department store across the street as people dashed
in to do their last minute shopping. Augusta sat at the
kitchen table, her lovely face a stony mask. Tears fell
upon the letter spread out in front of her. The news it
contained was not good. Robert wasn't coming home.
Robert didn't love her.

She sat for a long time. She knew what she must do.
She folded the letter and put it back in the envelope.
There was another letter with it. It was the one she
had sent to Robert, telling him she was pregnant. He
had sent it back with his letter. Augusta rose and went
to the telephone. She dialed a number and waited. Fi-

nally, Jerod answered. Augusta smiled faintly and then worked up a slight sob in her voice.

"Jerod? Oh, hello, darling. Listen, I... I...there is something I need to tell you. Can you come over right away?"

She waited a moment until Jerod answered.

"All right, darling, I suppose I can wait until then. But come as early as you can. It's very important. Yes, dearest, I'll see you at five."

Augusta hung up and smiled. Jerod was on his way. She went into the bedroom and got the small box down from the top shelf of the closet. She put the letters inside and then set it back on the shelf. Then she began to look through her clothes.

What shall I wear to bait the trap?

She looked through several dresses.

Too hot, too naughty, too revealing... Wait, here's what I need.

She pulled the white dress down and held it in front of her as she looked in the mirror. It was modest, came below her knees and the neckline was high. Her long, blonde hair and her stunning figure would make her look like a Christmas angel.

Perfect! The innocent virgin, all in white, confesses her sin. If Jerod doesn't fall on his knees and beg me to marry him...

By five o'clock, Augusta was ready. She had not put on makeup because she wanted her face to look pale. Her blonde hair framed her lovely face and the white dress was exactly right. At five minutes after five, the doorbell rang.

We'll train the young man to be more prompt after we are married, won't we?

Augusta went to the door and opened it a crack. Jerod St. Clair stood in the hallway, an anxious look on his face.

"I'm sorry I'm late, Augusta. Traffic was terrible."

Augusta managed a wan smile. "It's…it's all right, darling. I…"

And then she burst into tears.

Jerod took the sobbing girl into his arms. "Why, Augusta, what's wrong?"

"I'm so ashamed, Jerod. We should have been more careful…"

"More careful?"

Augusta pulled Jerod inside and closed the door. She took a deep breath, and then turned to Jerod. "Yes, more careful."

She paused and then put her face in her hands and began sobbing again. "I'm… I'm…pregnant, Jerod."

Jerod's face was a study in bewilderment. "Pregnant? But when…how? We never…"

Augusta pulled away and looked at him, trembling. "You don't remember?"

Now Jerod really looked confused. "Remember?"

Augusta began reciting the story she had come up with. Her voice was pitched with just the right combination of sultriness and shame. "It was in October. We went to the Stork Club. We were tipsy when you brought me home and you fell asleep on the couch?"

Jerod smiled and looked embarrassed. "Yes, I made rather a fool of myself."

"Well, the truth is, Jerod, you didn't stay asleep."

"I didn't?"

Augusta turned back to Jerod and put her arms

around his neck. "No, you did not. In the middle of the night you came into my bed. I didn't realize what was happening until you were kissing me."

She moved up close to him, very close. "You were so strong, so wonderful, I... I couldn't resist you. We..."

Jerod's face told her she had won. It flushed red and then white. "We did? And you got...well, in a family way?"

"Yes, and now I don't know what to do."

She flung herself on the couch and began sobbing. Jerod stood helplessly watching her. Finally her sobs slowed.

"New York society is not very kind to girls who get in trouble. I expect... I'll have to leave here, find one of those homes for unwed mothers. I'll have to give the baby up for adoption."

She choked back a sob.

Jerod pulled her up gently and held her tight. "Oh, no you won't!"

Augusta smiled with her face buried in his shoulder, but she put fear in her voice. "I won't?"

"Of course not! Don't you see, Augusta? I'm wild about you. I've loved you since the day we met. I truly don't remember that night, but if you will do as I ask, I'll make it up to you."

Jerod dropped to one knee. "Augusta, will you marry me? I love you and I won't let our baby go without a name. Please, Augusta, say you will marry me."

Augusta looked down at the trembling young man. "Do you really mean it, Jerod? You want to marry me, even after..."

"Yes, my love, I'll marry you today if you want."

Augusta took Jerod by the hand and pulled him up. She pulled herself into his arms and clung to him. "Oh, yes, yes, I will marry you. Oh, I thought you would hate me."

"Hate you? Augusta, you're the most incredible girl. You're beautiful and intelligent, and… Well, I just have to be with you always."

Augusta sprang the trap. She looked into his eyes, parted her lips, and pitched her voice slightly lower. "Jerod, darling, there's one more thing."

"What, my love?"

"Ever since that night, I can't get you out of my mind. Your kisses, your strength, I'm obsessed with you."

Jerod looked at her again and she could see the passion in his eyes. "Do you mean… I mean, do you want me like I want you?"

"Yes, Jerod, I'm crazy about you. I want to show you how much I love you."

"Oh, Augusta, I've dreamed of this."

Augusta dropped her eyes. "Please, Jerod, I need you. Can we, I mean… If we are going to be married, and I'm already… Well, won't it be all right? I love you so. I want to give you something, and this time you'll remember."

She pulled him after her as she turned toward her bedroom. Jerod followed her like a lamb to the slaughter. There was a slight smile on her face as she walked before him to her bed.

February 24, 1945

Augusta put the telegram from the war department down. She felt the baby move inside her. She held up her hand, and the huge diamond ring sparkled in the light. She smiled. This was perfect. She was a war widow. Pity and compassion would solidify her position in New York society. And she would win Robert back. She would have to tell Max and Margaret, of course. They would be devastated, but the baby would bond them all together so tightly. Perfect!

With my blonde hair, black should be most becoming.

She smiled. She couldn't have planned it better herself.

Randall read through more entries. They detailed different attempts to see Robert or entice him to come back to New York. After the baby was born, Augusta tried to use the boy to bring Robert home, but Robert was steadfast in his refusal. Augusta even tried to go to Lancaster to see him, but Robert arranged to be out of town. A year passed. And then Augusta received a surprising note from Robert asking her to meet him.

July 4, 1946

Augusta took one more look in the mirror. Everything was perfect. Her hair framed her perfect face and the dress was just the right mixture of modest and sultry. Her eyes, her strongest feature, were large, luminous pools of indigo blue. She smiled, and the effect was dramatic. She was a beautiful woman. She called a taxi. She mustn't be late, Robert was waiting.

When she arrived at the Stork Club, Augusta went inside. The maître d' saw her right away. "Mrs. St. Clair, how nice to see you. Mr. Robert is waiting for you."

Augusta followed Angelo to one of the small booths

in the back. Her heart leapt. Robert was waiting for her, his red hair like a flash of fire. He saw Augusta and stood. He did not smile, motioned her to a seat and reached out his hand to greet her.

"What, no kiss or hug, Robert? After all, we are family."

Robert ignored her rather pointed remark. "Augusta, I need to talk to you about that. I chose this place because I don't want a scene."

"Why, Robert, what could be so serious that it would cause me to be upset?"

"Augusta, I want to talk to you about Francis."

Augusta leaned closer. "You mean your son?"

"That is debatable. Paternity blood tests are unreliable when it comes to brothers. Jerod and I have the same blood type, O negative. So even a paternity test will not prove which one of us fathered the child."

Augusta stiffened in her chair. "And I'm telling you, Robert, that you are the father of my son. I never slept with Jerod before I got pregnant."

Robert sighed. "Look, Augusta, I'm going to be very blunt. You are a manipulating, greedy woman who will do anything to get what you want. My brother wasn't three days in his grave before you were writing me, calling me, wanting to see me. What kind of woman are you?"

Augusta's face flushed. "I'm that way because I love you, and I never loved Jerod. I only married him so I would have a name for my baby. Obviously, it doesn't matter to you what happens to girls with no money who get into trouble. You weren't man enough to take responsibility and Jerod was. So I married him. Now I can take care of my child without having to take some awful kind of work…"

"…not fitting to the style of life to which you have become accustomed? Augusta, I pity you. I will always believe that Jerod fathered your baby. You have his money so you don't need me to support you. We should just go our own ways. You'll be fine."

Augusta lowered her voice and put a pleading tone in it. "But, Robert! I love you. I don't care if you don't marry me. I just want to be with you."

Robert took a conciliatory tone. "Augusta, that will never happen. The truth is, I've met someone. She's carrying my baby and we're going to be married."

Augusta felt as though Robert had punched her right in the face. She gasped and struggled to catch her breath. "Who…who is she?"

Robert looked down. "She's Amish. She's a wonderful girl, honest and true."

"You mean unlike me, Robert?"

"Yes, Augusta, she's not like you at all. Her name is Rachel. I'll marry her as soon as she says yes."

Augusta could tell he was not lying. A dead feeling crept into her heart, and then rage rose up and almost choked her. She leaned close to Robert and her words were icy daggers. "You will rue the day you ever set eyes on her. You and all the St. Clairs will learn that I am a woman who never forgets. You…you…you get me pregnant and then you leave me for some country slut? I don't think so. You think your life will be wonderful? Well, I'm telling you that you and Rachel and your child will have nothing but sorrow. I will personally see to it. You proud, arrogant St. Clairs! I will destroy you all."

She stood up, picked up her water glass, and threw the

contents in Robert's face. Then she turned and marched out of the room, followed by the murmur of voices and curious stares.

Chapter Twenty-Nine

The Plan

Gerald St. Clair sat on his bed with his head in his hands. Fear gripped him. He knew that his grandmother had been deadly serious when she threatened his life. And what did she mean when she said she had taken care of other St. Clairs? And now she was going to kill Rachel. He hated the idea, but he was deeply afraid of his grandmother.

Gerald went into the bathroom. He was about to begin shaving when there was a knock on his door. When he answered it, Gordon Randall was waiting.

"Good morning, Mr. St. Clair. May I come in?"

Gerald hesitated. There was something creepy about Randall that frightened Gerald. Randall pushed past and shut the door behind him. He handed Gerald a small plastic vial filled with oval pills.

"These are the pills Dr. Newberry prescribed for your wife's pregnancy. They are fifty-milligram vitamin B6 tablets. For our purposes however, they've been dipped in an arsenic solution. These will help her morning sickness for a few days. But then she will start going downhill. It will look like a bad case of the flu. Give them to her with a glass of ginger ale about an hour after she gets up. Simple, tasteless, and painless…at first."

Gerald stared down at the bottle. Suddenly he knew that he couldn't go through with this. "How long will this take, Mr. Randall?"

"About ten days."

"Will she suffer much?"

"In the last few days, she will be very sick, but she will sink into a coma and be unconscious most of the time. Does that bother you, Mr. St. Clair?"

"It's just that I have never done anything like this and I'm a little nervous, that's all."

"You're not backing out, are you?"

Gerald felt sick. He wanted to run away, get out from under his dominating grandmother and this dangerous man. His hand trembled and the pills made a slight rattle in the bottle. Randall noticed. He stepped close to Gerald.

"When I was in Vietnam, there was a village in Quang Ngai Province that was supplying the Vietcong with food and weapons. I was a CIA dark ops advisor embedded with a small group of hand-picked mercenaries in a company of US soldiers. I had orders to make an example of the village, so we massacred everyone— men, women, and children."

Gerald could feel his hands shaking.

"What's your point, Mr. Randall?"

"My point is that we massacred those people on my orders. The regular soldiers were uncertain about killing civilians, but I was not uncertain. I had my orders and I carried them out. Those soldiers knew that my men and I would kill the first soldier who balked. This situation is no different. I have a job to do here. Don't balk at any of this or your life won't be worth a dime. Do I make myself clear?"

Gerald knew that Randall was telling the truth, but he had to make sure. "My grandmother wouldn't let you do anything to me. I'm her lottery ticket."

Randall smiled. "You just don't understand, do you, son? If you don't play this the right way, you will become expendable. Your grandmother will do anything to accomplish what she wants. She's like a black, evil, monstrous old spider—spinning her web. She has planned this very carefully and I'm here to see that her plans are carried out. To me, there is no difference between the operation in Vietnam and this one."

Randall smiled, but there was no warmth, only cold steel. He turned and left. Gerald stared after him, the bottle of pills held in nerveless fingers. He shut the door, his heart pounding.

How am I going to get out of this?

Rachel knelt beside the toilet. The paroxysm of retching had passed, but she still felt weak and disoriented. Augusta's doctor had visited the day before, and after a cursory examination, he told her that she just needed to get some rest. He wrote a prescription for some medicine for the morning sickness and left. Rachel rolled off her knees and leaned against the wall. She really did feel terrible. There was a knock on her door. She dragged herself to her feet, wiped off her chin, and went out into her room. The knock came again.

"I'm coming!"

Rachel opened the door to find Gerald standing there with a tray.

"Can I come in?"

Rachel stepped aside and Gerald entered. He set the tray down and turned to Rachel. There were two white pills and a glass of golden-colored liquid on the tray. "I brought your pills. The ginger ale will settle your stomach."

Rachel stared at Gerald suspiciously. He seemed kind and solicitous, but she didn't trust him. Her thoughts went back to Capri.

He just wants to keep me from divorcing him, so he's pouring on the charm. I've seen this before.

"Thank you, Gerald."

Gerald paused a moment and then he took her hand. There was a troubled expression on his face. "Rachel, I'm sorry that I have been so callous. It's just that I never met anyone like you, a girl who was not just some tramp. You're real and honest and good, and I don't know how to deal with honesty and goodness. I…well, I'm sorry."

He turned to go, but Rachel took his arm.

"I'm sorry, too, Gerald."

"Sorry for what?"

"I'm sorry for the way I've used you to get what I wanted. I just wanted to get away from my papa, so when all this happened I rushed ahead. Now I see that the cost has been terrible."

A tear ran down her face. "I'm supposed to be a Christian, but I threw all that away for the money. I forgot that nothing is worth more than a relationship with God. In the last few days, I've been praying again, and the Lord has really helped me to see what a fool I've been. Now I'm pregnant and I've hurt you and… Oh, Gerald, please forgive me."

Gerald looked away. "Rachel, I don't know much about God. When I was a kid I always liked church and being there made me feel peaceful and safe, especially after my parents died. But I don't know what you mean when you say you have a relationship with God. That just sounds so strange to me. And shouldn't you be the one forgiving me? After all, I seduced you under false pretenses and now...well, you are in real trouble."

"Trouble?"

A nameless dread came over her, and her heart began to pound.

Gerald turned back to her and took her arm in a powerful grip. "Yes, Rachel, trouble, dangerous trouble. You need to—"

Just then there was a knock on the door.

"Rachel, it's Augusta. Can I come in?"

Rachel stared up at Gerald. A terrified look came over his face.

"I need to what, Gerald?"

Gerald looked at the door. "Ah...nothing, Rachel, never mind."

The knock came again, more insistent.

"Rachel?"

Gerald let Augusta in. "Hello, Grandmother. I was just bringing Rachel her pills."

Augusta looked at Gerald curiously and then turned to Rachel.

"How are you feeling this morning, my dear? I'm so excited for you and for us. Another generation of St. Clairs, and I get to see it. I really never thought I'd be a great-grandmother. How delightful!"

Then she scowled. "Gerald also told me that he's

been a very naughty boy and that you're thinking of leaving us. Are you?"

Behind Augusta Gerald was shaking his head, his face pale. Rachel hesitated. "Well… I'm willing to at least talk about it."

Rachel could see the relief on Gerald's face.

Augusta smiled. "Excellent, Rachel. Now be a good girl and take your pills. You'll feel much better."

She turned to go. "Come, Gerald, we must let Rachel get her rest. I'll have cook send up something light, Rachel."

Augusta and Gerald went out. Before he closed the door, Gerald turned and gave Rachel another strange look. Rachel picked up the pills and took them with the ginger ale. In a moment, her churning stomach settled down. She went back to her bed to lie down.

I wonder what that was all about.

Gerald St. Clair followed his grandmother down the hallway. He felt hot and sweaty and flushed. She had almost caught him telling Rachel that they were poisoning her. His grandmother put her hand on his arm.

"I understand that Mr. Randall delivered my message, Gerald. I meant every word of it. Do not stand in the way of me getting what I want. You will be very, very sorry if you do."

"Just what do you want, Grandmother? And I don't believe that you would kill me, not if you want to get your hands on all that money."

Augusta smiled her icy smile and turned to go. "Sometimes money isn't everything, Gerald."

Daniel looked through the bushes at the house. He had not seen Rachel outside for days. He had to see her, but he had no excuse to be in the house. And those men, what were they doing here?

What can I do, Lord?

He began walking back to the barn. As he came around the corner, he ran right into Gerald St. Clair. The two men collided and Daniel was knocked to the ground. Gerald reached down to help him up. "Wow, sorry, I didn't see you. Are you all—"

As Gerald looked at Daniel's face, a light of recognition dawned in his eyes. "You look very familiar. I know you work here, but haven't I met you somewhere else?"

"No, I don't think so."

"What is your name?"

"David, my name is David."

"No…it's not David."

And then the penny dropped. "Wait…yes, I met you in Paradise. You're Rachel's friend. Dennis."

Daniel shook his head. "I don't know what you mean."

Gerald held onto Daniel's arm. "Dennis…no, Daniel. You're Rachel's Amish friend, Daniel. You were with Rachel the first time I met her. But you were dressed in different clothes. And you didn't have a beard."

Gerald looked around and then lowered his voice. "What are you doing here?"

Daniel looked for a way to escape, but Gerald held his arm with a grip of steel. Daniel capitulated. "All right, Mr. St. Clair, you're right. I'm Daniel."

"But what are you doing in Connecticut?"

Daniel looked Gerald straight in the eye. "I was worried about Rachel, so I came here to look out for her. You and your grandmother are not nice people and Rachel is my friend. I got a job working in the stable. And now there is something going on that is very strange.

Two nights ago I saw three men with guns arrive here. Is Rachel in danger? What are you up to?"

Gerald pulled Daniel close. "Yes, Rachel is in danger. And if anyone hears me telling you that, I'm as good as dead."

"Dead? Are you serious? What is happening here?"

Daniel could see both fear and resolve in Gerald's face.

"My grandmother wants all of Rachel's money. But she's not an heir. And I can't get it if Rachel divorces me. The only way I can is if Rachel dies without children. My grandmother has hired a man to kill Rachel. He's ruthless. They have started giving Rachel poison. I thought I could go along, but I can't. Rachel is good, she's beautiful and…and I've fallen in love with her. And there is a complication."

Daniel looked Gerald in the eye. "I know. Rachel is pregnant."

Gerald almost choked. "How…?"

"I heard you and your grandmother in the barn. I didn't hear everything, but I did hear that part."

Gerald put his face in his hands. "If they kill her, they'll kill my child, too. I can't let that happen. But I don't know what to do, and I need help getting Rachel away from here."

It was Daniel's turn to grip Gerald's arm. "This is unbelievable! How could you do such a thing?"

Gerald shook his head. "I thought the money was everything. But something Rachel said has been bothering me."

"What did she say?"

"She told me I could have a relationship with God. Ever since she said it, I can't get it out of my head. This morning I realized I'm a worthless human being, and now my grandmother wants to make me into a murderer, too. I just can't. I have to get Rachel out of here. Will you help me?"

Daniel nodded. "What can I do?"

"I can't talk any more now, but can you meet me here tonight?"

"What time?"

"Around eleven. I have to be careful because my grandmother has men watching the house. They will stay until Rachel is dead. You must be very careful. These men are trained professionals and they won't hesitate to kill us. My grandmother has something very evil planned for Rachel, and I think I'm on her list, too. I think it's much deeper than just getting the money, but I don't know all the details."

Daniel could sense the urgency in Gerald's voice.

"I'll be here at eleven."

Chapter Thirty

Suspicion

Augusta picked up her private intercom and called out to the caretaker's cottage. A male voice answered.

"Yes?"

"I need to speak to Randall."

There was a moment's silence and then Randall came on the line. "Good morning, Augusta."

"Randall, something is going on with Gerald. I found him with Rachel this morning, and he looked very guilty. I'm sure he is going to betray us."

"Well, he will at least try to wiggle out of his part in all this. He's weak and cowardly and has no stomach for this kind of operation."

"What should we do?"

"I'm already on it. My men are watching him. He won't leave or mess up our plans. He is a liability, of course. I assume you will want to deal with him at some point."

"Yes, but not until he is vested with Rachel's inheritance. When he turned twenty-one, I had Gerald sign over all his powers of attorney and make me the sole beneficiary of his will. He was too eager to start spending his trust fund to pay attention to the legal details. But if he dies before Rachel, there will be no money for me to inherit. And even then, I think we should wait awhile before we arrange something special for my darling Gerald—give everything time to cool down."

"We might have to keep him on ice until then."

"Whatever needs to be done, that's up to you. There should be plenty of ways to keep him quiet."

"Not a problem. He will be a grieving husband who has locked himself in his room and is not receiving visitors. After a few weeks, the unexpected death of his lovely young bride will unhinge his mind until, being unable to face life any longer, he will drive out to a remote spot on his magnificent estate and shoot himself in the head. The authorities will put the whole matter down as a suicide. And the billions will be transferred to the grandmother's bank account."

Augusta smiled at the scenario. "Really, Randall, you are quite ahead of the game."

"I try to be."

Augusta was quiet for a moment.

"Augusta, you still there?"

"I'm just wondering, how difficult would it be to turn him into a vegetable without killing him. I mean, someone in a comatose state but totally aware of everything going on around him. He could just sit there day after day while I did whatever I wanted. It would be very fulfilling to see him suffer as I have suffered."

"You, Augusta?"

"It's just a thought—the musings of an old woman

who has endured much at the hands of this cursed St. Clair family."

"I can arrange for any outcome you desire—a coma, a vegetable, or just dead. But as you add degrees of difficulty, you add more to the cost. So that's totally up to you. But adding Gerald to my list is going to cost you double my fee for Rachel. And I will need half up front, as usual."

"No problem, Randall. I will have a check for you this afternoon."

The line went dead. Augusta put the phone down and walked over to a mirror on her office wall. She pointed a finger at her own reflection.

"Be very careful, old girl. You're almost there. In a little while, all the St. Clairs will be dead."

Augusta laughed out loud.

Gordon Randall picked up a small bag and headed outside. He didn't want to make his next call on a line that Augusta might be monitoring. He walked into the woods, pulled a wireless handheld phone out and dialed a number. In a moment, the hissing voice of Michel Duvigney answered. "Well, Randall, how are we doing over there?"

"Everything is going as planned. Rachel will be out of the way in a few days and then we'll deal with Gerald and Augusta."

"I assume you have a plan for that?"

"Augusta is already counting the money she'll get when Rachel dies and her grieving grandson commits suicide. What she doesn't know is that you have lost or spent all her money, so there won't be any coming. You need to put some money into Rachel's account so that the pressure will be off you for at least a week. Then when Rachel is dead, I will send tapes to the police that reveal Gerald's part in murdering Rachel and Augusta's complicity. The police will find the medicine bottle with the poison in it and Gerald's fingerprints on it. Rachel will be exhumed and the coroner will find that death was caused by arsenic poisoning, not Asiatic flu. As a murderer, Gerald will be disqualified from inheriting the money and will spend the rest of his life in prison. Augusta will also go to prison. You will never be audited and the missing billions remain missing."

Duvigney actually laughed, although it sounded more like someone dying of tuberculosis. "Brilliant, Randall, I'm delighted."

"Thank you, Michel. I will keep you informed."

Randall turned off the phone, put it back into the bag with the tape recorder, and walked back to the cottage.

Michel Duvigney sat quietly for a few minutes, thinking about what Randall had said. Then he picked up the phone and dialed a number.

"Rose, here."

"Rose, I think Randall is double-crossing me. I found out that he has been making incriminating tape recordings of Augusta St. Clair. That means he has also been making recordings of my conversations with him. If those conversations ever leaked to the police or the press, it would be very disadvantageous for me. Be ready to eliminate him as soon as the project in Greenwich is completed. How many days until the girl is dead?"

"Three or four."

Duvigney nodded. "Good. As soon as you can verify

that Rachel St. Clair is eliminated, take care of Randall. Does he have any idea that you're a double agent?"

"Colonel Randall trusts me implicitly."

"Good. You'll be paid the usual fee and, Rose, be very careful. Randall has eyes in the back of his head."

"I can read the Colonel like a book. He trained me."

"Well, be careful anyway. Be sure you recover any tapes or information that will be incriminating to me."

Duvigney disconnected from the call. He smiled and spoke to himself. "Money always trumps loyalty…"

Then he dialed another number. A woman came on the line.

"Charlene Esperanto here."

"Charlene, it's Michel Duvigney. Have you accomplished the task I requested of you?"

"Yes, Michel. We have tracked Randall and discovered both the attorney that he would use to deliver any incriminating evidence he might have collected and the safe deposit box where it is kept. When should we move on it?"

"Wait until I hear from Rose. As soon as Randall is dead, I will call you and you will get rid of the attorney. And what is the bank?"

"Manhattan Trust."

"Good, I will have my man there clean out the safe deposit box as soon as Randall and the attorney have been eliminated. You'll hear from me within five days."

Duvigney hung up the phone. Then he made one more phone call to the Manhattan Trust Bank. When he had passed on the information and instructions to his contact there, he went to the wine bar, got out the bottle of Le Voyage de Delamain Cognac and poured himself a drink. He held the snifter to his nose and reveled in the delicious bouquet. Then he raised it in a silent toast to himself. If all went as planned, he wasn't going to have to give up his expensive little habits after all.

A cold, bitter wind cut the night air like a scalpel. The moon was a slim crescent and the pale light did little to illuminate the grounds of the St. Clair mansion. The temperature had dropped again. A million stars set against the indigo backdrop twinkled in the high canopy of the heavens, but the effect was not delightful. Instead, it was almost ghastly. Daniel King walked toward the horse barn. It was a few minutes after eleven. He slipped inside the open barn door and stepped into the shadows. He waited for almost twenty minutes. Finally, he saw Gerald slipping down the path from the house. Gerald stepped inside and whispered in the darkness. "Daniel?"

"Here, Gerald."

Daniel pulled Gerald into the shadows. Gerald was trembling. "Sorry I'm late. I had to wait until Randall's men went for coffee. I think my grandmother is suspicious because she's had those men watching me more closely."

"I'm glad you were able to get out. How will you get back in?"

Gerald shrugged. "I'll just tell them I went for a walk, if it's any of their concern."

Daniel put his hand on Gerald's shoulder. "It is very brave of you to go against your grandmother and her evil plans. You have to gather your courage and trust God."

In the dim light, Daniel could see a puzzled look on Gerald's face.

"You talk like Rachel does, Daniel, but I don't understand what you mean. You both act like God is a real person."

"Oh, but He is a real person. And He's helping us right now."

"What do you mean?"

"Rachel is His daughter. He's concerned about her safety. He has moved on your heart to save her. Don't you see?"

"You mean these feelings that have been bothering me are from Him?"

"Have you been feeling guilty?"

"Very guilty."

"So think about it, Gerald. You married someone you don't love, just to get her money. She became pregnant and now you're feeling guilty, probably for the first time in your life. I would imagine you have gotten other girls pregnant and not given it a thought."

Gerald stood silently for a long moment.

"You're wrong about two things, Daniel. I have felt guilty before—not for a long time, but I have. I used to feel guilty when I was a boy and the priest talked about sin and doing the wrong thing. But after I came to live with Grandmother, I learned to never feel guilty about anything I did."

"What is the other thing I'm wrong about?"

"You said I don't love Rachel, but I do. She's different from any girl I've ever met. She's strong, and sweet and pure. Well, she was…before…"

Daniel put his hand on Gerald's shoulder. "I understand, Gerald. I love her, too. So we must find a way to save her. Tell me where she is."

Gerald pulled Daniel to the door of the barn and

pointed at a wing of the house. "She has her own suite in the east wing. It's on the ground floor and she has a set of French doors that open out into the gardens. But those men are watching everything very closely. It will be hard for you to get to her."

"First of all, you've got to stop giving her the poison. Then you have to let her know I'm here and that I will come for her tomorrow night. Can you do it?"

Gerald nodded. "I'll slip her a note when I bring the pill in the morning. I'll tell her not to take it and that you're coming at midnight. I'll tell her to leave the patio door unlocked and that you will knock twice."

"Good, good, Gerald. Will she be able to walk?"

"I think so. We've only been giving her the poison for two days but Randall wants her to die in three more days so the dose has been strong. But the good thing is they can't give it to her all at once or it won't look like she died of the flu."

"All right. If she doesn't take it tomorrow, she might feel better. I'll figure out a way to get her off the estate between now and tomorrow night."

"Can you drive, Daniel?"

"Yes. I learned during my *Rumspringa*."

"Rumspringa?"

"Yes, that's when we get to go out and see if the Amish way of life is really for us."

"Okay, then. My car is parked in the garage. It's a white Bentley. Here are the keys. If you go right down the path from Rachel's room you'll come to the garage. This key opens the door. And this big one is the ignition key."

Gerald started away and then he turned. "Thank you

for being here, Daniel. I don't know why you would do such a thing…"

"I prayed, Gerald, and this is what the Lord told me to do."

"Well, however it happened, you have to get her out of here. If you don't, my grandmother will have us all killed." He turned and slipped away into the darkness.

Chapter Thirty-One

The Fading

The next morning Gerald came to Rachel's room with her pills and the ginger ale. He was shocked when he saw her. Rachel looked very sick. Her face was pale and her hair was wet plastered against her skin. There was a rash on her neck and left cheek. He knelt beside her bed and took her hand. As he did, he pressed a piece of paper into it and folded her hand around it. Rachel started to say something but Gerald gave a slight shake to his head. Then he spoke loudly. "How are you this morning, Rachel?"

"I don't feel well at all, Gerald. I've been throwing up a lot. I have a terrible headache and I feel very weak."

Gerald glanced around. He leaned closer to Rachel to kiss her cheek and as he did he whispered in her ear. "Read the note and don't take the pills."

Then Gerald leaned back from the kiss and spoke loudly again. Rachel was staring up at him, wide-eyed.

"The doctor says it's some sort of flu, Asian or something. You need to get a lot of rest and drink fluids. And take your the morning sickness pill."

Gerald stood up. "I hope you feel better soon, Rachel."

His lips mouthed the words "the note," and then he turned and left.

Rachel waited for a few minutes and then turned over to face the wall. She opened the note and read the words.

Don't take the pills. They're poison! Try to eat something today. Daniel is coming to get you at midnight. Leave your patio door unlocked and be ready. He will knock twice.

Rachel's heart leaped.

Daniel! Daniel is here. Oh, thank you, Lord!

She began to weep. As she did, she heard a noise and turned over. Two men were standing by her bed. One was powerfully built and towered over her. There was another man standing beside him. He looked familiar. Then she remembered. Gordon Randall.

"Hello, Rachel."

Rachel's heart skipped a beat. "Hello, Mr. Randall. What are you doing here?"

Randall smiled, and the look in his eye sent a cold chill down Rachel's back.

He reached over and pried her hand open. The note fell out onto the bed.

"I see Gerald has given you a message."

"Let go of me! You're hurting me!"

Rachel began to struggle and scream. Randall put his hand up and covered her mouth. There was a piece of cloth in the palm of his hand with a faint chemical odor. Then the lights went out.

* * *

Randall picked up the note and scanned it. He turned to the second man. "Go get Augusta. I need her now!"

The man hurried out the door. In a few minutes, he returned with Augusta trailing behind.

"What's this all about, Randall? Why, what's happened to Rachel?"

"Good morning, Augusta. We have a slight change in plans. You see, Gerald was planning to help Rachel leave, and I made an executive decision. I need a room where we can lock her in."

"We have a secret safe room downstairs."

Randall motioned to the second man, and he picked up Rachel like an empty sack. The two men followed Augusta down the hall. She stopped in front of an un-decorated section of the hallway wall and flipped open a large, ornamental light switch cover. Behind the cover was a keypad. Augusta punched in four numbers and a section of the wall slid back, revealing a room. She went in and motioned the two men inside.

The room was small and sparsely furnished. There was a small kitchen area and a desk with a phone. Two beds stood against the wall. A couch completed the furnishings.

Randall pointed to the first bed. "Put her there."

Randall's cohort laid Rachel down. She was still un-conscious.

Augusta watched with alarm. "Now what do we do, Randall?"

"We keep going only instead of keeping her in her room, we keep her here until she's too sick to get up. When she's in the last stages, we put her back in her own bed where someone can find her after she's dead.

We'll have to dose her intravenously because Gerald warned her about the pills. My men will watch the house. According to Gerald's note, someone named Daniel is coming at midnight to take her away. I assume that would be Daniel King. He'll find someone else there instead."

Augusta gave Randall a puzzled look. "How do you know about Daniel King?"

"Augusta, you pay me well to do my job. I know every detail about the subject of my investigations. Daniel King is a neighbor of the Hershbergers and has known Rachel since she was a small girl. That is the only Daniel that Rachel would know. Now, is this room perfectly secure?"

Augusta nodded. "Yes. You have to know the code to open the sliding panel."

"What about that phone?"

"It's a direct line to the Old Greenwich police station."

Randall reached down and pulled the phone cord from the wall. "Not anymore."

Randall turned to the other man. "Headley, no one comes in or out of the grounds without my knowing about it. And I want you to be ready in Rachel's room at midnight to intercept our would-be rescuer."

"Affirmative."

Headley turned and left the room.

Randall turned back to Augusta. "Does anyone else know about this room?"

"Only Gerald and my butler."

"Good. Tell your staff that Mrs. St. Clair is very ill and she is not to be disturbed. I don't want anyone going to her room. Is there a bathroom in here?"

Augusta pointed to a door at the back of the room. "Through there."

"Good, we have everything we need. No one comes in or out of this room except me."

"That's fine, Randall. But what about Gerald?"

"Gerald will stay under 'house arrest'. My man will be stationed by his room, and he will remain there until this is over."

"Fine, do what you have to do. This whole thing is very upsetting. I didn't know it would get so…so complicated."

"You're not getting cold feet are you, Augusta? We can't back out now."

"No, no, Randall… I will be fine. I think I'll go have a drink. Just let me know when it's over."

"Fine, Augusta. A drink is probably a good idea. I'll drop by later to collect my check."

Augusta left. Randall pulled a small walkie-talkie from his pocket and spoke into the microphone.

"How's everything going with our little backup plan, Jamison? Both of the St. Clairs are getting antsy. Gerald has already betrayed us and I can see that Augusta is beginning to crack. The probability that she might turn on us is high."

The speaker crackled and a tinny voice answered. "Don't worry, our presents for the St. Clairs are being placed right now. This property has at least five propane tanks that I counted. If they explode, the house will go up like a torch. But I don't understand, Colonel. Why blow the place up?"

Randall chuckled. "Most likely we won't. But there is another party involved. My professional sense tells me he is preparing to double cross us. I have some very incriminating tapes linking this man to a desperate plot to eliminate the St. Clairs. When I send them to the police, along with a note describing the location of the bombs, some very uncomfortable light will be shed on our man's schemes—just a little payback to Michel Duvigney for thinking he could betray me."

"Good, very good."

Randall smiled and clicked off the device.

Rachel awoke with a pounding headache. She was lying on a bed in a room she did not recognize. She sat up and swung her legs over the edge of the bed. The room began to spin and she nearly blacked out again. One of her legs suddenly cramped and the pain was so excruciating she almost cried out. She could feel her stomach begin to cramp. She looked around desperately and saw an open door that looked like it led into a bathroom. She lurched to her feet and stumbled toward the door. Before she could get there, she fell to her knees and vomited. Her stomach twisted and she retched until she was completely empty.

She crawled into the bathroom and found some toilet paper, which she used to wipe her mouth. Then she pulled herself erect at the sink and ran cold water into the basin. She dipped her hands into the water and splashed it on her face. She staggered back into the main room and collapsed on the bed.

As she lay there, she heard a click. Randall and the other man entered the room. Randall was smiling but it reminded Rachel of a shark. The other man had something in his hand. It looked like a hypodermic needle.

"Hello, again, Rachel. Sorry about the heavy-handedness in your room, but I have a job to do. You see, you have become a real problem for the St. Clairs."

Rachel looked into Randall's eyes. There was an evil there that chilled her heart. "Are you going to kill me now?"

He nodded to the other man who felt for a vein on Rachel's arm and then inserted the needle. "It will take a few more days, Rachel, but yes, I am going to kill you."

Daniel King crept up the steps to the French doors that led into Rachel's room. He tried to be absolutely quiet, but the hard crust on the snow crunched under his feet. The new moon was up and a low scud of clouds dimmed its already wan light. He knocked twice on the glass door. There was no answer. He knocked again and then tried the handle. It was unlocked and the door swung open. He stepped inside into the dark room.

"Rachel, are you here?"

Daniel heard a noise and then something went over his head from behind and tightened around his throat. His hands went to his neck. There was a thin cord there and he could not get his fingers under it. Whoever was holding it was incredibly strong. Daniel turned his shoulder against his assailant's chest. He got a little leverage and threw himself against the attacker with all his might. The assailant lost his footing and stumbled backwards through the open door. The noose around Daniel's neck loosened a tiny bit, and he could breathe again.

Daniel reached up and grabbed his opponent's wrists. He struggled to break the man's hold, but he felt himself weakening. Then he remembered something that he used when he had to lay a horse down. He pulled forward with all his might until he felt the man resisting. Suddenly, Daniel planted his feet and pushed his body sharply backwards. As he did, he reached under the man's knee and pulled it up.

His attacker slipped on the icy crust of snow and fell heavily against the wrought iron bannister that ran around Rachel's patio. Daniel felt the cord on his neck release and slide off and he turned quickly. His attacker was lying awkwardly against the pointed fence. The man's mouth opened, he jerked spasmodically, and then went limp. Daniel took some gasping breaths. Then he cautiously moved closer.

The man had slipped and fallen against one of the decorative wrought iron posts, and it had rammed upward into the back of his head. His body hung limply against the fence, and he did not move. Daniel grabbed the assailant's arm and felt for a pulse. There was none. The man was dead.

A shock went through Daniel's frame.

I have killed a man!

And then he remembered why he was there. He ran back to the open door and ducked inside. He waited until his eyes adjusted to the dark and then he looked around the room. The bed was empty. Rachel was gone! He stood there desperately trying to decide what to do. Suddenly, he heard a noise from somewhere in the house and panic gripped him. He ran out the door, and stumbled down the steps. His heart was a sledgehammer in his chest and then the reality of what had just happened swept over him and he fell to his hands and knees and vomited. He crouched in the snow like an animal, shaking, and then he struggled to his feet and leaned against the house until the sickness passed. He turned for a moment, looking back at the mansion that was looming above him like a dark, evil castle in the pale moonlight. "I'll come back for you, Rachel. I'll get help. Hold on!" Then Daniel King turned and ran into the darkness.

Chapter Thirty-Two

Hopeless

Gordon Randall stared at the body hanging limply on the wrought iron bannister, the garrote still clutched in one hand. It was clear what had happened. He could see the marks of the scuffle in the snow and the place where Headley's boot had slipped. He motioned to the two men with him, and they lifted Headley off the fence and carried him into Rachel's room.

Randall pointed to the bathroom. "Grab a towel and wrap it around his head. And then put him in a blanket and take him to the cottage before it gets light."

Randall shook his head in disbelief. Headley had been his best man since the days they fought side by side in the jungles of Vietnam. It was almost beyond comprehension that a highly trained, Special Forces soldier had been taken out by an Amish farm boy. Randall went back to the patio and shined his flashlight around. It was still well below freezing, so the blood from the wound had coagulated quickly and there was only a small amount on the patio to be cleaned up. Randall looked at his watch. It was 1:30 a.m. The moon had gone down, so there was little chance that anyone would see them. His men picked up the body and carried it to the patio door.

"Walk along the edge of the patio under the roof where there's no snow. I don't want to disturb King's tracks."

The three men muscled the body along the edge of the patio until they reached the path. The grounds crew had cleared the bricks of snow and the men did not leave any tracks as they carried Headley to the SUV. They put the body in the back.

Randall turned to the third man. "Rose, I want you to go back and sanitize the room. Wipe down the fence and make sure there is no blood anywhere. Step in Headley's tracks and leave the mark of your boots, but don't obliterate the boy's tracks. We have to have evidence he was here. We'll tell the police that you were the one who fought with King. Knowing the local boys, they won't get here until tomorrow and maybe not even then. After you're done, lock the room up tight. We've got to get some more men out here, so call some men you can trust and have them drive up as quickly as they can. I need at least two, three would be better."

"Got it."

Randall and Jamison climbed into the SUV and headed toward the cottage. Jamison shook his head. "It must have happened fast. Headley was good, real good."

Randall nodded. "It looks like the kid got him out the door and then Headley slipped on the ice. This really messes things up. The kid is on the loose, Gerald is unconscious in his room, we have a dead body on our hands, and Augusta is getting nervous. It's not so simple anymore."

"What are we going to do, Colonel?"

"I'll call the local police and tell them there was an attempted kidnapping here, and they should be on the lookout for Daniel King. I'll give them a scenario that King can't turn over and the police will buy. Deranged ex-boyfriend shows up at mansion and tries to kidnap the girl but is driven off by security guards. I want everything to look normal if the police show up. If they catch King, it will take him a while to get them to believe the truth. By then, the girl will be dead and we'll be long gone. Then Augusta can deal with the police."

"Okay, I'll handle it."

"Good, now let's get Headley into the cottage and we'll pull this operation back together."

The phone rang at the Old Greenwich police station. Sergeant Oliver Cromwell Franklin jerked awake at his desk and looked up at the clock on the wall. It was 3 a.m. Sergeant Franklin picked up the phone. "Greenwich Police, Sergeant Franklin, how can I help you?"

"Sergeant Franklin, this is Gordon Randall. I'm head of security for Augusta St. Clair. We've had an attempted kidnapping here at the estate. The man escaped and I think he's headed your way. He's on foot."

Sergeant Franklin groaned. Why did this stuff always happen on his shift? And why at the St. Clairs'? "Do you know who it was, Mr. Randall?"

"Yes. The intruder's name is Daniel King. He's an ex-boyfriend of Gerald St. Clair's new wife. He followed her here from their hometown. He got a job in the St. Clair stables. Then tonight, he snuck into Rachel St. Clair's room. He was ranting and raving about getting her away where she would be safe. When my man heard Mrs. St. Clair screaming and broke into the room, King fought with him and got away.

"Mrs. St. Clair is very upset over the incident, and she's suffering from the flu. I have our men on guard so it's pretty well buttoned up here, but you should put out an APB for King. He's tall, blond hair and beard, and dark clothes. And Sergeant, he is definitely dangerous."

"All right, Mr. Randall. Thanks for the call. Are you sure everything is okay up there?"

"Perfectly, Sergeant. I've called in more men and have them patrolling the estate. A squirrel couldn't get onto the grounds without us knowing it. Oh, one more thing."

"What's that, Mr. Randall?"

"When you catch him, Augusta would appreciate it if you did everything you could to keep this incident quiet. She wants him locked up tight. Do you understand?"

"I sure do, Mr. Randall. You let Augusta know that we'll catch this guy and keep him tucked away good and tight. As soon as we find King, we'll let you know. There are not too many places he could hide."

"Good, Sergeant, very good."

The line went dead. Sergeant Franklin picked up his dispatcher microphone. "Hey, Gary, you awake?"

A voice crackled in the speaker. "Very funny, Sarge. It's freezing out here. Just driving around keeping the car warm and waiting for this miserable shift to be over. What's up?"

"Just got a call from the St. Clair place. They had an attempted kidnapping by a disgruntled ex-boyfriend of Gerald's new wife. He got away, and he's on foot.

He's probably headed into town—tall, blond kid with a beard. And don't take any chances. He got in a fight with one of the guards out there and beat him up, so consider him dangerous."

"Right, Sarge. I just passed the St. Clair place and I'm coming in on Field Point Road now. We'll check along the road all the way into town."

Daniel King walked down the road toward Greenwich. He was still in shock from the events of an hour before. The lights of a car approaching from the direction of the St. Clair estate reflected off the trees ahead of him. Daniel slipped into a clump of shrubs under the trees and waited for the car to go by. It was going slowly and someone was shining flashlights into the trees on both sides of the road. Suddenly, Daniel's insides twisted and his heart started pounding.

Maybe it's those men. They're looking for me!

Daniel drew back into the heart of the shrubs. The car pulled up nearby and stopped with the motor running. It was a police car. Relief swept over Daniel. He was about to step out when he heard something in his spirit.

Stop!

He stopped dead in his tracks. Then he heard the radio crackle and a tinny voice came on.

"Gary, if King puts up a fight, use whatever force is necessary to stop him. Do you understand me?"

"Sure, Sarge, I get you. A tough customer, eh?"

"Yes, and according to their man, Randall, very dangerous. So when I say whatever force is necessary, that's what I mean. If he struggles, defend yourself."

"Okay, Sarge."

Daniel moved back into the bushes and then peeked through the branches. The police car was about fifteen feet away. The officer took his gun out of his holster and chambered a round.

They're working for Augusta, too! They would kill me if they had to.

Daniel pushed further back into the brush and stood as still as he could. The two officers in the car swept their flashlights over the sides of the road and then drove slowly on toward town. Daniel watched them go and then crept out of his hiding place.

Augusta has this town under her thumb. Lord, I need help.

Suddenly Daniel remembered Willy, the stationmaster.

Willy liked me. And he didn't seem too fond of Augusta St. Clair. Maybe he can help me.

Daniel headed toward town. He stayed along the edges of the road in the shadows, carefully watching for more cars as he went.

Willy was nodding in his chair in front of a decrepit old television set in the office at the Old Greenwich station when he was awakened by a noise. At first he thought it was the wind rattling the windows, but then he heard it again.

Tap! Tap! Tap!

He swiveled around in his chair. There was someone at the side door. Willy got up slowly and looked through the glass. It was the young man that he had sent out to the St. Clair estate. Quickly, he opened the door. "Well, well! Dan-David. What are you doing here? Come in, before I lose all the heat."

Willy pulled Daniel inside. Then he turned to look

at the young man. "You don't look so good. What's going on?"

Daniel sank down on a bench that was against the wall. "I'm in trouble, Willy. But worse than that, my friend Rachel is in great danger. They're going to kill her. I've got to help her."

"Whoa, hold on boy! Who's going to kill her?"

"Augusta and her professional killer, Gordon Randall."

Willy shook his head. "Now, son, you're a little upset…"

"But I'm not crazy, Willy. I'm an old friend of Rachel's. I've been kind of…well, watching over her out there. Gerald recognized me. He was terrified of his grandmother and her killers. He told me everything. They're killing Rachel for her money. They want him to help them, but he couldn't go through with it. I was going to get her out of there tonight, but there was a guy waiting in Rachel's room. He almost killed me, but I got away. I think he's dead."

Willy looked at Daniel closely and then went to the cupboard and got down a mug. He poured a cup of coffee from an old ceramic pot on a hotplate on the counter and handed it to Daniel. "Drink this, boy. Tell me your real name, and then start from the beginning."

Daniel took the coffee gratefully and then told Willy everything that had happened since he went to work for the St. Clairs. When he got to the part about being attacked in Rachel's bedroom and the death of his assailant, Willy's eyebrows went up and he whistled. Then Daniel told him about the conversation he had heard on the police radio.

"Right, Oliver Cromwell Franklin and his local

thugs. Those boys are sold out to Augusta St. Clair—have been for years."

Daniel put down his mug. "Willy, I have to call Sheriff Bobby Halverson. He lives at the Hershberger place in Paradise. That's Rachel's folks. He's an ex-cop and a decorated World War II vet. He'll know what to do."

Willy pointed to the wall by his desk. "Phone's right over there, Daniel." Just then, the lights of a car pulling up in front of the station flashed on the wall. Willy looked out the window. Quickly, he turned back and whispered to Daniel. "It's Gary Parkins, Franklin's right-hand man. You gotta get out of here. There's no place to hide. Go to my place on Railroad Street—number 432." Willy reached in his pocket. "Here's the key. Go out the back, cut down by the pizza place and keep walking. It's on the corner a block down. Do you have the number for this Sheriff Halverson?"

"I don't. You'll have to call information. He lives on Old Leacock Road in Paradise, Pennsylvania. His name is spelled H-a-l-v-e-r-s-o-n. You have to help, Willy."

Willy could see a flashlight approaching the front of the station. "I'll call him, Daniel. Now go, quick! Before these morons catch you." He shoved Daniel out the back door and went and sat down at his desk.

Just then the door opened and Gary Parkins called out. "Willy? Willy? You in here?"

"I'm in the back where it's warm, Officer Parkins." Willy glanced out the window. Daniel was gone.

Part Three

A Wind from the Sea

Mighty Angels of grace and hope
lift the heart of the sailor
and the fear that claimed his heart,
The tossing storm waves that carried him away,
Fade like the morning mist and are no more...
A sea change carries him back to shore,
Now from the crest of a wave he sees the haven
and his dear wife and child waiting by the fireside.

Home from the Sea—
From The Journals of Jenny Hershberger

Chapter Thirty-Three

First Light

The single lamp on the desk shed a soft light in the room. Rachel St. Clair lay on the bed. Her head throbbed and her pajamas were soaked with sweat. She groaned and tried to sit up, but the room began to spin and she almost threw up. She collapsed back on the bed.

"Help me, Lord…please help me!"

Rachel!

Rachel's parched lips moved and she whispered an answer.

"Is that you, Lord?"

Fear thou not; for I am with thee: be not dismayed; for I am thy God: I will strengthen thee; yea, I will help thee; yea, I will uphold thee with the right hand of My righteousness.

Then the lamp seemed to flood the room with brilliance. Rachel reached her hand toward the light.

"Danki, leiber Gott!"

Then the light dimmed again and Rachel faded into darkness.

* * *

Willy looked up to see Officer Gary Parkins standing on the customer side of the counter. Willy nodded. "It's a little early to be buying a ticket isn't it, Gary?"

"I'm not here for a ticket, Willy. I'm looking for..." Parkins glanced down at a piece of paper in his hand and then back up. "I'm looking for a guy named Daniel King. He tried to kidnap Rachel St. Clair. He brawled with the security guards and escaped. Seen any strangers around tonight?"

"Nope. No strangers tonight."

"Well, when's the next train due?"

"Two hours from now. What's this guy look like?"

"He's tall—blond hair and a short, blond beard. He was wearing jeans, a navy pea coat and a black watch cap. We consider him very dangerous."

"Yeah, officer, he must be if he fought his way off the estate. I'll keep an eye out."

"Okay, Willy. Say, you got a snort for a policeman who needs to warm up a little?"

Willy shook his head. "I gave up drinking last week. Doctor's orders."

Officer Parkins mumbled under his breath and headed for the door. "Don't forget to call me if you see anyone." The door slammed shut.

Willy reached into his drawer and pulled out a bottle of Southern Comfort. He took a pull and put it back. "Yeah, right, officer. I'll call you when I really quit drinking."

Willy waited until the lights of the police car disappeared. The clock on the wall read 5 a.m. Then he picked up the phone and dialed information.

"Information, what city, please?"

"Operator, I need the number for Bobby Halverson in Paradise, Pennsylvania."

"How do you spell that, please?"

"Halverson, H-a-l-v-e-r-s-o-n."

"Thank you, just a moment please."

Willy waited.

"That number is 717-687-2233."

"Thank you, operator."

"You're very welcome, sir. Have a nice day."

Willy dialed the number. It rang four times. "Come on, Sheriff! Pick up! Pick up!" The phone clicked over to an answering device. Willy's heart sank.

"Hi! This is Bobby Halverson. I'm not in right now, but leave me a message and I'll get right back—" In the middle of the message, there was a click and a voice came on the line. "Bobby Halverson, it's too early to be calling. What do you want?"

Willy almost cheered. "Sheriff Halverson, this is Willy Oxendine. I'm the stationmaster at the Old Greenwich train station and I'm a friend of Daniel King. He's in serious trouble here in Connecticut. Something about how the St. Clairs are trying to murder his friend Rachel. You have to come here immediately. Rachel is very sick and Daniel says she doesn't have much time…"

The bleary voice on the other end of the line interrupted. "Whoa, slower, Willy, I just woke up. Now what's this about Daniel and Rachel?"

Willy took a breath. "Daniel King came into the station early this morning. He was on the run. He's been working at the St. Clair place, keeping an eye on Rachel, he said, and he found out about a plot to kill Rachel for her money. He tried to rescue her but they were on to him. He barely got away. He's says they're poisoning

Rachel and she's only got a few more hours left. I can't call the local police because they all work for Augusta. Can you get up here?"

"I hope this isn't a joke, Willy."

"Honest, Sheriff, it's all true. My phone number is 203-525-4415. I met Daniel a few weeks ago. I got him the job out there. He's a good kid and I know he's not lyin'. You've got to help him, Sheriff."

"Okay, I'm coming up there. Should take me about three hours. Where is Daniel now?"

"I have him hidden at my house. Meet me at the station. It's right downtown. Then I'll take you to him."

"Okay, I'll see you soon."

The line went dead.

Jenny Hershberger sat in front of the fire. A bitter cold had engulfed Pennsylvania, and the fire fought weakly against it. Jenny had awakened at midnight with a deep need to pray for Rachel. She went out to the front room where she had been weeping and praying ever since. Now it was early morning. Jenny had her mama's old Bible. She opened it to the flyleaf.

Jerusha Hershberger 1937, from her grandmother, Hannah Hershberger

There was great comfort in holding the old Bible. Her mama and her *grossmutter* had both held this book. Her fingers moved over the worn pages, and without looking for any verse in particular, she flipped open a page. It was Proverbs. Her eye caught the first verse on the page.

Trust in the LORD with all thine heart; and lean not unto thine own understanding.

In all thy ways acknowledge Him, and He shall di-rect thy paths.

Jenny looked in wonder at the verse. It was as though *du leiber Gott* had spoken directly to her heart.

Suddenly, the door burst open. Bobby Halverson stood there. The look on his face was grim.

"Bobby, what is it?"

"Where's Jonathan?"

"He's lying down."

"Take me to him."

Jenny led Bobby down the hallway to her bedroom. Jonathan was lying on the bed reading his Bible. When Jenny and Bobby came in he laid the Bible down. A puzzled look came over his face. "Hello, Bobby, what's going on?"

"Jonathan, you've got to get up and get dressed. Rachel is in desperate trouble. I just got a call from Willy, a friend of Daniel King. Daniel told Willy that Rachel is being poisoned by the St. Clairs. We've got to go get her, now!"

A pained look came over Jonathan's face. "I can't go, Bobby. Rachel is shunned. The *Ordnung* says…"

Jenny looked at Bobby. His jaw was working. He walked over to the bed, grabbed Jonathan by his shirt and dragged him up to a standing position. Jenny cried out. "Bobby, what are you doing? Jonathan isn't well…"

"Stay out of this, Jenny." Bobby pulled Jonathan up close. "To hell with the *Ordnung*, Jonathan! This is your daughter who's dying. Now get your clothes on. You are coming with me if I have to kick you down the hall!"

Jenny couldn't believe this was happening. She tried to pull Bobby's hands away, but Bobby's grip was like a steel trap. "Let him go, Bobby! Let him go! You'll hurt him!"

Then Jonathan took hold of Jenny's hands and put them away from Bobby's. He looked into her eyes and a sad smile came on his face. "No, Jenny, don't. Bobby is right. I've been hiding behind the *Ordnung* too long, and you've been helping me. I know you mean well, but you can't protect me anymore. Rachel's in danger and I'm her father. I've got to go, no matter what."

Bobby let Jonathan go. "That's my boy. Now get moving."

"Give me five minutes."

"Okay." Bobby turned and walked out of the room.

Jenny's heart was pounding. Then a conversation she had with Rachel before all this happened came back to her. It was the day Rachel left. They had been standing in Rachel's room while she packed and Rachel's frustration and anger had poured out on Jenny....

"When he left us, Mama, everything changed. We went back to Ohio and you were so sad for so long. Everything was about you, your sorrow, your grief. What about my grief? You thought I was doing okay but I was not. And you were so lost in your own pain that you had no time to really find out how I was feeling. At least I had Grossdaadi and Grossmutter, and they helped me for a while. Then they died and I was so afraid."

"Afraid, Rachel?"

"Yes, Mama. I was afraid—afraid you would leave me, too. I used to wake up at night feeling like someone was standing on my chest. I just knew something was going to happen to you and then I would be alone. And then he came home and it did happen."

"What happened, Rachel?"

"You left me, Mama."

"But how? I was right here all the time."

Rachel's voice rose. "No, Mama, you were not. Suddenly we had a stranger in our house and everything was about him. Poor Jonathan, he's not well. Poor Jonathan, he shouldn't be disturbed. You never had time for me anymore, and I hated that. It was like I was a stranger, standing out on the porch and looking into this house where all this love used to be, but I was out in the cold and you both were inside."

As Jenny remembered Rachel's words, she felt as though she had been slapped. Rachel was right. She had protected Jonathan and tried to heal him in her own power. She had forgotten the lesson the Lord had taught her so long ago; to trust in Him alone and stop living life in her own strength. Jenny put her hands to her face and burst into tears. Jonathan turned as he was buttoning his coat. He came to Jenny and took her in his arms. Jenny sobbed. "I'm… I'm so…so sorry, Jonathan."

"Sorry for what, my darling?"

"Rachel… Rachel…was…right. I left her. I've been so focused on saving you that I… I…left her…alone."

Jenny felt strength flow back into Jonathan's arms as he held her tight.

"I know, Jenny. And I'm sorry, too. I've been so afraid of living that I've been like a dead man; to you and to Rachel. Now maybe *du lieber Gott* is giving me another chance; a chance to live again. Pray for us, my precious wife. We'll find her."

Bobby's voice came down the hall. "You can do that when we bring Rachel home! Let's go!"

Jonathan kissed Jenny and walked out the door. Jenny looked down at the Bible lying on the bed.

There was a bookmark in it. She picked up the Bible and opened it at the marker. Jonathan had been reading in Proverbs. The first verse leapt out at her.

Trust in the LORD with all thine heart; and lean not unto thine own understanding.

In all thy ways acknowledge Him, and He shall direct thy paths.

Sergeant Oliver Cromwell Franklin was very grumpy. He had just hung up from a nasty phone call with Gordon Randall. Randall had been a little perturbed that the police department had not found Daniel King, and he let Franklin know that his job was on the line if they did not find King soon. He also demanded extra police patrols around the St. Clair estate, which put a strain on Franklin's manpower. In fact, it meant that Sergeant Franklin would have to go out in a patrol car himself, a job that he thought he had left behind. He flipped the switch on the dispatch microphone. "Parkins! Parkins, are you there?"

Parkins came on. "Yeah, Sarge, I'm here."

"Any sign of King?"

"Not yet, Sarge. I'm just about to go off shift."

"Yeah, well get your tail back in that car. Nobody goes off shift until we find Daniel King. I'm coming out there myself."

Parkins snickered. "Got a phone call from Augusta, eh, Sarge?"

Sergeant Oliver Cromwell Franklin snarled back at his officer. "It was from her security man, Gordon Randall. Now listen up, smart guy. You're in this as deep as I am. Don't forget about the nice vacation to Aruba that Augusta popped for last summer. That wouldn't look very nice to the local yokels, would it? Or any of the other little perks over the years."

"No, Sarge."

"Right! So I suggest you find that kid. And keep your smart remarks to yourself."

"Okay, Sarge, okay. Sorry."

Oliver Cromwell Franklin lowered his voice. "Look, Parkins. There's something going on out at the St. Clairs', and if it blows up in our faces, we can kiss our jobs goodbye. So just find that kid and put him on ice. Do it now!" Franklin switched off the CB before Parkins could answer.

Chapter Thirty-Four

Deep Games

Gordon Randall looked at his watch. It was 8 a.m. Rose and Jamison were with him in the SUV. "Things are out of control here, guys. First, Gerald betrays us, Headley is killed, and Daniel King escapes. He either found a hiding place, or he's trying to get back to Rachel. We need to accelerate the schedule."

Jamison scowled. "What's plan B, Colonel?"

"The girl has to die today unless…"

"Unless what, Colonel?"

"I've got some business with Augusta before that happens. I want the girl alive until it's settled. If Augusta doesn't go for my proposal, Rachel is our ticket out of here. What about Gerald, Sergeant?"

"I've been giving him barbiturates, so he's out of it. His fingerprints are on everything."

"Good. Has the girl gone into a coma yet?"

"No, but she's very weak. She couldn't walk three steps. One more injection and she's a goner."

"Okay. What about Headley?"

"The basement of the cottage is like a meat locker. He'll keep until we leave."

"Good, Jamison. Are the other men here?"

Rose nodded. "Affirmative. They're at the cottage, waiting for orders."

"Okay, I want them patrolling the gate and the service road. Keep everyone out of the St. Clair estate, and no cops. They can patrol outside but nobody on the grounds. We should be out of here by ten, leaving Augusta and Gerald holding the bag. And there will be a big bonus for you guys."

Jamison smiled. "How big, Colonel?"

"One hundred thousand each."

Rose's face was impassive.

Randall picked up a briefcase from the seat next to him. "I've got one more card to play with Augusta and then we'll put this operation to bed." Randall got out of the SUV. "Okay, Jamison, I want you to watch Gerald and the girl."

Jamison nodded.

"Rose, you're a rover. Patrol the grounds and stay visible so that the staff knows there is a security team here."

"Got it, Colonel."

"Oh, and one last thing. Is the nuclear option set?"

Jamison handed Randall a paper bag. "All of the propane tanks are set with a charge of Semtex and a wireless receiver. These are the detonators."

Randall slipped the package into his pocket. Jamison headed for the mansion, and Rose drove away. Randall watched them go. His professional instincts were on high alert. The operation had gone south. It was time to play his trump card and get out before the police showed up.

I'll keep the girl alive and force Augusta to sign over the securities. The last thing she wants is the police talking to Rachel.

The wind picked up as Randall walked to the main house. Snow was falling, hard, icy snow that stung his face. There was a storm blowing in off the Atlantic. In the distance, he could hear the sound of heavy surf pounding against the point. The whole area would be shut down by that afternoon. Randall liked that. After he had squeezed Augusta for the securities, he would send the incriminating material to the police. They would find Gerald unconscious in his room, Rachel and the glass and bottles with Gerald's fingerprints in her room, and the taped conversations with Augusta. His team would leave under the cover of the storm.

Randall entered by the side door and headed for Augusta's office. He went in without knocking. Augusta was sitting at the desk with her head in her hands. When she heard Randall enter, she looked up. Her face was a question mark. "What's going on, Randall? Did you know Daniel King was here? How did he get away from you?"

"Yes, Augusta, I know. Daniel King was supposed to be eliminated by my man. Unfortunately, Headley underestimated the boy and got himself killed."

Augusta's eyes widened. "Killed? But...but how?"

"They were on the patio and Headley slipped on the ice. He fell backwards against a wrought iron post."

Augusta stood up from her desk. "Gordon! You promised this would go off without a hitch. Now Daniel King is loose out there." She sank back into her chair and put her face back in her hands. Then she looked up at Randall. "I want that girl dead."

Randall nodded. "Yes, I wanted to talk to you about that, Augusta." He opened his briefcase and took out a small bundle. "I think you should look at these first. I did a little exploring here a few nights ago and came up with some very interesting items. I took photos and printed up some copies. My originals are in a safe place."

Augusta took the bundle from Randall and rolled off the rubber band. She began to leaf through them. After a moment, she looked up at Randall. He had never seen such a venomous look. Augusta was trembling. "Why, Gordon, you clever boy. You broke into my office."

"Yes, and I photographed everything—the diary, the letters, the photos, the papers. I finally figured out what you're really up to, Augusta."

"And what would that be, Gordon?"

"It's never been about the money. It's always been about Robert St. Clair."

Augusta's face hardened, and her eyes focused somewhere beyond Randall. She whispered the name. "Robert St. Clair, my dear Robert." Then her eyes focused again. "Yes, Gordon, it has always been about Robert. He was so different from Jerod. He was a real man, strong, beautiful, and powerful. You know nothing about how I felt about Robert."

"You hated him, I know that."

"No, I loved him."

"You hated him with all your heart."

Augusta's eyes narrowed. "Well, I suppose you could call it a love-hate relationship, Gordon. What's that to you?"

Randall pulled out the pictures of Robert, Rachel, and baby Jenny. "These are the pictures that Robert sent to his father in 1948, the ones you said you never found. You stole these from Max. You knew all along what Rachel Borntraeger St. Clair looked like. When she showed up in New York, you were ready for her. And you hated her. You had her put out of the hotel and you hired Joe Bender to degrade her, get her strung out on heroin. You didn't want her dead. You wanted her to suffer, like you had suffered."

Augusta sighed and then tittered. It was a strange, grating sound. "Well, Gordon, you're very astute. You probed and you dug and you sneaked and you kept at it and you struck gold, didn't you? You've discovered my little secrets."

She got up and walked to the window. The snow was now blowing wildly across the grounds of the estate. "Everyone has a purpose in life, Gordon. You are a professional killer. That's what you were born to be. You can't be anything else. I wondered what my purpose was for a long time. I knew I wasn't supposed to be a dumpy housewife with a stupid husband and screaming brats. I was meant for greater things.

"And then the day Robert St. Clair rejected me, everything became perfectly clear. We were at the Stork Club and Robert told me he was going to marry that Amish whore. He went on and on and then I couldn't hear him anymore because there was another voice speaking to me. And I knew who it was. It was God himself, and in that instant, I knew that I had been called to serve God in a wonderful way. I had been chosen to be his hand of vengeance against the St. Clair family. And I have performed my duty. Well, not quite all my duty."

She turned back to face him.

Randall stared at Augusta. The mask had come off and Randall was looking at the real Augusta St. Clair—a conniving, climbing, murderess named Francine Bosnan—a woman capable of anything, a woman who was totally insane. The thought chilled him. He took a stab. "Max and Margaret, Robert's parents?"

Augusta nodded.

Another stab. "Your own son, Francis, and his wife?"

Augusta shrugged. "He was Robert St. Clair's son, and I hated him as much as I hated Robert." Augusta sat down and put on the glasses that hung on a chain around her neck. The change was startling. She looked like a prim, maidenly schoolteacher. She looked up at Gordon and spoke in a businesslike manner. "Well, Gordon, you didn't do all this sneaking for fun. What do you want?"

"Money, of course."

"How much?"

"One million dollars."

Augusta stiffened. "That's a lot of money."

"Really, Augusta? I know about the Swiss accounts under the name of Francine Bosnan. You've been siphoning Gerald's money for years. There's eighty million in Zurich and two million in New York. I also saw the list of negotiable securities, which are right here in the Greenwich bank, within a fifteen-minute drive. So call your banker and get him here with enough securities to meet my price. I get the securities, you get the photos, Rachel dies, and my men and I disappear. You take it from there." He glanced at his watch. "It's eight-fifteen. You have one hour."

"And if I don't comply?"

"My men and I take the girl to the hospital and then

we'll make all the other incriminating evidence available to the police and the FBI."

"Incriminating evidence?"

"The evidence that shows your complicity with Gerald in the plot to murder Rachel. Then when you are answering some very probing questions, your diary shows up in the mail at the D.A.'s office, and then the police will be looking into the murders of Robert St. Clair and the rest of his family. I cover all the bases. You should have learned that about me."

"Yes, Gordon. I have certainly been remiss."

"You have one hour, Augusta."

Willy was dozing at his desk when the creak of the front door woke him. He looked up at the two men coming to the counter. One was older but his hair was still sandy with a touch of gray at the temples. He carried himself like a military man. He wore a short green flight jacket with a sheepskin collar and a Stetson hat. Hanging at his side was a service revolver. The man with him was Amish, but the look in his eye was grim. He was tall, with long dark hair and a beard. A faint scar ran along the side of his forehead. The two men stood at the counter. Outside, the wind began to howl.

"You gotta be Sheriff Halverson."

"That's me, Willy. This is Jonathan Hershberger, Rachel's father."

"You made good time, considering the storm."

"We got in just ahead of the front. It's really blowing up a mess out there." Bobby looked around to see if anyone else was there and then spoke quietly. "Where's Daniel?"

"He's at my place, a block away."

"How do we get out to the St. Clair place?"

"It's out on Field Point Road but you can't get in that way. Augusta's security boys have buttoned that place up tight. If they see Daniel, they'll arrest him."

"How do we get in, then?"

"You've got to go out on Long Island Sound by boat. My cousin, Frank, has a Boston Whaler and he'll take you. It'll be tough because the wind is really starting to blow. But you can make your way along the shore and stay out of most of it."

Bobby glanced over at Jonathan. He was staring at Willy and there was anguish written on his face. "Out on the ocean? Long Island Sound?"

"Yes, sir, Mr. Hershberger. It's not far. The St. Clairs have a covered boathouse, and it's only a short walk to the house… Why, what's wrong, Mr. Hershberger?"

Jonathan's eyes had a strange look. He passed his fingers over the scar. They were trembling. He sat down on a bench and put his face in his hands. "I can't go out there, I just can't."

Bobby stepped over to Jonathan and put his hand on his shoulder. "Jonathan, we've been friends for a long time so I'm going to speak straight to you. I once had a discussion like this with Jenny's father, Reuben. He didn't think he could go into battle. He was afraid. But in the end, he went, and he saved my life. You have to put everything aside, all of the past, all of the terrible things that happened to you out on that ocean, and think only of Rachel. If we don't go now, she will die. That's the bottom line."

Jonathan took a deep breath, almost a sob. Then he slowly lifted his head. As Willy watched him, a change passed over his face and a fire kindled in his eyes. He stood up. "You are right, Bobby. We'll say no more about it. Let's go."

Bobby turned to Willy. "Can I use your phone?"

Willy pointed to the desk.

Bobby dialed a number. When a man answered, Bobby quickly filled him in on the situation. Then he shook his head. "Over an hour, Jerry? That's too long for us to wait. Rachel may be dead by then. We're going after Rachel. You get out to St. Clairs' as fast as you can. We'll hold the fort until then."

Bobby hung up the phone and looked at Jonathan and Willy. "That was my friend, Jerry Carlson, head of the Connecticut State Police. He's at Milford, but it will take an hour to get here. We have to go get Rachel on our own."

Bobby looked out at the gathering fury of the storm. "It doesn't look good out there, Jonathan, but suppose we put our trust in this God of yours and see what happens."

Jonathan smiled and turned to Willy. "Take us to Daniel, Willy."

Chapter Thirty-Five

The Greatest Trial

Daniel King, Jonathan, Bobby, and Willy stood on the dock looking at the old Boston Whaler as it rode in its moorings. Willy's cousin, Frank, motioned to the men to come aboard. They clambered over the side onto the deck. Waves from off the sound were starting to move into the harbor and boats up and down the quay were pitching and rolling in their slips.

Frank slapped the side of the boat. "She's old, but she's the most seaworthy craft on the sound. It's just a short run down to St. Clair's boathouse on the North Shore. We'll slip this baby right inside, and nobody will be the wiser."

Jonathan walked to the bow of the boat and looked out over the water. Grey-green, choppy swells rolled toward him from off the Atlantic. A mist rose from the water. The waves were endless, moving toward him out of the mist and disappearing away toward the unseen horizon. It was dark, so dark, and the strange smell of the salt water was overpowering and somehow terrifying. A stiff breeze drove the icy spray off the tops of the waves into Jonathan's eyes. He raised his hand to wipe his face. He was in the darkness and the cold and the spray and the waves, the endless waves, rolling, rolling, rolling by… He was lost, gone, alone on the bridge of a ghost ship that cut through the waves like a sword…

"Jonathan, are you all right?"

Jonathan jerked around. The hand on his shoulder did not belong to his father. His father was dead. The hand on his shoulder belonged to his old friend, Bobby Halverson. And then Jonathan knew he wasn't lost. He was here with his friends, and they were going to save Rachel. Jonathan passed his hand over his eyes. "Bobby! I… I kind of got lost there for a minute…"

Suddenly, a large wave came straight in and the boat jerked hard. They heard a cry, then a thud and a groan behind them. Bobby and Jonathan looked around. Frank was lying on the deck, holding his arm. Daniel was bending down to Frank. "Are you okay?"

Frank groaned. "I think I broke my arm. Ooooh!"

Bobby went over and checked out Frank's arm. Bobby looked up at Willy. "Willy, Frank did break his arm. You're going to have to get him to the hospital."

Frank grimaced in pain. "But what about the girl, Sheriff? She's going to die if you don't get her."

From behind them came a voice, soft but unafraid. "I'll take them, Frank."

Bobby looked up at Jonathan. "Are you sure, Jonathan?"

Jonathan nodded. "Look, Bobby. I grew up on Long Island Sound. I've been up and down every inch of the north shore in a boat just like this. We've got to get Rachel, and I'm the only one who can take us. You and Daniel couldn't sail your way out of a paper bag."

Bobby laughed. "You're right about that, pal."

Jonathan looked back out at the sea. "Besides, I won't let this ocean beat me again."

Bobby slapped Jonathan on the back. "Okay, Jonathan, let's do it then."

Willy helped Frank onto the dock. He stood morosely, holding his arm.

"Sorry, fellas. I let you down."

Jonathan took the wheel. "Frank, we're good. I know these waters and Daniel can show me the boathouse. We'll be back with Rachel before you know it."

He spoke to his crew. "Bobby, you and Daniel cast off those two hawsers…those ropes."

Jonathan stood at the wheel, his dark hair flying in the wind as he eased the boat out into the wild waters of Long Island Sound.

Gordon Randall watched the storm through the window of the cottage. The wind had picked up in intensity. Through the blowing snow he saw a figure approaching. It was Jamison. He came inside banging his arms across his chest to get warm.

Randall looked at his watch. It was 9:45. Augusta was half an hour late.

Jamison got right to the point. "Colonel, Augusta tried to buy me off. She said if I would kill you she would give me the securities. She has them, but she hasn't called you yet. I played along and said I'd do it. She cackled like a chicken. She's coming unglued."

"Jamison, this whole operation is coming unglued. Augusta is extremely dangerous and Daniel King is out there somewhere. He has to have contacted someone by now. We've got to get out of here, before the whole thing blows up in our face."

"It's not Augusta you have to worry about, Colonel."

The two men turned. Rose was standing in the entry-way. He was holding a pistol equipped with a silencer. Randall saw the look in Rose's eye, the connection between brain and trigger forming, and knew he was about to be shot. It was a skill he had developed over the years and it had saved him many times.

He pushed Jamison to one side and at the same time leapt the other way. Rose hesitated for a split-second deciding which man to shoot and then shot at Jamison. That gave Randall time to drop his arm. The concealed throwing dagger slipped into his hand, and with a flip of his wrist, the knife flew through the air and caught Rose in the neck. Rose looked at Randall in surprise and then collapsed. Randall kicked the gun away. Rose's eyes were glazing over.

"Who paid you, Rose? You might as well tell me, because that knife has killed you."

Rose grimaced and then gasped. "Duvigney."

Then his eyes closed and he was gone.

Jamison was clutching his arm.

"Are you okay, Jamison?"

Jamison grimaced. "The bullet caught me in the fleshy part of my arm. It went clear through but I think it broke the bone. Thanks for pushing me out of the way. He had me for sure."

Randall pulled off Jamison's coat and rolled up his shirtsleeve. Blood poured from the wound and the arm was indeed broken. Randall went in the kitchen and grabbed some kitchen towels and a wooden spoon. He used the spoon as a splint, set Jamison's arm and tied a compress over the wound. "That should keep it from bleeding." Jamison put his coat on over the bandage. Then Randall used the other towel as a sling. "You okay?"

Jamison winced, but nodded. "It doesn't hurt too bad, but it will need a cast soon. Say, Colonel, if Rose was working for Duvigney, that means the guys he brought in are working for Duvigney, too."

Randall nodded. "That's right. So we have three guys working for Duvigney and the cops working for Augusta. I think we need to redefine the mission."

Randall grabbed his briefcase and opened it. He took out some small cassettes and put them in Rose's pocket. Then he took out the two detonators, put one in Rose's hand and wrapped the hand and the thumb around it. "We take the girl with us and use her as a shield. If they try to stop us, we use our detonator to blow the propane tanks, and in the confusion, we get out. When the cops get back here, they find Rose with the cassettes and the detonator. They'll think Rose blew the tanks before he died. The tapes will implicate Duvigney in the plot against the St. Clairs. Then we'll send the D.A. the info on Augusta. It will take them a while to sort everything out but Duvigney and Augusta will both be in deep water. We'll just have to cut our losses and disappear."

Jamison shook his head. "It's a good plan, Colonel, but there's only the two of us and my arm is broken. There's three of Rose's men and all of Augusta's cops. We'll never carry that girl out to the car and be able to cover ourselves at the same time."

Randall scowled. "You're right, Jamison, we're in a real bind here."

Randall took a pair of binoculars out of his case, walked to the window, and scanned the grounds. He could not see the front of the house, but he knew the men were there. He swung the glasses toward the back of the estate and then stopped in amazement. Out on the storm-tossed waters of Long Island Sound was a small boat. It was heading in toward the St. Clair dock. There were three men on the boat. "Halverson."

Jamison walked over to the window as Randall pointed. "What did you say, Colonel?"

"Out there, on the sound, there's a boat coming in and Sheriff Bobby Halverson is on board with two men. I think we may have just gotten our help."

Bobby Halverson watched as Jonathan eased the boat out into the sound from the protective confines of Greenwich Harbor. The wind began to blow straight in at them. The six-to-eight-foot waves were running before the wind in a chop that was like riding a bucking bronco. Jonathan looked at Bobby. He shouted over the wind. "There's only one way to get through this! I've got to power the boat up and jump the tops. It's going to get rough so hold on tight."

Bobby held onto a stanchion and nodded to Daniel to do the same. "Whatever you have to do, Jonathan. You okay?"

Jonathan smiled and in that smile, for the first time in years, Bobby saw his friend. He glanced at Daniel and saw that he was holding on tight and then turned back to Jonathan and nodded. "Cut 'er loose, cowboy."

Jonathan pulled back on the throttle and the boat picked up speed, heading straight into the waves. As the speed increased, the boat lifted up out of the troughs and began to skip along the tops of the waves. Soon they were flying along, lifting off from the top of one wave and crashing down onto the next. Bobby looked at Jonathan. He was staring up into the sky and shouting something, but the wind snatched the words away, and Bobby didn't catch them. Jonathan's hair was flying in the wind, and he stood strong and powerful against the storm.

After about twenty minutes, Daniel yelled and pointed toward the shore. Through the spume and the spray, they could see a large, brick boathouse nestled on the shore in a protected cove. Daniel shouted over the wind. "That's the St. Clair place. Take her right inside and we'll be out of the wind."

As they entered the cove, the waves dropped down and Jonathan was able to navigate safely into the large boathouse. He pulled the boat up to the dock and Daniel and Bobby jumped over the side and made the boat fast to the pilings. Jonathan stood staring out at the ocean. Then he clambered over the side onto the dock.

Bobby pulled his hat off and knocked the water off against his leg. "Boy, quite a place the St. Clairs have here." He turned to Jonathan. "Say, what were you yelling out there?"

Jonathan grinned. "I was yelling at God. I told him that if He wanted to kill me in the ocean, after all, there wouldn't be a better time to do it. And if it was not yet my time, would He mind helping me get this tub into safe harbor. Looks like it was not my time."

Bobby looked at Jonathan's face. Years of pain and sorrow, fear and confusion, had been washed away by the fierce blast of the storm. The man who stood before him was the Jonathan Hershberger he knew and loved.

Bobby put his hat back on. "Well, let's go find Rachel. And keep an eye out for Randall and his men."

"You won't have to go far to find me, Sheriff."

The three men turned. Two men walked out of the shadows. One had his arm in a sling but his good hand held a large pistol. The other man was Gordon Randall. Bobby's heart sank. Then Randall nodded to the other man who holstered his pistol. As Bobby, Daniel, and Jonathan looked on in surprise, Randall lit a cigarette.

"Sheriff, I know we've been playing on two different teams here, but Jamison and I find ourselves in a tight squeeze. So we came out to make a deal with you. Rachel is not in her room. She's hidden in a safe room and I am the only one that can get you in. She's very sick."

Daniel lunged at Randall, but Bobby held him back. "Yes, she's sick because you've been poisoning her!"

"That's true, son, but we were only doing what Augusta paid us to do. It was nothing personal, believe me. Now the game has changed and we find ourselves in need of some help. And then you show up. It seems that timing is everything."

Bobby nodded. "Go on."

"Here's the deal. We give you the girl and you take us out of here. We have an SUV and the sheriff can get us past Augusta's cops out front. We have another car in town. I've got the information the doctors need to save the girl. As soon as we're at the hospital, Jamison and I walk away and you never see us again. But you have to decide now so you can get the girl out of here. Once you're there, you give the doctor this." He showed Bobby a note and a small glassine bag with pills in it. "This will tell him exactly how to treat the girl. She will probably live if we go now. What do you say?"

Bobby looked at Jonathan and Daniel. Jonathan concurred. "Rachel's life is more important than anything, Bobby. We have to do what he says."

Bobby nodded. "Lead the way, Randall."

Chapter Thirty-Six

The Truth Will Set You Free

The five men left the boathouse and made their way to the east wing of the house. Randall led them in the side door and moved silently down the hall. They came to the secret room, and Randall keyed in the combination. The door slid silently back and Randall looked inside, and then turned to the men. "Rachel isn't in here. Augusta must have taken her."

Daniel grabbed Randall by the arm. "How could she carry Rachel by herself?"

Jamison spoke up. "I didn't give Gerald his drugs yet this morning so he could have been alert enough to help. She must have forced him to carry her."

Randall saw something on the floor. "Someone vomited here. Augusta's taking Rachel back to her room. She wants the perfect scenario. Rachel dies in her bed, her grieving husband commits suicide by the bedside, Augusta leaves the country and lives off the eighty million she stole from Gerald."

The men made their way to Rachel's suite. Randall

motioned for them to move to either side of the door.
Then he slowly opened it. Rachel was lying in the bed.
She looked like she was sleeping. Her face was pale
and her hair was matted against her head. Gerald was
standing next to her holding her hand and Augusta was
holding a gun on him. When Augusta saw Randall, she
shoved Gerald aside and jammed the barrel of the gun
against Rachel's head.

"Well, well, Gordon Randall. I thought Mr. Jamison
was going to take care of you."

Randall stepped into the room. "Some of us retain
a sense of loyalty, Augusta."

Augusta saw a movement outside the door. She
pressed the gun tighter against Rachel's head. "Everybody inside or the girl dies. Move!"

Daniel came into the room, followed by Bobby and
Jonathan.

"Well, Daniel King! Uh, uh, don't come any closer.
I will shoot her if you take one more step."

The men halted. Augusta looked at Jonathan. "And
this must be Rachel's papa." Augusta snickered. "You
certainly don't look non-violent."

Jonathan stiffened. "Where my daughter's life is concerned, you might be surprised what I am capable of."

Augusta motioned for the men to stand against the
wall. Then she began a weird singsong chant over Rachel. "Dearly beloved, we are gathered here today to
celebrate cleansing the earth from the stain of the St.
Clair family. Rachel and Gerald will be crossing over
today and soon all the St. Clairs will be gone." She
snickered again. "Except me, of course, but then I'm
not really a St. Clair, am I?"

Randall looked at Gerald. He was staring at his grandmother in disbelief. Randall took a chance—anything to keep the crazed woman talking. "Gerald, why don't you ask your grandmother what she did to your family? It was all done so brilliantly, and I'm sure she wouldn't want her secrets to follow her to the grave, would you, Augusta?"

Augusta looked at Randall. The gun was still pressed against Rachel's head. "It was brilliant, wasn't it, Gordon?" She turned to Gerald. "Yes, my darling grandson. You should hear all about it. All these years, you thought I loved you, that I was just a doddering old grandmother with a few peculiarities. Shall I start with your grandfather, Robert?"

Gerald's mouth dropped open. "What?"

"Yes, Gerald, your grandfather, Robert St. Clair. Jerod St. Clair wasn't your grandfather. Robert St. Clair fathered my child. But he rejected me and married that Amish tramp. And then God told me that I would be his instrument in wiping out the St. Clair family. Robert didn't understand that a woman's love could turn to deep hate if she's wronged. What is that old saying, 'Hell hath no fury like a woman scorned'?"

Her eyes narrowed. "How could he marry her instead of me? She gave him a daughter. I gave him a son. I gave him everything—and he spurned me for her, that Rachel Borntraeger."

Randall moved an inch to his left, trying to get into a position to get the jump on Augusta. Jamison saw it and moved slightly to his right. "Tell Gerald what you did to Rachel, Robert's wife."

Augusta smiled as if reliving the memory. "I should have killed her like I killed Robert. But I wanted her to suffer horribly. When I saw her, I knew her right away. I had Robert's pictures. I got them from Max. Joe Bender worked for me. It was easy to get Rachel addicted to heroin. The heroin was her escape. And I loved that. I wanted her to stay alive, a slave to drugs, knowing that Robert was dead, and that she would never have him."

Gerald's hands were shaking. "You killed Robert St. Clair?"

"Ah, yes, Robert. Of course I killed him. Did he really think he could spurn me and walk away? Did he really think he could leave me for that little slut? Bender said it was easy. He stole a truck, waited for Robert to go to work and then Bender ran him off the road into a tree. Robert's car exploded. He roasted in hell before he died. That was the best part."

Bobby Halverson spoke up. "Joe Bender worked for you? He was your hit man? You had Robert St. Clair killed and Joe Bender did it?"

"Yes, Sheriff. Didn't dig that one up when you were looking for Jenny's parents, did you?"

Bobby shook his head in disbelief. Augusta looked at the men and smiled seductively at them. The effect was repulsive. "Bender would do anything for me. He loved me. I could get any man to love me…except Robert. I… persuaded Bender to kill Robert. Robert had it coming. Everyone thought Robert was such a nice man, but he didn't hesitate to climb into my bed or seduce Rachel Borntraeger. But it's not just Robert I swore revenge on. I have taken care of all the St. Clairs."

Randall spoke. "Gerald, she had your grandfather Robert's parents killed, your great grandfather and great grandmother."

Gerald stared at Augusta. She nodded.

"Well, actually, Gerald, I killed Max and Margaret

myself. Nobody ever noticed the little mark where I injected the air bubble into his neck. They all thought it was a stroke. And Margaret. That was a lot of fun. I would show her the pictures of her granddaughter and tell her that the little girl had been run over by a car. It didn't take long until she had a heart attack and died."

"And who else, Augusta? What about Francis and his wife?"

"Oh, Francis! That was so easy. They had been drinking. My agent lured them off the trail, suffocated them and buried them in the snow. They didn't find them until spring."

Gerald moved closer. "You killed my father and my mother?"

"He was Robert's son, the devil's spawn. I couldn't let him live, now could I?"

Randall pressed the attack. "Why didn't you just confess that Gerald is Robert's grandson? Wouldn't the DNA prove it?"

Augusta snickered. "Without Robert the DNA could only prove that Gerald is a St. Clair. But there was nothing left of Robert, was there? Gerald didn't have the Key so it would have been my word. But it was never really about the money…"

Augusta tittered.

Randall nodded toward the bed. "And now you're going to kill Rachel."

"Oh, that's not all, Gordon. You forget Robert's daughter—she's a St. Clair. She won't escape me."

She gave Gerald a venomous look. "And then, of course, I have to do something about Gerald, don't I?"

Randall looked at Bobby and Jonathan. They were

staring at Augusta in shock. Randall kept going. "Jenny Hershberger, too? Augusta, you are insane."

"No, Gordon—bitter, thwarted, frustrated maybe, but not insane. Otherwise I wouldn't have worked so hard to get my hands on the money. You see, when I'm finished all of Robert St. Clair's heirs will be dead and I'll have the money."

Jonathan stepped forward. "If you hurt Jenny..."

Augusta waved the gun at him and then quickly put it back to Rachel's head.

"Oh, didn't I tell you, Mr. Hershberger? I've already dispatched my messenger."

Jonathan looked desperately at Bobby. "Bobby..."

Bobby shook his head and motioned Jonathan back.

Randall looked at Augusta. "I hate to burst your bubble, Augusta, but there's something you are not aware of. There is no money in Robert St. Clair's trust. Duvigney spent it all."

Augusta's face twisted in disbelief.

Randall nodded. "Yes, Augusta, the money's gone. When you killed Robert, Duvigney didn't know about Rachel Borntraeger St. Clair and her daughter, Jenny St. Clair, because you kept that a secret and they had disappeared. Duvigney thought Robert's trust was a dead end, no heirs, no disbursement. So he spent it. It's actually kind of funny. Something else you don't know is that I've been working for Duvigney all along to set you and Gerald up for the murder of Rachel. Then when Gerald went to prison, he couldn't inherit and so your demands for the St. Clair fortune that wasn't there would cease and Duvigney was off the hook. I also recorded your part in the plan. You would have ended up on death row next to Gerald. But then Duvigney tried to have me killed, which means that I'll just have to make sure that his part in all this comes to light, too. I'm sure the St. Clair board of trustees won't be happy about the missing money. If they don't have him killed, he will end up in prison with you."

Augusta hissed. "Why, that sneaky rat. I suspected something, but I never thought he spent all of it. That's why he was stonewalling me."

As Randall had been speaking, Gerald slowly moved closer to Augusta. When Randall mentioned Duvigney, her attention was diverted for a split second. Gerald leaped at Augusta and grabbed her arm. He jerked it away from Rachel's head and held it against his own body. They wrestled for the gun.

Gerald began shouting at Augusta. "You're insane, Grandmother! I've known it for years, but I was always too afraid of you to say anything. You killed my parents. You killed my real grandfather. But you are not going to kill Rachel."

They struggled violently for the gun. Suddenly, the gun went off. Gerald's body jerked and then with one violent shove, he threw Augusta against the wall. Her head smacked against the corner of a mirror with a sickening sound. She went limp and slid down the wall. The gun dropped on the floor. The men rushed forward. Gerald sank down on the bed next to Rachel, holding his chest.

Daniel grabbed him. "Gerald, Gerald!"

Gerald looked down. The front of his shirt was soaked in blood. He looked at Daniel. "Take care of her, Daniel."

He smiled and started to fall over. Daniel knelt on

the bed next to him and held him up. "Wait, Gerald! You saved Rachel. Let me help you."

Gerald tried to lift his head. "Grandmother's killed me, Daniel. I'm going."

Daniel pulled Gerald closer. "Then you need to give your life to God before you go. You saved Rachel, now let God save you. Just ask him to forgive you, quickly Gerald, while you still can."

Gerald gasped. "Yes, Daniel. Ever since we talked, I've known that you were right. I asked Him to forgive me, and I…believe…"

He choked, and a bloody froth colored his lips. "Tell Rachel that for the first time in my life I loved someone, truly and deeply…"

And then it seemed as though an ethereal light illuminated Gerald's face, and he smiled at Daniel. "Take care of her, Daniel."

Gerald's eyes closed and he slumped against Daniel. He was gone.

Daniel laid him down next to Rachel. He turned to Bobby. "There's nothing we can do for him now. We've got to get Rachel to a hospital!"

The spell was broken and the men leapt into action. Randall took charge. "I'll go get the car and bring it around to the back. You men carry her down. Hurry."

Daniel and Jonathan wrapped the blanket around Rachel and Daniel picked her up. Bobby looked at Randall.

"Which way?"

Randall nodded toward the hallway. "Down the stairs, turn left, go down the hallway until you see the first outside door. I'll be waiting there. Hurry!"

Chapter Thirty-Seven

Rescued

Rachel opened her eyes. She was being carried. Slowly her eyes focused on the one who was carrying her. She reached her hand up and touched the face. The unfamiliar beard was soft under her fingers. It was Daniel. His strong arms held her tight, and she felt safe. When he felt her hand, Daniel looked down at her. Rachel could see the love in his eyes.

"Daniel, are you married? You have a beard."

Daniel smiled and pulled Rachel closer. "No, Rachel, I'm not married."

"How did you find me? Why are you carrying me?"

"We're taking you to the hospital. You are very sick. Your papa is here."

Rachel turned her head. Her papa's face swam into view, but it was a different face. It was the face she remembered—a face she had not seen for a long, long time. She could not see Richard Sandbridge, just her precious papa.

"Papa, I'm so sorry. I…"

Jonathan took Rachel's hand. "It's not your fault, *dochter*, it is mine. And when you are well, we will talk. Right now, all I want is for you to get well. Just hold on and stay with us."

Rachel could see the love in her papa's eyes. It was the last thing she saw before the world around her faded into darkness.

At the bottom of the stairs, they turned left and followed Jamison down the hall through the door. The wind and snow tore at them. Randall pulled up in the SUV and climbed out. Bobby slid in behind the wheel. Jonathan opened the back hatch and Daniel laid Rachel down. Daniel crawled in next to her. They all climbed in and Bobby headed for the front gate.

They could see only about twenty feet ahead through the driven snow. A picture came into Bobby's mind. He was sitting in the cab of an old snowplow. Reuben Springer was sitting next to him. They were plowing toward an old, deserted cabin in the woods. The wind was howling and the snow was blowing sideways through the dark and twisted trees...

"Bobby, you okay?"

Bobby turned. The Amish man sitting next to him was Jonathan, not Reuben. Bobby pushed his hat back on his forehead. "Yeah, Jonathan, I'm good. Just thinking about another time I was on a rescue mission in a blizzard."

"When you and Reuben saved Jerusha?"

"Yep. That was a long time ago."

Then they were coming to the gate and there was a police car blocking the way. They rolled to a stop. A short, stout man climbed out of the car and another police car pulled up. The policeman started toward the SUV.

Sergeant Oliver Cromwell Franklin had been out in the storm for three hours and for the last two he had been parked in front of Augusta St. Clair's house trying to keep from freezing. He was very cold and very cross. He saw an SUV coming through the blizzard. There were several men in the car. The SUV pulled up to the gate. Franklin pulled his coat collar up around his pudgy neck and climbed out of the car. He waved at Gary Parkins who was parked down the road. He waited until Parkins arrived and then crunched through the snow to the driver's side of the SUV. The man behind the wheel rolled the window down. There were two men in the front, two in the middle and a man in the back next to someone rolled up in blankets. Franklin realized the man in the back matched the description of Daniel King. His hand went to his pistol.

"Say, what's going on here?"

The man behind the wheel looked up at him. He was an older, sandy-haired man wearing a Stetson hat. The sandy-haired man opened his jacket. Pinned to his vest was a silver sheriff's badge. Next to it was a combat medal. Franklin looked closer. It was the Silver Star. There was a police-issue revolver strapped to his waist. The sandy-haired man smiled.

"My name is Bobby Halverson. Sheriff Bobby Halverson. The reason you can still call me Sheriff is because the citizens of Wayne County, Ohio, saw fit to bestow the title on me permanently in light of my long service to them. We have a very sick girl in the back. Her husband and his grandmother have poisoned her. Daniel King tried to rescue Rachel but was prevented. He called me for help, knowing that he could not trust you or the local police. We had to sneak in by boat.

These men are Augusta St. Clair's security chief and his assistant. They discovered the plot to kill Rachel and offered to help us rescue her. The three private security men who are helping you guard the house are in on the plot and should be arrested. Now, if you will move your car, we need to get this girl to the hospital, fast!"

Franklin looked in the window again. He pointed to Daniel and fumbled at the snap on his holster. "You fellas don't seem to realize the bind I'm in here. One of our most prominent citizens has filed a very serious complaint against that man back there, Daniel King. She—"

The sandy-haired man interrupted.

"You are to arrest Daniel King and keep him quiet, and you're buying into it because she owns you."

Franklin felt heat infuse his face. "Say, you can't talk to me like that!"

Bobby Halverson got out. He put his finger in Franklin's face. "Let me explain something to you. The grandfather of the girl in the car was a Congressional Medal of Honor winner who single-handedly turned the tide of the battle for Henderson Field on Guadalcanal. This man next to me is Rachel St. Clair's father. The current police commissioner of New York City and I served as officers together on the board of the Fraternal Order of Police. Colonel Jerry Cowell of the Connecticut State Police is on his way here from Middleton with twenty of his troopers to take over this investigation. And we have a sick girl who will die if you don't get your fat behind out of the way. You should be arresting Augusta for the murder of her grandson, and the attempted murder of Rachel St. Clair. You also need to round up the three men who are on the estate as guards."

Bobby continued. "If you want to buck me on this, I

will make some phone calls and the bigwigs who show up here will make Augusta St. Clair look like a pussy-cat. If Rachel dies while I'm doing that, I will person-ally beat you to a pulp. When you recover, you will find that your next position will be as a weather balloon op-erator in Goose Bay, Labrador, if you're not in jail with Augusta. Am I clear?"

Oliver Cromwell Franklin looked at Sheriff Bobby Halverson. There was a fire in Halverson's eyes that guaranteed the truth of what he was saying. The fight went out of Franklin, and his shoulders dropped. He was about to start back to his car when he heard a voice.

"Just stay where you are, officer. We have some busi-ness with Colonel Randall."

Franklin turned. Three men armed with nasty-looking automatic weapons were standing behind Par-kins. "Get out of the car, Colonel."

Randall started to open the door. Just then the blast of a bullhorn cut through the wind.

"You men there! This is Colonel Jerry Cowell of the Connecticut State Police. You are surrounded. Lay down your weapons, put your hands behind your heads, and kneel down. Now!"

Oliver Cromwell Franklin looked toward the sound of the voice. As he watched, several tough-looking State Troopers materialized out of the storm. They were armed with shotguns and rifles. The three men dropped their weapons and did as Colonel Cowell told them. Then a tall man with a bullhorn walked up to Sheriff Halverson.

"Bobby, what's going on here?"

"Jerry! It's pretty complicated, but first of all I have a very sick girl here, who will die if I don't get her to the hospital." Bobby nodded at Sergeant Franklin. "The sergeant and his men have been obstructing us on the orders of Augusta St. Clair, who just shot her grandson, Gerald. She is still in the house. Gerald is dead. Those three men are in on the plot. These two men are helping us. I need to take them to the hospital with me so they can talk to the doctors. I know that's a lot to digest and there's a lot more, but I can sort it out with you later. Right now we have to go!"

Colonel Cowell nodded and turned to one of his men. "Take your cruiser and escort these people to the hospital." Colonel Cowell pointed to the three men on their knees and motioned to some of his troopers. "Take these men into custody!" Then he turned to Franklin. "You! Get your car out of the way but give me your pistol first, and then I want you and your men to accompany me to the house."

Franklin stood in bewilderment, watching his world come crashing down. Then he handed over his gun and got in the police car. When he had moved his cruiser, Colonel Cowell motioned to Bobby.

"Get the girl to the hospital and then call me when she's in good hands. I'll need you to debrief me on everything that's happened here."

Bobby shook the Colonel's hand and then jumped in the SUV and followed the trooper toward town. Oliver Cromwell Franklin shook his head and wondered how cold Goose Bay, Labrador, got in the winter.

Chapter Thirty-Eight

The Road Home

Bobby followed the State Patrol cruiser through the blinding snow. As he drove, he remembered a day over forty years earlier when he had taken another precious girl on a race for life. For the first time in a long time, Bobby prayed.

"Lord, I have a girl here who is very sick, just like my little Jenna so long ago. Please let this time be different. Please let Rachel live."

In twenty minutes, they pulled up in front of Greenwich Hospital. Daniel climbed out with Rachel in his arms. He and Jonathan headed for the emergency entrance. Gordon Randall handed Bobby the folded piece of paper and the glassine envelope.

"This note will tell the doctor exactly what Rachel is suffering from and there are some of the pills in this bag. Follow the directions and there is a good chance Rachel will live."

Bobby grabbed Randall by the coat collar and stared at him. "I'm letting you go because we made a deal.

If Rachel dies, I will hunt you down. If I were you, I would retire."

Randall smiled. "I think I'll take your advice, Sheriff. Now you should go help the girl."

Bobby turned and ran into the hospital.

Randall turned to Jamison and noticed the sour look on his face.

"This operation sure blew up in our faces, Colonel. All that work and nothing to show for it."

Randall reached into his coat pocket and pulled out an envelope. "Not exactly, Sergeant. Before I got the car, I broke into Augusta's office and grabbed these. They're the securities. Augusta signed them over. I think it's time for us to become beach bums in Costa Rica."

Jamison smiled. "I'm with you, Colonel Randall."

"Is the back-up SUV still parked downtown?"

"It's in a garage about ten minutes from here. We have supplies and a medical kit."

Randall nodded. The two men disappeared into the falling snow.

Bobby ran through the door. Jonathan and Daniel were arguing with a nurse. Bobby ran up to her and showed her his badge.

"Get me a doctor, quick!" he shouted at her. "This girl is dying."

The nurse dropped her paperwork and got on the intercom. In a few minutes, a white-haired man came down the hall.

"I'm Dr. Wilson," he said. "What seems to be the trouble?"

Bobby handed the note and the glassine envelope to the doctor. "This girl is suffering from acute arsenic poisoning. She needs treatment immediately. The exact poison is in this envelope and instructions for treatment are in this note."

The doctor pulled back the blanket and examined Rachel. He opened the note and scanned the instructions. Then he turned to the nurse. "Get a gurney in here, stat! Move this girl into the ER and start her on fluid and electrolyte replacement immediately. I want her stomach pumped as quickly as possible, and I want her chelated with dimercaprol."

The nurse motioned for another nurse to help. They grabbed a gurney and Daniel laid Rachel down. Then the two nurses pushed the gurney through the emergency room doors.

The doctor shook his head. "She's in bad shape. I'll do the best I can."

Daniel took hold of the doctor's arm. "There's something else, Doctor. She's pregnant."

The doctor frowned. "That's not good. I might save the girl, but the baby...well, that would take a miracle."

The doctor pointed to the waiting room. "I'll let you know their status as soon as I can." He turned and followed the nurses.

Jonathan took Bobby aside. "Bobby, what about Jenny? Augusta sent someone to hurt her."

"Jonathan, I'll call the local boys in Paradise and get them out to the house. In the meantime, we'll leave Daniel here with Rachel and drive home."

Bobby went to the desk and asked for a phone. In a few minutes he returned. "The police in Paradise will send some men out to the house to guard Jenny. I talked to Jerry Cowell. He's dispatching three cruisers to get us through to the Pennsylvania state line. There will be some Pennsylvania boys there to take us into Paradise. We'll meet the troopers at my truck."

Bobby shook Daniel's hand. "Daniel, Jonathan and I have to see about Jenny. Will you take care of Rachel?"

Daniel nodded and looked at Jonathan. "That's all I've ever wanted to do."

"*Das ist gut*, Daniel. We'll call as soon as we know what's happening."

Bobby grabbed Jonathan's arm. "Come on, pal. We got a long drive ahead of us."

Then he and Jonathan headed out the door.

Colonel Jerry Cowell and his men entered the St. Clair estate with drawn guns. They found the frightened staff huddled in the kitchen. A tall, dignified man approached the Colonel.

"I'm the butler. We heard a gunshot and screaming upstairs."

Colonel Cowell motioned to one of his men. "Take them out and put them in the cruisers. I want them taken into town along with Sergeant Franklin and his men and held until I get there. Are there any other buildings where people might be hiding?"

The butler pointed out the back window. "There's a caretaker's cottage just through those trees. The security men have been using it."

Colonel Cowell signaled to two of his men. "Go out to the cottage and check it out. We'll go upstairs and see what's happening with the St. Clairs."

He pointed to the butler. "I need you to show me where you heard the shot."

The two men left by the back door while Cowell and his men followed the butler down the hall to the stairs.

The man stopped. "Go up the stairs and turn left down the hall. You'll pass another set of stairs and then you're in the east wing. Ms. Rachel's room is two doors down."

The state police crept silently up the stairs. They came to a room with the door partly open. From inside they heard a weird, crooning. Slowly, they pushed the door open. Augusta St. Clair was sitting by a man who was obviously dead. She was caressing the man's forehead and singing. "Rock-a-bye Gerald, in the tree top, down came the cradle, Gerald and all…" And then the old woman giggled.

Colonel Cowell spoke. "Mrs. St. Clair?"

The old woman turned. Her coiffed hair had fallen apart and she had a vacant stare. "Mrs. St. Clair? Oh, no, I'm Francine, Francine Bosnan. I'm not a St. Clair. They're all dead and I'm alive. Gerald's dead, and Rachel will soon be dead, and then Jenny and then they will all be dead. No more St. Clairs…all gone…all dead."

Colonel Cowell moved up beside the old woman. "Augusta St. Clair, I am arresting you for the murder of Gerald St. Clair. Stand up and put your hands behind your back."

Out in the cottage, the two state policemen entered with guns drawn. The body of a man was lying by the front door. He had a throwing dagger in his throat. One of the troopers took a small box with a flashing light on it from the dead man's hand. There was a button below the light.

"I wonder what this is."

His partner started to speak. "Don't press—"

The first policeman pressed the button. There was

a short series of beeps and then a roar as the propane tanks around the house exploded.

Colonel Cowell and his men were thrown to the ground by the force of the explosion. One of the men crawled to the window. "The house is on fire, Colonel."

"Get everyone out, now!"

Colonel Cowell turned to assist Augusta. She was gone.

Augusta ran down the stairs to her office. Behind her, she heard the pounding steps of a state policeman in hot pursuit. She pulled open the door, ran in, and slammed it in the trooper's face. "Can't get in, can't get in."

The trooper pounded on the door. "Mrs. St. Clair, come out. The house is on fire."

Augusta ignored him. Her safe door stood open. She ran inside and opened her lockbox. Inside, she found the diary and the pictures. She laid them on the desk and spread out the photos. Outside, the policemen shouted but she took no notice. She reached in her desk, and pulled out some lipstick and smeared it on her mouth. Then she went to the mirror. "Here I am, Robert. Aren't I beautiful? More beautiful than her? Why did you choose her, Robert? I gave you a son…"

Augusta could hear the troopers trying to break down the door but it was solid steel. She heard someone shouting that the whole east wing was on fire. She smiled when she heard Colonel Cowell order his men out. Above her, she could hear the house groaning and cracking. The reflection in the mirror held her spellbound. She was young and beautiful again. She began to sway seductively, the picture of Robert St. Clair in her hand. "You're all dead, all the St. Clairs. You should have chosen me, Robert."

Above her, a circle of fire began to eat its way through the ceiling. The chandelier crashed down as the support was eaten away by the flames. Augusta looked up as the ceiling began to fall. She held up the picture and screamed. "Robert St. Clair, I'll see you in hell."

As the whole east wing collapsed in a roar of fire right on top of her, the last thing Augusta saw was the face of Robert St. Clair smiling at her.

Bobby and Jonathan drove east behind the police cruisers. The storm was blowing itself out, and the weather was clearing. They met their escort at the Pennsylvania border and drove on toward Paradise. The snowplows had been out but it still took them four hours to get there. They headed toward the farm, followed by the police cruisers. A local police car was parked in front of the house, but they didn't see anyone on guard. Then Bobby saw someone lying off to the side of the house. It was a local policeman and he was groaning and holding his head. Bobby grabbed him. "Where's Jenny?"

The policeman pointed. "She's in there. Someone knocked me out."

Bobby and Jonathan ran into the house. Outside, the wail of sirens proclaimed the arrival of the state police.

Jonathan shouted. "Jenny? Jenny, where are you?"

There was a faint cry from the back. The two men ran down the hall and burst through the door. There was a man in the room. He was holding Jenny from behind and had a gun at her head. "Don't come any closer or she's dead."

Bobby stepped forward. "There are a dozen state policemen outside. You wouldn't get two feet out the door. And besides, Augusta St. Clair won't be paying you, she's been arrested."

The man smiled. "I already got my money, mac. Now I'm taking the woman out of here. As soon as I'm clear, I'll turn the lady loose."

Bobby could see the lie in the man's eyes. Jenny moved her head and then she suddenly grabbed the man's arm. Bobby and Jonathan jumped him as Jenny pulled the gun down. There was a roar as the gun went off, and Bobby felt a blow to his side, like someone jabbing hot icepicks into his hip. He crumpled in a heap.

He saw Jonathan's dark hair fall over his face as he fought ferociously with the killer. As Bobby watched, the scene changed. He was in a trench on top of a hill on Guadalcanal. He couldn't move. Above him, a tall, dark-haired Marine was fighting hand-to-hand with a crush of Japanese soldiers. Bobby called out. "Reuben, Reuben…" And then everything went black.

Rachel opened her eyes. She was in a dark room lying on a narrow bed. Everything was blurry and it was hard to see. There were tubes attached to her arms and up her nose. Next to her on a stand were several pieces of equipment that were either softly beeping or showing jagged green lines on small screens. She had a terrible headache and her stomach felt sore. There was someone seated next to her bed. It was Daniel! She tried to speak, but the tubes were in her way.

Daniel saw Rachel move and took her hand. "Don't try to speak, Rachel. Just rest. We got you here in time, but you must save your strength. Close your eyes now and sleep."

Rachel squeezed Daniel's hand but when he tried to

take it away, she would not let go. She closed her eyes. Daniel was with her, and the Lord was with Daniel.

In another hospital room in Lancaster, Bobby Halverson lay in a bed. Beside him sat Jonathan and Jenny Hershberger. Jenny was crying. Bobby slowly opened his eyes and smiled. He reached over and patted Jenny's hand. "Don't worry about me, kid. This old Marine is too tough to kill."

Jenny took Bobby's hand. "Oh, Bobby, we were so worried."

"What happened after I passed out?"

"Jonathan grabbed the man and knocked him out. I guess he wasn't expecting an Amish prize fighter."

Jonathan reached in his pocket. "Here's something the doctor gave me. He dug it out of your hip when he got the bullet out."

He leaned over and handed Bobby a twisted shard of metal. "This is the shrapnel that's been in your hip since 1942. He figured you might want it as a souvenir."

Bobby reached out and took the chunk of metal. "Well, I guess this story has come full circle. I've got a special place for this, Jenny, right next to a picture of your father. How is Rachel doing?"

Jenny patted Bobby's arm. "She's alive and slowly getting better. The doctor told Daniel that she and the baby have a fighting chance. Daniel's with her and that's the best care she could have right now. We are going tomorrow. We are confident that the Lord will keep her."

"Me, too," Bobby said. "Me, too."

Chapter Thirty-Nine

Home from the Sea

On a cold morning in early January, an ambulance drove slowly up the gravel drive from Leacock Lane and stopped in front of the blue farmhouse. Jonathan and Jenny were standing on the porch with two other Amish men. Bobby Halverson sat in a chair, his dog, Rufus, lying next to him. The driver and an attendant got out and opened the back. Daniel King climbed down as the two men pulled a gurney out and extended the legs. The girl on the gurney stirred and a wan smile crossed her pale face. The attendants rolled the gurney up the path and lifted it onto the porch. The girl raised her hands and Jenny reached down and took them, pulling her girl into a warm embrace. Rachel was home.

While the attendants wheeled Rachel inside, Jonathan and Daniel conversed with the two elders of their community, *Bischopp* Hochstetler and Daniel's father, Jonas King. The *Bischopp* put his hand on Jonathan's shoulder. "*Und so*, your *dochter* has come home? And what of her *Englischer* husband?"

"Her husband is dead, *Bischopp*. It was a terrible tragedy."

"But Rachel is still pregnant with the man's child?"

Jonathan nodded. "It is a miracle that the baby is still alive. The doctors don't know how the poisoning affected the child, but Rachel is a very strong girl. She was in intensive care for a month. Then we brought her to a care facility in Lancaster for three weeks. She is healing from the arsenic much quicker than expected, and we pray that the baby will be born undamaged."

"And has Rachel repented of leaving the church?"

"We have not yet had that conversation. We only want to see her get well."

The *Bischopp* turned to Daniel. "*Und Sie, junger Mann?* You violated the *meidung* when you followed Rachel. That put you under the *bann* also. What do you have to say for yourself?"

Daniel took a deep breath. "I do not regret following Rachel. I believe the Lord told me that she was in great danger, and she needed me to look after her. I am sorry that I violated the *Ordnung*, but if I had to do it again, I would. *Gott bringt Rachel in meinem weg.* He gave her to me to love. If she stays under the shunning, then so be it, I will be shunned also."

Jonas King put his arm around his son's shoulder. "I was *sehr böse*, very angry, when Daniel ignored my counsel. But because of Daniel, Rachel is alive. If he had not listened to the Lord, she would be dead. Now I am very proud of my son and will support him in whatever he does."

The *Bischopp* looked back at Jonathan. "And you, Jonathan? Rachel is still under the *bann*. If she stays here you are violating the *meidung* also. Would you and your wife risk being excommunicated from the church?"

Jonathan nodded. "*Bischopp* Hochstetler, I know this is difficult for you, but, although I love the ways of the Amish and know that the *Ordnung* protect us, I believe that grace will trump all. In the last few days I have been touched by *die hand des Gottes*, and the old wounds and fears are gone. I am Jonathan Hershberger again. Not the foolish hippie, or the *Englischer*, Richard Sandbridge, but the Jonathan Hershberger who came to love Jenny Springer and the Amish way. And out of that love came my girl, Rachel. Her well being is the most important thing, no matter what her decision about the church. So she will stay here until she is well enough to decide about her life. If we are excommunicated for that, well, so be it."

There was a cough behind them and they turned to see Bobby Halverson leaning on his crutch. He hesitated a moment and then spoke. "Gentlemen, I am not Amish and I don't mean to intrude, but I have something to say here. I live on this farm because I have no other family except the Hershbergers. I have been a friend of this family for over forty years. During that time I have always called myself an agnostic because I was never really sure if there was a God. I should have known better, because as I look back over my relationship with Reuben and Jerusha, with Jenny and Jonathan and now Rachel and Daniel, I realize that I have seen the hand of God at work through them many times."

Bobby put his hand on Daniel's shoulder. "I watched God work in this young man's life to save a girl who is more than precious to me."

Bobby looked at Jonathan. "When we were out on

the ocean and Jonathan became the captain of the ship, I saw God reach out of heaven and heal a man that has been lost for many years."

Bobby looked straight at the *Bischopp* and Jonas King. "So, while you are considering what to do, you might factor in that a man who has never really believed has come to realize that I was a fool. In the lives of these two men, I have come to know that God is real and that He sent His son for me, too. And I'm a better man for it."

Jonathan walked over and embraced his old friend. He whispered in Bobby's ear. "Well, you old prodigal. Tonight we kill the fatted calf."

Bischopp Hochstetler looked around and smiled as he shook his head. "*Ja, das ist ein Rätsel.* It seems I have a small rebellion on my hands. And yet I, too, see the hand of *Gott* in all these things." He pulled Jonas King aside and spoke to him for a moment. Jonas nodded in agreement and then the *Bischopp* turned back to the men. "We will put any decision on hold. While not setting aside our *Ordnung*, I believe, as Jonathan says, we must allow for the grace of God to work its healing now. Rachel may stay at home until she is well enough to decide what she will do with her life. Daniel, you are on probation, under your father's watchful eye. You may come and care for Rachel, as you are needed, for who are we to deny a calling that God has made so plain in your life. We will talk of these matters more when Rachel is well."

The *Bischopp* turned and walked out to his buggy. He climbed in, waved to the group on the porch, and then drove away. Above them, the ragged clouds opened, and for the first time in days, the sun shone through to warm the land and the hearts bound to it.

* * *

And so the days passed. January was a cold, snowless month, and Rachel was still so weak that she was most often confined to her room. She would sit in her rocking chair with her mama's shawl wrapped around her. Outside her window, the bleak fields were locked in the grip of winter's death, and as she watched the unchanging landscape, her mind lay in a strange dormancy, with only the promise of the baby growing within her, bringing a small sense of life to the cheerless days.

Daniel would come as often as he could to sit with her and talk, mostly of his work on the farm and the new foals born to his father's mares. Rachel would sit quietly and listen, but for the most part, she did not enter into the conversation. A deep darkness lay on her soul, as though she were floating far down under the sea where only a few rays of sun could penetrate to the depths.

One day she looked up at Daniel and spoke quietly. "I am ruined, Daniel. Because of my stubbornness and unforgiveness, I have destroyed my life. I am not worth your love and the care you give me. You should go home and stay away. Leave me to my fate."

Daniel patted Rachel's hand and smiled. "I am your truest friend, Rachel. I will never leave you or forsake you, no matter what you have done or what you say."

Rachel looked at Daniel's face. It was a strong and handsome face—the face of a true and noble man, and Rachel could see that he was telling her the truth. And in that moment, she had a glimpse that perhaps…perhaps something might be made of the disaster she had brought upon herself.

Early in April, on a still, dark night, Rachel awoke. Something was happening in her body, and she knew what it was. She called out in the darkness. "Mama! Mama!"

She heard the sound of her mama's feet coming down the hall and then the door opened and Jenny came in holding a lamp. "What is it, *dochter*?"

"It's my time, Mama. I feel the contractions and my water broke."

Jenny went to the door and called to Jonathan. "Get up, Papa, you are about to have a grandchild."

Jonathan came into the room. He was buttoning his shirt. "I need to get the nurse from the birth center. I will go now. It shouldn't take long. I'll ask Bobby to drive me."

Jonathan left and Jenny turned to Rachel. Rachel turned her face toward the wall. Jenny came and sat by her daughter's side. "What is it, Rachel?"

Rachel sobbed. "I am so ashamed, Mama. I am having the baby of a man that I did not love. I gave myself away for money. I feel so sorry for this baby because I will have to leave here and my baby will not have a father."

"Why will you have to leave, my darling?"

Rachel turned back to Jenny. "I am not worthy to stay. I have disgraced myself, and you, and I am not worthy to be loved by anyone. I will go and live alone with this bitter fruit of my own making."

Before Jenny could answer, Rachel gasped. Jenny held her hand. "A contraction?"

"Yes, Mama."

"Well, let's get ready for this baby. It's coming soon."

Daniel stood with Jonathan and Bobby on the porch. The sun was just coming up over the eastern hills, and the sweet fragrance of apple blossoms from the orchard filled the air. Out in the fields of the Hershberger farm a light mist clung to the trees and rose from the ground like gentle fingers reaching toward the awakening sun. Above their heads in the plum trees by the porch, tiny pink flowers were alive with brilliant color as they painted the day with God's palette. Stillness lay on the land. From within the house, they heard Rachel give a great cry. Then the silence of the dawn was broken by the lusty cry of a newborn baby. Daniel looked at Jonathan in apprehension.

Then the screen door flew open and Jenny stood there, breathless. "It is a boy, Jonathan, strong and big. He is fine and the nurse says he will live and not die."

Daniel looked at Jenny. She smiled. "Rachel is very tired, but she is well."

Daniel took his hat off and held it in his hands, nervously shifting from one foot to the other. "May we, I mean, can I…"

"Yes, Daniel, you may go in and see Rachel."

"May I see her alone for a few minutes?"

Jenny looked at Jonathan and then nodded her assent.

Rachel lay still and quiet, her eyes half-closed and her dark hair spread out against the white sheets. The nurse stood holding a bundle in her arms. Rachel could see the tiny arms waving and her heart filled with a love she had never known before. She reached up. The nurse put the baby down beside her and Rachel took the newborn into her arms. She could see Gerald in the small face and she thought back to all that had happened to her in the last year. Then the door opened quietly and Daniel stood there. The nurse nodded to him. "I'll let you speak with her for a moment while I go clean up. Do not excite her. She is very tired. It was a hard labor."

The nurse left and Daniel came and looked down at Rachel. Without thinking, he reached out and stroked her brow.

Rachel looked up at him. "The baby is well, Daniel."

Daniel nodded.

"You have been so good to me, Daniel. Why have I been so blind?"

Daniel touched her lips and silenced her. Then he knelt down beside the bed. He took her hand in his. "Now, Rachel, you will listen to me for once in your life."

Rachel stared at him.

Daniel went on. "I have loved you since we were children. God has put you in my way, and there is nothing I can do about it. You are going to marry me and this baby will be my son. His name will be Levon King and he will be Amish and his children will be Amish."

Rachel started to protest. "But, Daniel, I am not good enough for you to love me. I am ruined. I can't give you what I should have, my purity…"

Daniel looked at Rachel. "I, too, am ruined, Rachel."

"What do you mean, Daniel?"

Rachel could see Daniel struggling with himself. Then he spoke, so quietly she almost could not hear.

"I killed a man."

Rachel's eyes opened wide. "Daniel…when?"

"When I came to rescue you there was a man waiting in your room. We fought and I killed him. I violated the deepest tenant of our faith. So, we are both broken. But don't you see? That is where *du leiber Gott* wants us to be—having nothing in ourselves and putting our lives in His hands. Rachel, He has given you to me and me to you. We are broken and hopeless, both of us faithless. But it is His plan for us to be together for the rest of our lives, depending on Him and helping each other to walk each day in faith and love. Now, say that you will marry me, and let me be a father to this boy."

Daniel reached over and tenderly touched Rachel's face. Then quietly and gently he leaned down and kissed her. Rachel felt a stirring in her heart that she had never felt before and her arm went around Daniel's strong shoulders and then she was kissing him back with all the strength and passion and love that was in her.

And like the golden sun that awakens the day after a long dark night, the strength of Daniel's love for her poured into Rachel's heart and the emptiness and despair were swept away by the power of God reaching through Daniel to her. And like a flash of lightning on a hot summer night, the truth came to her. She loved Daniel. She had always loved Daniel and now their love would somehow make everything right again. And she would be Amish, and her son would be Amish, and she would live her life with this man, and the mighty angel that had turned her away from the gate of the garden would lower his flaming sword, and she would return with joy to live again in Paradise.

Epilogue

The Rest of the Story

The tall writer put down the last page of the manuscript and looked up at the clock. It was four-thirty in the morning. He had been reading since six o'clock the night before. He took a handkerchief out of his pocket and wiped his eyes. Then he turned to the phone, picked it up, and dialed a number. The phone rang a few times, and then a voice came on the other end.

"Who's calling me at four-thirty?"

"I finished the manuscript. It's an amazing story. It's so far outside anything she ever wrote before. I couldn't put it down."

The writer could hear the interest in the other man's voice. "That good, huh?"

"That good. She's a brilliant writer. The literary world lost an icon when she handed these manuscripts over to me."

"How long will it take to re-write it?"

"Not long. There's not a lot to do. It will be very hard not to just copy it word for word."

"No, don't do that. We need the man's point of view in this story. We need the adventure angle and the words and observations that only a man would see."

"Yeah, I know. I'll get to work on it right away."

"What else does she have?"

The writer shuffled through the stack of manuscripts. They were hand typed on a manual typewriter and then tied with a red ribbon.

"There's a story here about Jonathan's great-great-great grandmother. She was an Indian princess who converted to the Amish faith. And there's another one about a Polish princess who became the matriarch of the Hershberger family. Pretty heady stuff."

"Good. I'll call our publisher—at a decent hour—and tell him you're ready to go on to the next book."

The line clicked and went dead.

The writer picked up the manuscript he had been reading and started to tie the ribbon back around it. A handwritten note that he had not seen before slid out from between the pages. He picked it up. It was written in Jenny's smooth cursive and was addressed to him.

Dear Friend,

I just wanted to fill in a few of the details in the rest of Daniel and Rachel's story. They married and went to live on the King farm with Daniel's family. Jonathan, Bobby, and Jonas helped them build a fine house on the knoll by their tree. Daniel adopted the baby and he and Rachel named their boy Levon St. Clair King, in honor of Gerald. Interestingly enough, Levon was born with the Key, the birthmark above his heart—the same one that

The Amish Heiress

caused Rachel so much trouble. Someday there
may be another story there for you to write.

    A year after they were married, Jonathan re-
ceived an unexpected royalty check from a reprint
of one of Richard Sandbridge's old albums. With
the agreement of the elders of our church, Jona-
than used the money to pay Rachel's way through
a local veterinary school. Now our community has
a real Amish vet.

    Rachel returned to the church and as Jonathan
so lovingly put it, "Grace trumped all."

    I see that the first three books did very well.
I read them and I appreciate your honesty and
clarity in telling the story of my family. May the
Lord bless your further endeavors.

Jenny Hershberger

The writer remembered the day several years before that he sat with Jenny on the front porch of the old
farmhouse. Cups of tea stood on the small table in front
of them and a warm summer breeze had heralded the
coming of another beautiful evening in Paradise, Pennsylvania. He had come all the way from California to
meet her, and she had unfolded the story of her family
as she had unfolded the marvelous quilt that held the
secrets of the Hershberger saga. After she told the story
of her sister, Jenna, and of her husband, Jonathan, he
had asked her a question.

    "What about your daughter, Rachel?"

    Jenny smiled. Her *kappe* was slightly askew and the
rebellious curls, now turning white, fought to escape at
the urging of the evening breeze. And then the breeze

picked up and the golden light of the setting sun touched the leaves of the trees and they began to dance, and then they flamed into fire.

"It was hard for Rachel when her papa came home. She was fourteen, she was becoming a woman, and Jonathan had missed such a big part of her formative years. They were at odds for a long time. I think she felt like he came between her and me. Eventually, they found what they once had when Rachel was little, but it took circumstances far outside the boundaries of our quiet Amish life to heal Jonathan. And Rachel...well, Rachel went through her own trials before she came home. But then, that's another story."

The writer smiled as he remembered. He picked up the manuscript and looked at the title, *The Amish Heiress*.

Yes indeed, Jenny Hershberger. That was another story...

* * * * *

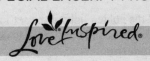
"Dating is so complicated."

"People are complicated, Noah. Every single person you meet
is dealing with something."

He asked, "How did you get so wise?"

"Never said I was."

"I'm being serious. How did you learn to navigate so seamlessly
through these kinds of interactions, and why aren't you married?"

Olivia Mae thought her eyes were going to pop out of her head.
"Did you really just ask me that?"

"I did."

"A little intrusive."

"Meaning you don't want to answer?"

"Meaning it's none of your business."

"Fair enough, though it's like asking a horse salesman why he
doesn't own a horse."

"My family situation is…unique."

"You mean with your grandparents?"

She nodded instead of answering.

"I've got it." Noah resettled his hat, looking quite pleased with
himself.

"Got what?"

"The solution to my dating disasters."

He leaned forward, close enough that she could smell the
shampoo he'd used that morning.

"You need to give me dating lessons."

"What do you mean?"

"You and me. We'll go on a few dates…say, three. You can learn how to do anything if you do it three times."

"That's a ridiculous suggestion."

"Why? I learn better from doing."

"Do you?"

"I've already learned not to take a girl to a gas station, but who knows how many more dating traps are waiting for me."

"So this would be…a learning experience."

"It's a perfect solution." He tugged on her *kapp* string, something no one had done to her since she'd been a young teen.

"I can tell by the shock on your face that I've made you uncomfortable. It's a *gut* idea, though. We'd keep it businesslike—nothing personal."

Olivia Mae had no idea why the thought of sitting through three dates with Noah Graber made her stomach twirl like she'd been on a merry-go-round. Maybe she was catching a stomach bug.

"Wait a minute. Are you trying to get out of your third date? Because you promised your *mamm* that you would give this thing three solid attempts."

"And I'll keep my word on that," Noah assured her. "After you've tutored me, you can throw another poor unsuspecting girl my way."

Olivia Mae stood, brushed off the back of her dress and pointed a finger at Noah, who still sat in the grass as if he didn't have a care in the world.

"All right. I'll do it."

Don't miss
A Perfect Amish Match *by Vannetta Chapman,*
available May 2019 wherever
Love Inspired® *books and ebooks are sold.*

www.LoveInspired.com

Copyright © 2019 by Vannetta Chapman

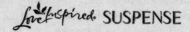

SPECIAL EXCERPT FROM

Love Inspired
SUSPENSE

*A K-9 cop must keep his childhood friend alive
when she finds herself in the crosshairs of a
drug-smuggling operation.*

Read on for a sneak preview of
Act of Valor *by Dana Mentink,*
the next exciting installment in the
True Blue K-9 Unit *miniseries, available in May 2019*
from Love Inspired Suspense.

Officer Zach Jameson surveyed the throng of people congregated around the ticket counter at LaGuardia Airport. Most ignored Zach and K-9 partner, Eddie, and that suited him just fine. Two months earlier he would have greeted people with a smile, or at least a polite nod while he and Eddie did their work of scanning for potential drug smugglers. These days he struggled to keep his mind on his duty while the ever-present darkness nibbled at the edges of his soul.

Eddie plopped himself on Zach's boot. He stroked the dog's ears, trying to clear away the fog that had descended the moment he heard of his brother's death.

Zach hadn't had so much as a whiff of suspicion that his brother was in danger. His brain knew he should talk to somebody, somebody like Violet Griffin, his friend from childhood who'd reached out so many times, but his heart would not let him pass through the dark curtain.

"Just get to work," he muttered to himself as his phone rang. He checked the number.

Violet.

He considered ignoring it, but Violet didn't ever call unless she needed help, and she rarely needed anyone. Strong enough to run a ticket counter at LaGuardia and have enough energy left over to help out at Griffin's, her family's diner. She could handle belligerent customers in both arenas and bake the best apple pie he'd ever had the privilege to chow down.

It almost made him smile as he accepted the call.

"Someone's after me, Zach."

Panic rippled through their connection. Panic, from a woman who was tough as they came. "Who? Where are you?"

Her breath was shallow as if she was running.

"I'm trying to get to the break room. I can lock myself in, but I don't... I can't..." There was a clatter.

"Violet?" he shouted.

But there was no answer.

Don't miss
Act of Valor *by Dana Mentink,*
available May 2019 wherever
Love Inspired® Suspense *books and ebooks are sold.*

www.LoveInspired.com

Inspirational Romance to Warm Your Heart and Soul

Join our social communities to connect with other readers who share your love!

Sign up for the Love Inspired newsletter at **www.LoveInspired.com** to be the first to find out about upcoming titles, special promotions and exclusive content.

CONNECT WITH US AT:

Facebook.com/groups/HarlequinConnection

 Facebook.com/LoveInspiredBooks

 Twitter.com/LoveInspiredBks